To Honor

Evergreen Point Book One

by

Rasha Selim

To Honor

Contact Information: info@thewildrosepress.com

Cover Art by *Diana Carlile*

The Wild Rose Press, Inc.
PO Box 708
Adams Basin, NY 14410-0708

Visit us at www.thewildrosepress.com

Publishing History
First Scarlet Rose Edition, 2019
Print ISBN 978-1-5092-2674-0
Digital ISBN 978-1-5092-2604-7

Published in the United States of America

One kiss, two destinies. Love or loyalty? Friend or family?

"You all need to take your shirts off," Susan piped up, pointing to my team. I turned in time to see her blush. She covered her mouth with a hand, shaking her head as if she couldn't believe what she said. I grinned at her cuteness and happily complied.

Grabbing the back of my shirt, I pulled it off in one motion. She gasped, and it pleased me knowing I'd shocked her. I quirked my eyebrows at my brothers in challenge. They followed suit, and the four of us stood bare-chested in front of the other team.

"Ew. Cover up. I'm going blind," Kate shrieked, yelping when Susan smacked her.

"I'm enjoying the view. Shut up," Susan whispered to Kate, but not quietly enough. We laughed, making her flush.

Her gaze lingered on me for longer than the others, and I fought the urge to puff up my chest and show off my abs. Leaning close so only she heard me I goaded her, "Sure you can handle my glistening chest, Susan? Wouldn't want you to fall over and hurt yourself."

She huffed at me but couldn't hide her deepening blush. "I'm going to make you eat those words."

"I'd rather eat something else," I said, knowing I crossed a line, but for once, I didn't care.

At her stunned gulp, I walked to my dad standing by the deck.

Dedication

For Susan

Author Acknowledgments

Writing is a lonely endeavor but it is by no means a solitary one. There are several people who helped, encouraged, and supported me.

My thanks go to all my girls, especially Susan and Jenn, laughs and dreams are shared with you. Susan, I hope Pax is all you imagined him to be. Jenn, my most dedicated supporter and loudest cheerleader. Bring on the party bus, chocolate cake, and wine!

Wild Rose Press for taking a chance on me, especially Judi. Your encouragement, advice, and support were invaluable.

Jen, Sara, and Michaele for listening to me and pushing me to get the manuscript finished.

Chad, you were so much more than a boss. A friend and a mentor.

Rita, my fellow expatriate, the hours we spent talking, the unrelenting support and encouragement you provided, the mumbled swears when I lost my way, for all that and more, I love you and hope you are at peace. I miss you my friend.

My husband and three beautiful boys for giving me the space to write, for understanding my style of crazy, and for holding my hand.

And finally, my readers for giving me some of your precious time.

Chapter One

Pax

"Pax, my office," my commanding officer, Billy, bellowed as I entered the firehouse at the start of a forty-eight-hour shift. I dumped my pack, containing clothes and other items I needed while on shift, inside the door and entered his office.

"What's up?" I appeared calm on the outside, but inside my stomach roiled. Being summoned into Billy's office was like walking into a principal's. I did not have much experience with the latter and didn't want to start a trend with the former.

"Have a seat, son." Billy's face showed no emotion, leaving me stumped. I sat in the old orange and green twill chair, faced his desk, and braced for the worst.

Surprisingly, he stood, rounded the desk, and propped against it. "Congratulations. You're my new second-in-command. Welcome to the ranks of management." The corners of his mouth lifted.

Months of anxious waiting evaporated, and the knot of tension in my stomach eased. With a wide smile of my own, I stood and accepted Billy's extended hand and stumbled when he pulled me into a hug.

Stepping back, Billy rested his free palm on my shoulder. "I'm proud of you, son. You've busted your butt for ten years, and the higher-ups are impressed.

You're the youngest firefighter given this command in the state of Washington."

"Sir, I'm honored to have their trust, and I'll keep working hard for the people of Bellevue." Overwhelmed with emotion, my voice cracked.

"Janice sent cupcakes for the celebration. Stow your gear and let's clue in the crew to their new boss."

I nodded, turned, and walked out of his office with a bounce in my step, and even though I struggled against it, my grin broadened.

The guys noticed, but I avoided their silent questions and hustled up the steps. The bunkroom consisted of twenty cots lining the two sides of the large open room, each one assigned to two firefighters on alternate shift schedules. Designated lockers held our belongings.

Reaching mine, I opened it and placed my bag inside. I'd unpack after the announcement. I couldn't wait to sink my teeth into one of Mrs. Walsh's delicious cupcakes, but the glint of a shiny key hanging on one of the three hooks caught my eye. A key I did not put there.

On my way back downstairs, Billy called the men into the gigantic kitchen, outfitted with two ovens and stove tops, two large fridges, and a twenty-foot wooden table with long benches for the firefighters. A team of three firefighters cooked breakfast and dinner on a rotating schedule.

Billy stood at the head of the table surrounded by my crew. I made my way into the room and stood at the other end and waited.

"I'm happy to say Mike has made a full recovery and is home," he started. The men burst into cheers at the good news. Mike was the second-in-command until he retired ten months earlier. Unfortunately, soon after, he'd suffered a minor stroke. For the past few months, I'd acted as second, walking in shoes far too big to fill. I respected the heck out of Mike more each day as I did his job. Now the job was mine, and I could create my own legacy.

"I'm proud to announce The Hulk is your new second," Billy said, using my nickname. The noise level erupted as each firefighter approached.

"Congratulations, man."

"Do I have to call you boss now?"

"Nobody better for the position."

I laughed with the crew, welcoming the one-armed hugs and slaps across my back. Relief coursed through my body the more the news settled in my mind. My promotion wasn't a guarantee, even with years of experience, and degrees in Fire and Ambulatory Science.

I turned at a squeal from the kitchen door. I groaned. Julie, a station bunny, hopped up and down begging for my attention. Since the day I sat with her while she cried, she fixated on me, coming by the station on the days I worked.

I didn't answer her calls, nor did I initiate conversation when she showed up, yet I couldn't shake her off.

She rushed into the room and flung herself against me. I wrapped my arms around her, keeping us from stumbling, but pulled away quickly.

"Oh, baby, I knew you could do it. Congratulations." She leaned in with puckered lips. At the last second, I turned my face and gave her my cheek.

"This is private, you shouldn't be here," I said. Putting my hand on her arm, I stepped back, adding distance between us.

"Oh, don't be silly. I'm here for you. You can use the key I left you and meet me at my place when you get off. We can celebrate the right way." She licked her lips, and I cringed. Her idea of celebration was not in line with mine.

Running my hand through my short hair, I groaned. I didn't know where she lived, and even if I did, I wouldn't visit her. "You can't go in the bunk room. It's reserved for personnel only. Julie, stop leaving me things. I've already told you, I'm not interested. I don't see us going anywhere." Repeating myself for what felt like the hundredth time my frustration grew. I led her out of the kitchen and through the front door. "You need to stop coming by."

As if I hadn't spoken, Julie placed her hands on my chest, rose on her toes, and whispered, "We're meant to be, Pax. The sooner you realize that, the sooner you'll be happy. Use the key. I'll make it worth your while." She tapped her hand against my chest, turned, and walked away before I could respond.

It was best since I had nothing more to add. At least, nothing nice.

Billy and my crew waited for me, annoyance plastered on their faces. They knew of my troubles with Julie and didn't appreciate her shenanigans. I ignored their unspoken questions and returned to my earned position.

"Janice made cupcakes. You have ten minutes to celebrate, then it's back to work. We still have our morning duties to get through," Billy said, as he waved a paper in the air. He exited with his treat and a smile to the crew's moaning.

Billy pushed us hard and maintained an efficient firehouse, but he was a teddy bear when it came to us firefighters. He treated us like we were his children, yet drilled us to perform our duties without slacking, not because of departmental regulations but because he wanted to ensure our safety.

I grinned, grabbed a cupcake, and sat.

"Man, talk about busting up a celebration," Beck said from beside me.

"Ten minutes? The trucks are clean, stocked, and ready for action," another piped in.

"Would it kill him if we took a day off?"

I gazed from one man to another listening to their grumblings. Each of their remarks, although in jest, made me think. For the first time in ten years, I understood Billy's gruffness.

"He's just being hard on us because you're his family. He's responsible for your safety. So am I. Let's eat, then get out there. At the end of the day, it isn't only about helping civilians. It's about making sure we all go home."

The men nodded, quieted by my heartfelt speech. I smiled and mentally patted my back. First day on the job and it felt good.

My phone rang, pulling me out of my thoughts. Seeing my cousin Caden's image on the display, I took my half-eaten dessert and returned to my bunk.

"Hey, what dragged you out of bed early?" I reported for my shift at six in the morning, not an hour Caden was usually awake.

"I'm on the East Coast. Not early here. Anyway, I felt the need to call. Everything okay?"

I laughed. Caden didn't ignore his feelings or premonitions. No matter what, he always acted on them. He swore he knew the moment the distracted driver hit his parents' car. I didn't argue with him since he tended to be spot on.

"I got the promotion."

"Hey, that's great. Next is commanding officer." Caden meant well, but he didn't know of my hesitations. Commanding officers, chiefs in other states, rotated shifts with their crew but didn't enter buildings. They were the ground control. Early on in my career, I wanted a position in upper management, but administration no longer held the same spark it once had.

"I'm good where I am. I still want to fight fires, not sit behind a desk."

"What about the arson and fire investigations position?"

"I still want that, but…" The longer I fought fires, the more my heart and soul craved the job. Helping people was what I did. Who I was. Anything else felt wrong.

"When will you be home?" I asked.

"A week tomorrow. Late Friday night."

"I'm working. Mom and Dad picking you up?"

"Nope. I'm taking a cab home."

We spoke for a few more minutes, making plans, before hanging up. I pocketed my phone and sat on my cot enjoying the silence. But it didn't feel right leaving all the work for my crew.

I joined them and checked our gear and trucks. An

hour later, my phone rang again. Smiling, I knew the news of my promotion had spread like a wild fire through the family grapevine. An image of Morgan's face lit the display, and once again, I headed back to my cot, answering the phone on the way.

"Hey, brother. What has you up so early?"

"Caden," Morgan grunted.

He didn't talk much, especially at seven in the morning. Morgan stayed up most nights working on his bike designs. He liked the silence the night hours afforded him.

"I'm assuming you've heard?"

He grunted again, and I imagined him sitting on his dock on Lake Washington, taking in the morning sky's changing colors. Of all my siblings and cousins, he lived closest to our parents, only a few houses down on Evergreen Point Road.

"Why'd you call if you're only going to grunt?"

"Too early. Thought you didn't want this promotion?"

"Yeah, I did." I stretched my legs out on my cot and covered my eyes with the back of my arm. I wished I had the privacy needed for the conversation. However, men came and went from the bunkroom. "I'm glad I got it, but I don't want to give up my time in the field."

"Your CO still goes out."

"He does, but he commands. I want to be inside doing what I do best." A juxtaposition of happy and troubled emotions ran through my mind. Neither taking a stronger hold.

"I get it. Mom's going to want to celebrate this weekend."

Sundays were family days. Unless on shift, I never

missed our gatherings. The eight of us, my three brothers and four cousins, got together at my parents' home for a day filled with grilling out and playing football.

"Yeah, I know. I'm going to ask her not to make a big deal of it. I'm not on shift. I'll be there. You?"

"Not sure. Susan's been sick for the past few days. I might hang out at her place."

I closed my eyes, and my heart clenched. Susan, my brother's best friend, was also the woman I loved. I couldn't pursue her because I didn't want to interfere with the bond between them, nor did I want to jeopardize my relationship with Morgan. I envied what they meant to each other. I'd declared her off limits and dated others, but never found a woman who captivated me the way Susan did.

"She won't go to a doctor, says it's only the flu. Can you check on her? Maybe she'll listen to you," he said, the frustration evident in his voice. Not many people provoked reactions from my brother, but Susan was one of them.

"I'll see what I can do." I'd ask a medic to go with me since they knew her. Susan came by the firehouse with food for the guys. Said it was her civic duty to ensure our well-being through our stomachs. I lived for the days when she came by and had wondered why I hadn't seen her in the past few days.

"Okay, thanks. And congrats. You'll make it work."

Morgan clicked off, and I climbed off my cot. First order of business, track down one of the guys. Susan's apartment building stood only two blocks away from my firehouse. Second, find Billy and ask his permission. I didn't foresee any issue with the request. He had a soft spot for Susan.

I hoped for a quiet shift even though they left me restless, yet the busy ones weren't any better. A busy one meant there were fires somewhere wreaking havoc on peoples' lives.

Unfortunately, I never got the chance to check on Susan. Two fires on the first day kept the crew and me hustling, but the fire on the second day would forever be ingrained in my mind, heart, and soul.

****

Susan

"Dump his ass," I said to my cousin Ann Marie. "How can you be so smart, yet be so stupid and stubborn when it comes to your love life? He's a douche and you know it. Why the hell are you still with him?"

"Don't get onto me about my love life. My arrangement works for me. I don't have time for more. I know he's an asshole, but he's giving me what I need, damn good sex."

"Oh my God. You did not just say that. Many other guys can give you the big O. Why him?"

As CEO and owner of a marketing company, Ann Marie knew what she wanted. A no-strings-attached good time. Me, on the other hand, I wanted a long-term forever kind of relationship. And I wanted it with the one man I could never have, my best friend's brother Pax.

"Enough about me. How're you feeling?"

"I'm still in bed. Don't have the energy to do much else." I dropped another tissue in my ever-growing pile on the floor. Grabbing another one, I held it to my nose, staving off the constant flow.

"Are you eating? Isn't the saying, starve a cold, feed a fever? I can be there in three hours."

My cousin lived in Seattle, but the distance didn't diminish our closeness. Dad and I lost Mom when I was only three. My extended family held a strong place in my heart. Ann Marie became a significant part of my life in our teenage years. We spent many hours on the phone talking, commiserating, crying, and laughing. When she graduated from college, she traveled the country before settling back in Seattle and creating her company. I stayed close to home and attended Washington State. I graduated with a business degree, and with advice and help from Ann Marie, I opened an animal shelter.

As a kid, I gravitated to abandoned animals. I wanted to give them food, love, and safety. My dad tried steering me in a different direction but eventually relented and allowed me to bring home many strays. I nursed them back to health and, although I wanted a house full of pets, I posted adoption flyers in my neighborhood. Seeing them become a part of a family always filled me with a deep sense of satisfaction.

"Hey, where'd you go?" Ann Marie said, stirring me from my musing. "You better be eating."

"Dad and Morgan have come by every day with food and advice. The way they're feeding me, I'll be as big as a whale before long." I patted my stomach although she couldn't see me.

"And Pax?" Ann Marie was the only person who knew about my feelings for Pax. I told her my secret when we were younger, and she encouraged me to go for it. However, she didn't understand chasing Pax had

10

the potential to backfire. My heart couldn't withstand losing what I craved most in my life. A family.

Hanging out at the Anderson home filled a void. I also didn't want to hurt Morgan, my best friend.

The boys had a pact about the women in their lives. So even though I wanted Pax, I couldn't have him. Ruining my friendship with Morgan or negatively affecting the relationship between the brothers was too great a risk.

Instead, I put all my energy into Kisses and Paws, my home away from home, and I was proud of my accomplishments. Most of the animals brought to me were cats and dogs, but I had the occasional reptile or other exotic creature. Many pets came to me with their apologetic owners in tow, but more often than not, I found them abandoned on the side of a road or at the shelter door. I worked with the wildlife preservation and animal control agencies in Bellevue to make sure they all got a second chance.

"He hasn't been by. Thank God. I don't want him seeing me like this. My nose's red, my eyes are puffy, and I haven't brushed my hair in days. I'm lucky if I can manage a shower."

"Have you called him?" The sound of a door slamming shut sounded on her end.

"No. Why would I?"

"Hold on a sec." Her muffled voice came across the line, but I couldn't make out what she said. "Sorry. I swear there are days I don't know how the company functions when I'm not around."

"Do you need to go?" She sounded exasperated, and I hated using her limited time.

"No. This is the most stimulating conversation I've

had all week. Anyway, back to what's important. Call him and entice him over to help soothe your sore body. He'd rub his hands all over you, working your muscles—"

"Stop. Now I'm all worked up. Bad enough I have a fever making me hot, but now my body's on fire and the only thing that'll help it cool off is a Pax rubdown. I can't believe you did that." My addled brain ran in overdrive with the appetizing picture Ann Marie painted.

"Ha. Once he hears your husky voice, he'll be right over with oil and massaging hands. Any man with a working dick wouldn't pass up that kind of invite."

I laughed, regretting it immediately. I clutched my throat pressing at the pain. "You can be so crass sometimes. What happened to the sweet, doll-playing Ann Marie?"

"She grew up and now works in a dog-eat-dog world. If you can't beat them, join them, is what I say. Besides, your mind is as filthy as mine. Don't go all good girl on me."

I did have a dirty mind, but it centered on one man. Oh, the things I imagined Pax and I doing to each other were X-rated. "Yeah, but I don't need to shout it from the rooftops."

Ann Marie laughed. "True. You always preferred leaving your wild side for his eyes only."

"Oh, stop. Anyway, I should go. I can't keep my eyes open. Call me tomorrow?"

"Sure, bitch. Sleep, eat, and fuck Pax, and you'll get through this."

"God, you're bad. Love you."

I disconnected the call and set the timer for the

next dose of my fever-reducing medicine. Placing the phone on the nightstand, I left the small light on. I didn't need to wake up in the middle of the night and fumble my way around in the dark. Although I improved each day, the three days I had already spent in bed worried me. I had faith in my staff, but I missed my animals.

Either way, the sooner I rested and got better, the sooner I got back to my life. Four hours later, I didn't wake to the alarm on my phone but instead to the one coming from down the hall.

Chapter Two

Pax

I ran up the stairs, ignoring my commanding officer's orders to exit. Flames lit up the sky escaping Susan's building. I hadn't seen her when I scanned the crowd outside. I also hadn't checked in on her the day before. Frantic to find her, I disobeyed orders. If something happened to her...no, I couldn't go there.

I focused on finding her. I couldn't question what I couldn't control and chose leaving the fire to my crew. I trusted them to guard my back. Susan needed my protection. I continued climbing to the fourth floor. Once there, I bent low maneuvering under the smoke line.

The fire originated on the floor above. The building's old age and wood structure didn't provide much stability. It raged fast and hot giving me little time to find her before the whole place went up in flames.

Fear made my heart beat erratically. Fear of getting to her too late. Fear of not finding her alive. Fear of never hearing her voice again.

With those thoughts, I forced my way to her apartment. Lifting my leg, I kicked her door in, the frame didn't resist. I jumped back as several overhead beams crashed around me.

I adjusted my Self Contained Breathing Apparatus,

SCBA mask, over my mouth, thankful for the clean oxygen. My gaze roamed over the apartment. Smoke overwhelmed my sight. Although futile due to my gear, I listened past the roar of the fire straining to hear a sound from Susan.

Nothing. Absolutely nothing.

"Susan. Where are you?" I mumbled into my mouthpiece seeing no point in yelling. Only my crew could hear me through the two-way radios.

I hunched down and walked through her apartment, minding my every step. I hoped the floor boards didn't collapse beneath me. I didn't find her in the living room, kitchen, or bedroom. I stood in the doorway of her room and questioned my earlier observations.

I turned and assessed my options. Smoke wafted around a closed door. The bathroom door. I sprinted down the hallway and skidded to a stop. I turned the knob with my gloved hand.

I found her curled in the bathtub. With a sigh of relief and silent thanks, I ignored my training and bolted for her. Her red hair covered her face, hiding her eyes. There were no signs of injury, yet also none of her breathing.

My heart thumped against my ribs. I feared my arrival too late. Between the thick smog and the sweat dripping down my face inside my mask, my vision blurred. I reached for her neck.

In my haste, I forgot to pull off my gloves. With frustration, I fumbled taking one off. Finally free, I reached down and relaxed only fractionally. A weak pulse drummed against my fingertips.

"I got you, baby. I'll get you out of here."

I calmed when her eyelids fluttered at my touch. I

blinked away a salty sting and took off my mask. I adjusted it over her mouth and nose. Her chest rose and fell a few times. Satisfied, I put it back on me before long, knowing I'd fail if I suffocated.

My glove and mask back in place, I reached under her lower back and knees and pulled her close. She tucked her nose into my uniform and draped her arms around my neck. The metaphorical weight on my chest lifted.

I sprinted through her apartment and back down the stairs.

"Pax, the building's going down, man. Where the fuck are you?" Other firefighters yelled into my earpiece. I rushed my steps and rounded a corner relieved to see Beck. He extended his arms, but I shook my head. Understanding, Beck turned and led the way out.

He pushed his way through the debris and I followed close behind. Fire licked our heels. I drew in a ragged breath, the exertion of carrying Susan, while in full gear, tiring me. I refused to give up and as light penetrated the thick smoke, I knew we were close. Loud creaks echoed overhead, and I pushed through with my waning energy.

Organized chaos greeted us outside. My crew worked hard containing the inferno. I didn't slow down my pace. The creaking grew louder pushing me. I increased the distance between the building and us. Once clear, I ran toward the EMS bus parked inside the safety perimeter.

I knocked off my mask with my shoulder. Susan stirred in my arms, coughed through several inhales, and hid her face further in my chest. I leaned in closer and listened to her smoke-induced raspy voice.

"I knew you'd save me. I love you," she said.

My heart rate quickened. I buried my nose in her hair and held onto words most likely not intended for me. Yet I couldn't find the will to care. Whether she meant them or not, I held her tighter not wanting to relinquish the feeling.

"Shush, baby. Your throat's dry. I've got you." I rubbed my cheek across the top of her head. Everything about the moment felt both right and wrong.

I reached the ambulance at the same time an emergency worker pulled out a gurney. I placed Susan on the bed and pulled away. Susan reached out and clutched my hand. "Stay." Desperation laced her voice, and I was powerless to reject her request.

"I'm not going anywhere," I whispered. Leaning forward I kissed her forehead. My gaze traveled across her face, saw beyond the tear-streaked soot, and committed the moment to memory.

Two EMTs rushed her through the ambulance doors and hooked her up to an oxygen line. They took her vitals, working around each other in a well-choreographed dance.

Susan didn't open her eyes but tightened her grip on my hand. The hold was awkward, and I shifted, realigning our hands. I twined our fingers together and relished her small fingers within mine. Closing my eyes, I savored the sensation.

They snapped open when she coughed. I scrutinized her for any signs of distress. Her eyes moved behind closed lids, but she slept through the commotion. I wanted nothing more than to see her sparkling hazel eyes stare back at me.

"Temp is one-hundred-three," one of the EMTs said. He hovered over her with a thermometer in hand.

"She has the flu," I told him.

"How many days has she been sick?" He pulled out an I.V. bag and needle. I sat back helpless. The confined space constricted my ability to help. It killed me inside. I couldn't reconcile my need to sit back and let them do their job with my desire to shove them aside and hold her.

"Not sure," I answered, as another answer came from behind me.

"She's been sick for five days."

My heart dropped. With Morgan's arrival, my presence was no longer needed. I knew I should have been happy to see him, but the devil on my shoulder wanted to kick him out. To tell him he was the one not needed. I wanted to be the one holding Susan's hand.

My gut wrenched when Susan stirred at the sound of his voice, reinforcing what I already knew. Susan and Morgan belonged to each other, and I had no right to come between them.

"Morgan?" she croaked out, opening her eyes for him.

I moved away as my brother came closer. "It's okay, Red. I've got you." Replacing me by her side he used the same words I had earlier. "Thanks for staying with her, man. I got here as fast as I could."

Swallowing my feelings and disappointment, I nodded. Before I gave in to my desire to hold her longer, I leaned down and whispered in Susan's ear. "Take care, beautiful." Inhaling, I filled my lungs with her scent before kissing her forehead.

Straightening, I let my gaze roam over her once

more. With my best poker face, I turned to my brother. "Let me know if you guys need anything. I'll call you if we can safely enter her apartment, but it's doubtful."

Fire engulfed the building, the distinct sound of metal bending penetrating the air. "It'll be sheer luck if the building doesn't collapse," I mumbled.

"Where're you going?" he asked, grasping my arm before I stepped out of the bus.

"She needs you. I'll only be in the way here. Besides, I have to join my crew. Take care of her." I walked away from the woman I loved and my brother without regret, but with sadness in my heart.

"Good one. Like she'll ever let me help her," he yelled at my retreating back.

I rushed back to my crew and headed to my commanding officer. Fury radiated off him. I deserved it. I disobeyed orders, yet I couldn't find the will to care. I did what I needed to do. Susan was alive and safe, and back in my brother's arms. Whatever Billy dished out in anger and instructions, I took without argument. I would change nothing if faced with the same circumstances again. "Everyone's out. Go help Beck, and I better see your ass there for the rest of the night." Billy's face reddened the longer he stared at me before he turned away. Whatever he planned would hold until we were back at the firehouse.

With a nod and one last glance toward the bus, I made my way back toward my second love; fighting fire.

****

Susan

Sounds of beeping and a quiet hum of florescent lights activated my confused brain. My eyelids heavy. I couldn't open my eyes.

Underneath the acrid smell of smoke, I got a whiff of Pax's scent. My focus too fragmented for me to determine if he was in the room, if I dreamed him up, or if his whispered, "Take care, beautiful," was only a figment of my imagination.

Concentrating took too much effort, but I reviewed the events of the day. I remembered the smell of smoke coming from the heat vents in the apartment earlier. With the effects of the medicine from the morning wearing off, the fever and chills had come back, but as the smell intensified, I realized I was in trouble. Too weak to leave, I grabbed my cell phone and it took every ounce of energy to crawl the several feet from the bedroom to the bathroom.

Once in the tub, I turned the water on, but nothing came through the pipes. Too tired to do more, I curled into a ball and prayed someone would find me—that Pax would find me.

Delirious when someone lifted me, I wrapped my arms around his neck and thought him familiar. I didn't have the strength to confirm my suspicions. Knowing I was in safe hands, I gave up my fight to stay awake.

I racked my brain over my rescue and a nugget of information pestered me. It felt like I had done something stupid, but the more I reached the further away it moved.

When I woke in the ambulance Morgan's concern-filled eyes met mine, I couldn't hold back my disappointment. I loved Morgan, but my mind and body kept reacting to the memory of Pax carrying me out of the building.

Overcome with sadness, I closed my eyes at the

beckoning tears. I yearned for Pax to be by my side, to hold me and make things right. However, my disappointment turned to anger. Angry with him for leaving me alone in the ambulance. Angry he didn't see fit to stay with me. I gasped at my ridiculous thoughts and willed my juvenile desires away. I should be admiring him. He did his job, and he did it well. Deep down I knew the fire demanded his attention, and I loved him more for his responsible and quiet sense of duty.

With thoughts of Pax tucked away, and Morgan by my side, I let my tired body win and fell back asleep.

****

I finally succeeded in prying my eyes open and looked around. I was in bed with an I.V. and oxygen tubes hooked to me. A pulse reader encased my finger and the beeps of my steady heartbeat from the monitor to my left comforted me. No longer burning up, sweat drying uncomfortably on my skin, I wanted water to ease my dry and scratchy throat.

The brightness of the room hurt, and I squinted. Through hazy sight, I focused on a blurry figure standing by the foot of the bed. Recognition only dawning through the sound of his voice.

"Hey, Red," Morgan said. "Welcome back. It's good to see you alive."

"Water...pl..."

He came around and reached behind my head helping me tilt forward before I finished my sentence. Morgan held a straw to my lips, and I sipped greedily at the ice-cold water. I moaned as it soothed my throat.

"Slow down, Red. You'll make yourself sick," Morgan said, as he pulled the straw away. He gently placed my head back on my pillow and grinned down at me. "Better?"

"Much better, thanks," I answered with a small smile. "What time is it?"

He pulled his phone from his back pocket and checked the time. "It's two in the morning. They brought you in last night at seven. Your fever's down, and since you have no lasting complications from smoke inhalation, the doctor said you can leave tomorrow. Well, later today, I guess."

I surveyed the room, taking in the generic surroundings. "Did they save the building?"

Morgan's gaze strayed across the room, not making eye contact with me.

"Morgan?"

Clearing his throat, he took my hand and sat on the edge of my bed. "Sorry, Red. There's not much left. Pax texted me earlier and said the building is closed for the time being. All the units ruined either by fire, smoke, or water." He leaned down, kissed my forehead, and made his way across the room where he paced in front of the door.

I closed my eyes against the onslaught of sadness, fighting back tears. I didn't own much, but I had a few irreplaceable mementos. "I don't care about the furniture or clothes. I can replace all of it. I want my mom's hope chest."

He stopped and faced me. "Don't worry. I'll talk to Pax and see if anything were salvageable."

Morgan resumed his pacing. He and Pax resembled each other. Both stood over six feet tall, with jet-black hair and hold-you-captive bluish-gray eyes. Pax was turning twenty-nine in a few weeks, and Morgan twenty-seven three days later. They worked hard, loved their family, and were loyal to a fault. Both loved taking risks, Pax with fighting fires, and Morgan with his motorcycles.

That is where the similarities ended.

Broad shouldered and built with muscles on top of muscles, Pax outweighed Morgan's lean mass. Morgan covered his body in tattoos while Pax had one on his right shoulder extending down his arm. They were my two favorite men. One I loved like a brother and the other I'd loved forever.

Morgan and I became friends in first grade after I knocked John Beach on his ass when he relentlessly teased Morgan about his glasses. I didn't have the best social skills at the time and preferred staying out of the way, but when the kid cornered Morgan, I jumped in without thinking. John grabbed me as he went down. I fell, bracing on my arm, and broke a bone.

Morgan became my self-imposed helper, carried my backpack, and walked me to and from my dad's car every day. He sat with me at lunch. He unpacked my food, put the straw in my juice, and opened any bags my dad packed.

It was sweet, but he wasn't trying to be. He took the blame for my injury, his guilt driving his actions. Assisting me helped him deal with the guilt of his perceived mistake. We became inseparable, and twenty years later, we were still best friends.

When I was eight Morgan invited me to his home. My dad didn't understand why I chose a boy for a best friend, but after days of begging and a conversation between our dads, he finally relented. He came with me the first time and ended up staying. He hung out with

Mr. Anderson while I played with Morgan in the backyard.

Mrs. Anderson returned home as we were leaving, with ten-year-old Pax, six-year-old Jesse, and four-year-old Foster in tow. I stood in awe. I knew Morgan had brothers, but I had never met them. Even though we attended the same elementary school, Pax was in fourth grade and in a different building.

I couldn't tear my gaze from Pax, and I might have drooled. My memories were fuzzy, but I remembered doing whatever I could to hang out at the Anderson home. My infatuation for Pax grew along with the fear and shyness to do anything about it.

Through the years, many of our friends thought Morgan and I were a couple. No matter the number of times we denied our relationship status, our friends labeled us as girlfriend and boyfriend.

One night, Morgan proposed we give in and date. Agreeing, I sealed it with a kiss before I lost my courage. We stood silent for a few awkward minutes then broke down laughing. Moments later, we calmed down and blurted, "That's like kissing my sister/brother." We were better as friends.

"Hey, Red?" Morgan asked, snapping me out of my memories.

"Sorry. I'm just tired." I rubbed a shaky hand down my face, realizing the truth behind my words.

"Rest. I'll be here when you wake up and take you to your dad's. He came by earlier, but I made him go home. He needed sleep," Morgan said. He sat in what looked like the most uncomfortable chair. He winked, as if reading my mind. "I've sat on a bike seat harder and for far longer. I'll be fine. I'll text your dad and give him an update. Mom's going over later in the morning to help him get your room ready. Sleep."

Unable to keep my eyes open, I closed them and relinquished control of my tired and aching body. I survived the fire, but I needed my strength to face the coming days. I dreamed of Pax sitting by my side, holding my hand, and pulling me into a hug. I relaxed and enjoyed my imaginary moments with him.

Chapter Three

Pax

Distractions plagued me throughout the rest of my shift. Since the fire at Susan's building was toward the end of my second day, I only had to return to the station house and complete paperwork. My body ached from the nine hours we fought the fire, and I couldn't concentrate, only wanting to leave and check on Susan before heading home. Even though Morgan's texts said she was stable, I wanted to see her. Unfortunately, I had a few more hours before I could leave.

Around me, the other firemen snored in their sleep. Every time I closed my eyes, images of Susan huddling in the tub, frail, and fevered, played a constant loop. I shuddered thinking of various negative scenarios.

Giving up on sleep, I rose and stripped off my clothes. I gathered my belongings for another shower. The smell of smoke still seeped from my pores. Down to my boxers with a towel and a change of underwear in hand, I headed to the bathroom. I stopped at the sound of approaching footsteps. I turned and found Billy silhouetted in the doorway.

"Anderson, get your ass in my office, now," he said, stirring several of the crew.

I hung my head, swallowed back the bile in my throat, and gave him a slight nod. I knew Billy needed to reprimand me for my actions, but I foolishly wished for a delay.

"I'll be down in a sec. Need to get dressed."

"You have one minute," he said, and walked away.

I sighed at his retreating back and hurried to my locker and grabbed a pair of faded, well-worn jeans and a gray T-shirt sporting the firehouse crest. I slid my feet into a pair of sneakers, foregoing socks in a rush to get to Billy's office. I ran down the stairs tripping over my feet. I didn't want to piss him off any more.

"Shut the door," Billy commanded, without tearing his gaze from the papers on his desk as I walked inside. Before I closed the door, he started. "What the fuck were you thinking? I didn't give the okay for you to go in, and I sure as hell didn't stutter when I ordered everyone to clear out."

I made to interject, but he lifted his hand silencing me. "Don't fucking speak right now. I can have your ass and promotion for this. You disobeyed a direct order. You not only put yourself in harm's way, but you also jeopardized your crew. I had to send them in after your sorry ass. You messed up, and I'm not letting this one go."

"Billy, I'm sorry for not following orders, but I'm not sorry for going in. A civilian needed our help. Susan needed our help." I played my only available card and hoped he didn't call me out on it.

He calmed at the mention of Susan and stepped around his desk, standing before me. Leaning back, he rested his ass on the edge of the desk and crossed his legs at the ankles. "I get that. But you should've talked to me. I'm not a heartless bastard. I would have sent someone with you. Instead, you ignored the rules we have in place. Those very rules are there keeping you

27

and the civilians we rescue safe." He pushed off the desk and rounded the corner. He settled back in his seat, pulled out a paper, and held it to me. "I'm putting you on warning. Another stunt like that and it'll be the desk for you for three months."

I breathed a sigh of relief. I hated desk duty, but a three-month probationary period was cake.

"However, your actions cannot go unpunished." He smirked. I hesitated to take the paper from him, but he wiggled it leaving me no choice. I took it and placed it on my lap without reading it. "The Community Outreach Picnic is coming up. No one's volunteered to oversee it yet. I believe this'll be the perfect opportunity for you to make amends."

I groaned. "Sir…"

"No." He held up his hands again. "I've made my decision. Have your ideas to me for the theme by the end of Friday shift, next week."

****

With little time left, I skipped the second shower. However, I took off my shoes and put on socks. Jokes and laughter dogged my steps as I left the firehouse. Secrets were hard to hold onto in the close quarters we shared, especially since the men liked to gossip like high school girls. I knew they taunted me in good faith, and under normal circumstances, I would join them. But I had somewhere else to be.

The rising sun colored the sky in pink and orange hues as I left the firehouse and climbed into my truck. If I had a minute, I might have stopped and admired the fresh, crisp morning air, but I didn't.

I texted Morgan before starting up the engine. He responded with Susan's room number. Within ten minutes, I walked through the front doors of the hospital. I may or may not have driven faster than the speed limit. Once inside, I made my way to Susan's room. I spotted Morgan sitting in the waiting room a few feet away. Veering, I went over to him instead.

Settling into the uncomfortable chair next to him, I laid my hand on his shoulder. "How's she doing?" I asked, holding my breath. My brother looked like he'd gone through hell and back. His hair stood on end as if he'd ran his hand through it numerous times, and his bloodshot eyes appeared tired.

"She's doing better. Her fever's down, and she didn't stir when the nurses took her vitals."

I closed my eyes in relief. "Have you slept yet?"

"Nah, man, I'm fine. I didn't want to leave her alone. Her dad came by for an hour when she was admitted, but I sent him home when it got too late."

"Why don't you leave too? I'll stay with her." I was genuinely concerned but, say what you will, I wanted time alone with her.

"You can't. You're tired, and it's been a long night for you." Morgan leaned back on the stiff chair and laid his head against the top.

I rubbed his shoulder. Any more display of worry or affection, and he would close off. "I'm good. I'm still running on a high. Go. I got this. Did the doctor say when they'll discharge her? Is she going to stay with you?" I asked, not sure I wanted to hear his answer to my last question.

He shook his head, and the tension left my shoulders. "She can leave today, but she's staying with her dad."

I stood when he did and followed him into Susan's

room. She slept soundly, and I smiled at her soft snores.

She was alive, and my shoulders sagged more. The knot in my neck eased seeing her, and I no longer cared my brother stood next to me. Ensuring her safe return to Morgan was not only the right thing to do, it was the necessary thing. I could never allow any force, including me, to break them apart.

"What the hell happened? She was sick when I talked to her yesterday. She couldn't even hold her phone long enough to talk to me. How'd she make it out?" Morgan whispered, as he kept his affectionate gaze focused on Susan.

"He carried her out," Rob said from the doorway, surprising Morgan and me.

Rob and Beck, two of my crew, walked into the room. "He didn't follow orders and ran into the falling building like the bullhead he is."

Morgan faced me, surprise clear on his face.

I shrugged, not needing or wanting my brother's thankful expression. Morgan didn't need to know I went in after Susan not for him, but for myself, and I didn't need my selfishness appreciated. "What? It's my job, man. I only did what everyone on my crew would have done."

Beck laughed while shaking his head. "Nah. You were in a league of your own yesterday. How did you know she was still in the building?" He looked over to Morgan. "We were given the order to evacuate, and this crazy one," he cocked his thumb toward me, "charges up the stairs instead of heading out. Our CO spat profanities faster than a sailor. He sent Rob and me in after him. But before we could assist, he," Beck said, pointing again at me, "had her, running fast with fire licking at his back. No sooner than we got out, the fifth floor collapsed, making every floor beneath it hazardous. If you ask me, he should get a medal, not punishment."

I jostled Beck's shoulder feeling uneasy at his praise. "I didn't follow orders, and even though it ended up well, it could have easily turned bad."

"Pax, shut up. I didn't know you saved her, and I for one am glad you didn't follow orders," Morgan said as he pulled me into a tight hug. Surprised at the rare embrace, I let him hold me for the few seconds. The only people he'd put his arms around were our mother, Kate, and Susan.

I wiped away a stray tear before anyone noticed. I cleared my throat and took a moment controlling the timbre of my voice before speaking. "She's your girl, man. She's family. There was no way I'd leave her in there. I swore an oath…"

Beck wrapped his arm around my shoulder. "Yeah? We all swore the same oath, yet none of us disobeyed The Bear. Take his thanks. Yesterday, Susan was lucky to have you in her corner."

After several minutes of tough guy talk and back slaps, Beck and Rob headed out. I sat in the chair by her bed while Morgan leaned in, kissing her forehead. It sparked a pang of jealousy, but I pushed it away. I wasn't lying before. Susan was his girl. End of story. I would deny myself and ensure my brother's happiness.

"I'm going to head home for a quick nap and a shower. I'll be back in a couple of hours," Morgan said as he straightened.

"Take your time."

He tapped my shoulder twice and left, closing the

door quietly behind him.

With no witnesses, I scooted my chair closer to the bed and pulled Susan's hand into mine. Raising our entwined fingers to my lips, I kissed each of her knuckles, then returned our hands, resting them on the mattress. I rubbed circles with my thumb along the inside of her wrist and let out a deep sigh.

Susan's presence and sure breathing calmed me, slowed my heart from its rapid and erratic rate. With the last of the adrenaline gone, fatigue took over. I rested my forehead on the cool sheets alongside our hands and allowed the miniscule proximity. In reality, I wanted to climb into bed with her, hold her, and feel her heartbeat against my cheek. Instead, I remained seated in the chair as close as I dared and once again thanked the forces that be I got to her in time.

For three hours, I perched on the edge of my seat, and listened to the monitors. Her chest rose and fell with each steady breath, and I felt her pulse against my fingertips. I dared not move, and the few times she stirred, her skin dampened with sweat, and I whispered reassurances. When she was restless, I ran my fingers through her hair and massaged her scalp as I had seen Morgan do many times. I relaxed as she calmed and smiled each time she squeezed my hand in response.

The few times I dozed off, images of her burning in the building plagued my mind, and I woke up agitated. The comfort of her hand in mine kept me sane. But the possibility of losing her would bombard me if I left her side. Even with her safely ensconced in the bed, I couldn't find any semblance of peace and wondered if keeping her close or seeing the department therapist would be better medicine for my battered heart.

Chapter Four

Pax

Every Sunday my parents, Emily and Ted, hosted a picnic during the warmer days and brunch when it got colder.

Having finished two more shift rotations busier than the one of Susan's fire, my body needed rest. I went home and slept for three hours, waking up in a cold sweat feeling like the room was caving in around me. Nightmares plagued my sleep since Susan's rescue. They kept me awake most nights.

Unable to fall back asleep I headed to my parents' home early, hoping company kept the 'what if' scenarios at bay.

As each of my brothers and cousins arrived, the noise level increased. Mom smiled contently watching her large family together under one roof. We lived near our childhood home, except Caden, my oldest cousin, lived on the road as a sports agent. My aunt and uncle, Karen and Dustin Sr., died in a car crash when Caden was twelve. My parents took him and his siblings in, ten-year-old Parker, nine-year-old Dustin, and three-year-old Kate. I was a year younger than Caden when they came to live with us and room assignments reconfigured, mixing us together to strengthen our bonds.

I shared a room with Caden. Morgan and Jesse

made up the second room, while Foster, Parker, and Dustin were in the third. They were inseparable. Kate got her own. Growing up, we tormented my mom with extreme activities and non-stop movement. We were close before the Jacksons passed away but living together cemented our brotherly bond. We were overprotective of Kate, not only because she was the only girl, but because she was the youngest.

Although my mom wanted to celebrate my promotion for the past week, I begged her to concentrate on Caden's return home instead.

Mom squealed at Caden's arrival, dropping the meat platter onto the closest counter. She ran to him, pulling him into a tight hug, and rested her head on his chest. Caden stood the tallest of us and engulfed Mom's petite frame in his arms.

After several minutes, she pulled away and wiped her tears with the back of her hands. Noticing the kids standing around watching her emotional display, she smiled wide and fumbled to speak. "What? I miss all of you when you're not here," she said as she patted Caden's chest. He wrapped an arm around her shoulders and kept her tucked into his side. Mom leaned in closer to him, and whispered, but not quietly enough for us not to overhear, "but you, I miss most of all."

I smiled. She said it to each one of us when she hugged us. My mom never had a favorite. She loved us equally and provided a rock-solid role model to live by. Her husband and kids were her world, family above all else.

I waited for my brothers and cousins to greet Caden before I made my way over. I clapped him on the back and came closer. He did his best hiding the sadness in his eyes behind a smile. But I knew him. He never spoke of it, but his parents' deaths weighed on him, and their loss played a role in the way he lived his life.

It wasn't the first time I thought he'd chosen a traveling job to escape memories of his parents and our hometown. He didn't share his feelings, ever, so I learned early on to be a quiet ear. In the eighteen years since his parents died, he'd only revealed his emotional state twice, and I planned to be there for him when he needed to do it again.

"Hey, old man. Good to have you home. How long this time?" I asked.

"Who are you calling old man? Isn't your birthday two months away?" He pulled me into a fierce hug. Caden never shied away from showing his affection. In the years he and his siblings lived with us, Caden held us close whenever we needed it. "I'm not sure how long I'll be home. I have to go south in a month."

"Mom'll be happy. She doesn't shut up about you when you're gone. It's always Caden this, or Caden that. I swear I'm tired of hearing about your sorry ass."

Caden yanked me into a light chokehold. I fought half-heartedly to get away. Using his foot, he dislodged me and forced my face into his armpit. He held onto the back of my head and rubbed against me. It was an old trick he used on me, and it never ceased to make me laugh.

"Shit, man, use deodorant," I joked. I could have maneuvered out, but the sound of my sibling's laughter made me happy. I reached my arm around his back and pulled on his pants, just like when we were kids.

"I'm not wearing undies. Not going to work," he grunted. I may not have been fighting him, but it still took a lot of strength to hold me.

"Gross, man. That's more information than I needed." Redirecting, I lifted my hand and yanked his hair.

With my face still in his pit, and his hair fisted in my hand we both yelled, "Mercy." He let go of me and we fell to the floor. "I missed you, man," I said, between laughs.

Caden sat up and rested his elbows on his bent knees. He eyed me from under his lashes and filled his lungs with ragged breaths. His face lost its red hue as he regained control. "I missed you, too, and congratulations."

I stood, extended my hand to him, and helped him to his feet. "Thanks. It means a lot coming from you."

He smiled in response, and together we headed out to the backyard.

****

"Pax," my mom yelled out the back door for me.

I stopped horsing around with my brothers, which gave them the advantage they needed to tackle me. I groaned when I realized my mistake a little too late.

"Mom," I whined from my prone position, "you distracted me." I stood and rubbed dirt off my clothes before I ran to the deck and jumped over the railing instead of climbing the steps.

My mom swatted me and laughed at my antics. "One day you're going to get hurt doing that, young man. This old heart can't take it."

I pulled my mom into a one-armed hug and kissed the top of her head.

"You're the youngest one here, Mom. There's no getting old for this lady," I told her. "What's up?"

"I forgot to buy Caden's favorite salad dressing."

"'Nuff said. I'll go to the store," I replied, kissing her again before running through the house and grabbing my keys from the table by the door.

With Caden home Mom treated him like a king. Since we all stopped by unannounced, she kept our favorites stocked. A thought struck before I made it out the door. I turned back and headed to the kitchen where my mother stood sheepishly.

"Hey, Ma? I was thinking. There's no way you forgot his salad dressing," I said, as I reached over and hugged her shoulders. "Why don't you tell me what this trip is really about?"

"You're too perceptive. I can't get anything by you, can I?" she responded and punched me in the stomach.

I hunched over and feigned a shortness of breath. She laughed, making my heart beat faster. I loved making people laugh, especially my mom.

"I need you to go convince Susan and her dad to come over. She's been given a clean bill of health, and it's been over a week since the fire," she said.

To be exact, it had been eight days, nineteen hours, and twenty-four minutes since my heart stopped beating, but who's counting?

I protested. The situation called for Morgan's help, not mine. "I've already talked to Morgan. He said he tried. She's sad. She needs her family right now."

"Mommmm," I grumbled, "what makes you think she'll listen to me?"

She smacked me again, harder this time. "She will

do anything you ask. She always has. She might be Morgan's best friend, but…"

I cocked my eyebrow at her hesitation. "But what?"

"But nothing. Go over there and convince her to join us. Her dad as well. I have an extra pie I made and hid from your father. You can take it home if you do it," she said, winking at me.

I groaned. I loved my mom's lemon pie. I'd do about anything for pie. "Fine. I'll see what I can do." I kissed her forehead then turned to leave. I beamed as I tossed my keys and left the kitchen. Mom had improved my day. I hadn't seen Susan since the morning after the fire.

"You'll always be my favorite," Mom yelled as I ran out the door. Before I got in my truck, she was at the door waving for me to stop. "Don't make it obvious," she said, when she got within whispering distance.

"Don't make what obvious?" my younger brother, Foster, asked as he rounded the corner of the house.

My mom startled and flushed at his appearance. I smiled at her inability to be devious. "Mom forgot Caden's favorite dressing. I'm going to the store for her, and she doesn't want me to make it obvious I'm her favorite, and she forgot about him," I joked.

Mom smacked me again, but a chuckle escaped her lips.

Foster looked from me to Mom and shook his head. "Whatever. Just hurry back. I'm starving."

"You're always hungry. You're still a growing boy," I jibed.

Foster, with his lighter blond hair and green eyes,

looked different from my brothers and me. His body more tanned, due to the many hours he spent in the sun. He lost weight since he injured his back while surfing competitively two years ago. Many months in rehab, and a couple of surgeries later, he'd made it back into the water but as an instructor. I was damn proud of him. He beat the odds. Doctors told him he'd never walk unassisted again, but he refused to listen to them.

"Ha, ha. There will come a time when I will make you eat those words, *big* brother."

Chapter Five

Pax

Susan sat with her head down and feet tucked under her on the front porch stoop of her dad's house, a large split-level, with red brick, black shutters, and a two-story porch. A well-tended, bright green lawn, with small flowerbeds along the walkway, led to the front steps.

I wanted to sit beside her, put my arms around her shoulders, and draw her to my side. Not only did I want her in my arms, but once there I knew I'd never let her go. Morgan's scowling face penetrated my thoughts and destroyed those images. I had no right fantasizing about her. It was a betrayal of my brother.

Yet I couldn't take my eyes off her. The sun glinted off her face, making her appear angelic. I debated taking my phone out of the glove box and capturing the moment. She was beautiful with her long red hair flowing over her shoulders, and my fingers itched to play with the strands. I wanted to fix whatever dimmed her light and bring back her smile.

I sat too long in my truck watching her, taking in her beauty, from her feet to the makeup free face. My skin heated when she spotted me. With a hesitant wave, she plastered on a small smile. Susan looked as Mom said. Sad.

Climbing out of my truck, I made my way over to

her. "Hey. Why so glum?"

"Hey, Pax," she whispered. "Today's Sunday. Why aren't you at your parents?"

"I came for you. Why aren't you at the picnic? Did Morgan forget to pick you up?" I asked.

Her eyes rounded, and she stood. In her haste, she stumbled, and I grabbed her hips steadying her. Through the thin cotton fabric of my shirt, the heat of her palms seared the skin of my chest. My heart rate skyrocketed, and I hoped she didn't notice. Over the years, I avoided touching her, because I knew the sensation would be addictive.

The unexpected contact tested my limits, and I held back a moan. I wanted to feel those hands on my bare skin. I grew hard, and I fought my instincts to pull her closer. I dropped my hands and stuffed them in my pockets.

She moved back, increasing the space between us. It wasn't what I wanted. I wanted her in my arms, my lips on hers, my hands on her hips pulling her back against my body. I struggled to get the ideas out of my head, willing my caveman thoughts back into their cave.

It didn't help when she flicked her hair off her shoulders, showing her long lean neck. I wanted to lick, kiss, and bite the skin where her neck met her shoulder, take my time exploring her, and finding out what made her whimper. The breeze wafted around us. It carried her scent of apple and cinnamon toward me, and I leaned closer.

"He didn't forget," she said, pulling me out of my haze and I quickly tilted away. "I didn't want to go." Her watery gaze swept past me.

Giving in, I cupped her chin, bringing her attention back. "Why not? You always come."

"It's family. I didn't want to intrude." She pulled her chin from my grasp. I stepped and closed the distance between us, not giving her a chance to draw away again.

"Bullshit. You're family. Have been for a long time."

Her gaze drifted over her shoulder.

"I can't. I promised Dad I'd make him dinner. It's in the oven."

"Your dad's always welcome. I know my dad would enjoy his company," I said. "Grab your casserole, seeing as how Foster never stops eating, and your food will be a perfect addition. We'll bring it with us. Mom always makes enough food to feed an army platoon, so two more mouths won't make a difference. Besides, my mom will be even more excited to have you guys over than she is to have Caden home."

"Okay, I guess."

I turned her and urged her into the house. She yelled for her dad telling him of the change of plans. I waited outside and listened to them moving about inside. A few minutes later, they exited, and I took the casserole from Susan while she locked the door.

"Hello, Pax."

"Sir," I said, with a tilt of my head. "Glad you could join us today."

"I can never turn down your mom's cooking." I followed them down the steps and to the truck where Mr. Hayes directed Susan to the front seat. I turned away keeping my smile hidden. The gleam in his eyes told me I failed.

****

Susan

I stood on the back deck watching the Andersons and Jacksons talk and play. My busy mind deprived me of the energy to join them. I needed more space for the animals at my shelter, but I didn't have a clue on how to raise the money or renovate the area.

"Hey. Whatcha doing?" Kate asked from behind me.

"Watching everyone." I kept my back to her. For all her aplomb, Kate was observant. I didn't need her seeing my fake happiness.

"Well, why aren't you over there giving my brothers hell? God knows they need it."

I adored Kate like a sister. Although five years younger than me, I envied her easy manner, and the way she took life on with a sense of freedom and fun. Kate loved life, chipper no matter the situation. You could never be sad around her, making her perfect for her current job. She waitressed at Parker and Dustin's bar while attending her last year in college.

"Just enjoying the beautiful scenery," I said without thinking. I bowed my head in embarrassment.

She giggled but let my remark go. Something told me she knew what I meant by beautiful scenery, but she was wrong. I wasn't watching Morgan. My focus was on Pax.

"How's the apartment hunt going? I'm happy you salvaged your mother's stuff."

"I couldn't believe it. The floors on the front side of the building collapsed. My bedroom in the back remained intact. Even with the water damage, my mom's box remained unscathed, and Pax found it. I don't know how I will ever repay him." My smile widened thinking of Pax and what he'd done for me.

"Your mom was watching over you and used Pax to keep you safe. He's not looking for payback. He does stuff like that because he likes seeing you smile." Her eyes widened, and she raised her hand to her mouth. "Besides," she continued, as she waved her hand, "Morgan explained the importance of the box to him. Once he knew, he went through hell finding it in the rubble." Again, she appeared shocked at her own words. She turned away, but not fast enough to hide her flushed cheeks. "We were all happy to hear you made it out okay, especially Mom. She loves you like a daughter."

I took a moment remembering my own mom. I missed her although I didn't recall much about her. What I missed most were the lost opportunities a girl had with her mother. Yet I was fortunate to have Mrs. Anderson. Over the years, she became more of a maternal figure than simply my friend's mom.

"I can help you in your apartment search or when you move in. The boys can help. You say the word and I'll get them together," she rambled on, pulling me from my melancholy.

"Do you need a drink? I want one but they all keep giving me this look as if I can't have one. Argh. It's so aggravating. I mean, I'm twenty-two and they still treat me like a baby. Maybe we should have a drink and show them how girls do it."

I laughed and turned, facing her. I placed my hand on her arm. "We better not. I have to figure some stuff out, and I don't want a fuzzy head or a hangover while I do it."

"What kind of stuff?" Kate placed her hands on her hips. The expression on her face told me I couldn't avoid answering. With a sigh, I motioned to the chairs at the edge of the deck.

I needed to talk to someone. I always felt better after I spoke my thoughts aloud. Morgan listened to me rant and rave the previous night but remained his usual silent self. He didn't give answers or solutions because he knew how much I hated his quick reactions and tendency to try to fix things. Kate, on the other hand, didn't hesitate to voice her opinion.

We sat and faced each other. I looked around, not because I didn't want anyone overhearing, but because my gaze never wandered from Pax for long. I spotted him talking to Parker and Dustin, and I settled into my chair.

"I've outgrown the shelter. I have too many animals and not enough space. With more coming in every day. I have enough land to build, but I don't have the money or the know-how." I moaned.

"Oh my God. Did you sigh?" Kate asked. "I can't believe Miss-Always-Look-At-The-Bright-Side is sighing. If I didn't know better, I'd say you're having a pity party for one."

My eyes widened in surprise. Kate tended to speak her mind. Usually she directed her craziness toward others, and for the first time since we became friends, she focused her no-filter words at me.

"All I'm saying is there's a solution for every problem. But you can't come up with one if you're all sad and internalizing. Think of what you need to get this done and then do it. Simple."

Standing, she tugged at my hand and pulled me

with her to the food table. "Come on. Let's eat and figure something out. I always think better after I've had one of Dad's burgers. I swear he puts smart spice in them making us all brighter. Whatever it is, it works. Besides, the hoard hasn't come over yet. There might be food left for us. They all eat like pigs. Have you seen Caden yet? My brother's put on another twenty pounds of muscle since the last time I saw him. Then there's Pax. He's intent on living up to his nickname. All he ever does is lift weights. Says he wants to be stronger to better help victims. Between the two of them, I think Mom's couch's going to collapse."

I stopped myself from laughing and placed my hand on her arm. "Breathe, woman," I demonstrated the art of taking in a deep breath. She copied my exaggerated motions, fighting back her laughter. I didn't know how she spoke so fast or for so long without inhaling. Pure talent. Or survival. It couldn't have been easy growing up with seven boys.

Chapter Six

Pax

I approached with my heaping plate of food to the only available seat at the picnic table. The one next to Susan. I looked around for another option and found none. Besides my mom and dad, my family sat around the table, talking and laughing.

I spotted my parents by the sliding door whispering to each other. Curious to know what they were up to I watched them from a distance. When Mom blushed and smiled, I turned away, not wanting to intrude on their private moment. I handled their affection fine, but I didn't need to think about what happened behind closed doors.

"Pax, take a seat," Kate said. She patted the empty spot beside her. Having no other choice, I squeezed into the miniscule space between her and Susan. Susan's light scent hit me like a ton of bricks. With great effort, I avoided touching her. I didn't trust myself if we made contact.

Mom and Dad joined us at the table. Mom sat on the other side of Susan while Dad stood at the head of the table. He raised his glass, and everyone followed suit and waited for Dad. He cleared his throat and reached his empty hand out to Mom. She grasped it with a grin on her face. He let his gaze roam across each of us before he spoke.

"To have each of you here today brings your mom and me immense joy. Caden," he said, pointing his glass toward my cousin. "We miss you. We're glad you're here today and look forward to your permanent return home. However, and as much as he hates the attention, we would be remiss if we didn't congratulate Pax on his promotion." He turned to me. "We admire you for your devotion and hard work. Mom and I are very proud of you." I nodded in acknowledgment. "We're also honored seeing the rest of you grow into fine young men and women. The road ahead is wide open and each of you has chosen a path unique and personal to you. We are proud of you all. Here's to many more years of adventure." He raised his glass higher. "To family."

A chorus of 'to family' rang out around the table and we took a sip of our drinks. Conversation picked up soon after, and the laughter of my family brought me a sense of calm and peace. Even as I sat aware of the heat coming from Susan's body, our arms accidentally rubbing against each other, I kept my head down. I knew looking at her would be my undoing, so it was best to focus on my food.

****

Susan

"Thank you for having my dad and me, Mrs. Anderson."

She patted me on the arm, admonishing me. "Hush, child. How many times have I told you to call me Emily?" she said. "How have you been? Is there anything I can do?"

"No, Mrs. Ander...Emily," I faltered, after she gave me her infamous frown. "Dad's been great. He's

48

helping me with the insurance company. We're waiting for the fire investigator to file his conclusions. Hopefully it won't be much longer."

"Have you asked Pax about it?"

"No." I turned to Pax sitting beside me. From the moment he sat down, I warmed from the heat of his body alongside mine and as each minute passed, I fought the urge to reach out and kiss him, but I discovered a few ways of "accidentally" rubbing my hand along his leg. If I could justify sitting on his lap without anyone's notice, including him, I would have.

I imagined straddling his legs, wrapping my arms around him, and sighing as he licked my neck. I would rub against every inch of his length. Lost in my fantasy I didn't register Mrs. Anderson's concerned expression until the heat of Pax's hand warmed my thigh. I grabbed my glass of lemonade needing a minute to cool off.

"Susan, are you okay?" he whispered. "Your face is red. How can I help?"

Lemonade spewed out my nose. My flush deepened. I imagined all the ways he could help. He tapped me on the back as Mrs. Anderson handed me a napkin. I dabbed my face and hid my reddened skin.

Once I gained control over my features, I turned and faced Pax again. My gaze landed on his, and what seemed like days, but was probably only seconds, we held each other's stare. I forgot about my embarrassment lost in his darkening eyes. Morgan's unsubtle coughing across the table pulled me away.

"I'm sorry. Don't know what came over me." I turned my attention back to Mrs. Anderson. I shook my head and remembered her initial question. "No, no, I haven't asked him."

She remained silent, watching me with interest, thinking through something I didn't want to guess at. With a slight nod of her head, she turned back to her plate.

"Morgan said you only wanted a box with your mom's keepsakes in it. Did you get it back?"

I smiled my first real smile since the fire. "Yeah, I did. It's the only reason I'm not losing my marbles over this fire. I may have lost everything else I owned but losing the last bit of Mom I had would have been too much for me to handle."

I appreciated Mrs. Anderson's sweet smile. I didn't want her pity. Moreover, she never gave it. She always provided a listening ear and a warm hug. She didn't replace Mom but became a person I always relied on. It further reinforced my reasons for not pursuing Pax.

"I met this wonderful young lady, Kristan. She has a place at Richard's Creek. Says she loves the security a gated complex provides." I knew not to interrupt Mrs. Anderson. She always had a point to make. "She moved in with a roommate, and they updated everything. She loves the proximity to both downtown and the water. A bit of both worlds, she says. It's close to where you lived. I can call her and see if she knows if there are any other apartments available."

Not sure about the idea, I agreed nonetheless. It didn't hurt for her to find out. "Sure. Thanks for thinking of me."

I fell silent and moved the food around my plate, lost in thought. My mind drifted between the shelter, my lack of solutions, and Pax's presence beside me.

His breath tickled the little hairs on my neck as he

spoke. "You need to eat."

I regarded him from under my lashes. I wasn't ready for the full force of Pax's attention on me. Even with my obscured view, I still fell into the depth of his stare. My gaze dropped to his lips as he placed a bite of potato salad into his mouth. How he made eating an erotic act I didn't know. At his quiet snicker, I knew my ogling hadn't gone unnoticed.

His proximity, unwavering attention, and smile tied me in knots. I couldn't look away or keep looking at him without doing something stupid. I bit my lip. Pax's breath hitched, and his eyes widened. He pulled my lip from between my teeth with his thumb, and I fought to hold in a whimper.

My body clenched at the minute touch. He smiled, and in that moment, I swore his gaze was carnal. Animalistic. My mind went blank, desire sweeping through my body. I lucked out when his brother, Parker, distracted him with a question. With his focus elsewhere, I took in a much-needed breath. It didn't help. All I smelled was Pax. All I felt was Pax. All I was aware of was Pax.

Mrs. Anderson put her hand on mine, drawing me out from my short-lived reprieve. "You will never fatten up, if you don't eat. No matter what's on your mind, food will help."

"I don't need to fatten up, Mrs. Anderson," I said, but then worried I offended her with my disinterest in the meal before me. "It's not the food, and you're right. I have a lot on my mind. I'm sorry."

"No need to apologize. Tell me what's got you worried." She set her fork down and turned to face me.

Much like Kate, Mrs. Anderson rarely took no for

an answer. This was one of those times I knew I couldn't wave her off. "I've outgrown my shelter. More people are dropping off strays every day, and I don't have the space. I can't turn them away. I have land, but I have no money to build, and I don't have the foggiest idea of what to build." *And I'm in love with your son. No, not Morgan. Pax.*

I stopped talking, out of breath, surprised that I divulged as much as I had. However, Mrs. Anderson tended to bring out the young, scared girl in me.

When she said nothing, I panicked and continued, "When I bought the building, Dad and Morgan made all the construction decisions. However, Dad's tired, and Morgan's busy with his bike designs. I don't want to ask either of them to put their lives on hold to help me out. Morgan said he'd give me a loan, but I can't ask him. Friends should never loan each other money."

Her eyes sparkled and crinkled at the corners. She laughed out loud, drawing the attention of her family.

"Sorry, sweetheart. I'm not laughing at you." She tapped her hand on mine. "You reminded me of me when I was your age. If you can't ask your friends and family for help, then what else have you got? Ted had this one friend. He asked him for money." Her eyes grew hazy, and she stared off into space, lost in her memories. "Ted didn't have much, but he was damn determined to help him. They struck a deal and shook on it. Ted loaned him as much as he could, five thousand dollars. It was a lot of money for Ted, especially since he was wooing me at the time." She blushed and fanned her face.

I took a bite of my salad, smiling, and listened to her story. "Anyway, they agreed to work through any complications, and Ted helped him further by being his partner. They started their small boating business and worked hard together. Ted made his money back within a few months and then asked me to marry him. One night the three of us went to dinner and Ted asked me to bring my sister. Karen met Dustin Sr. that night, and they fell in love. They got married before Ted and me. I was happy for her. For *all* of us. If Dustin Sr. hadn't approached Ted and Ted hadn't put his faith in his friend, things could have turned out differently. We were all busy and struggling to become financially secure, but friendship ended up becoming family. Do you understand?"

I nodded my head although I didn't see how her story related to my situation. My mind drifted and without rhyme or reason, I sought out Pax. He winked when he spotted me looking his way. The butterflies in my stomach took flight, and I spun away, my drink teetering on the table from my jerky movement. I reached out steadying my glass to Mrs. Anderson's quiet giggles.

"What you need is a plan. I'm sure when you sit down to it, you'll figure it out," she told me, patting my hand again. Gesturing with her other hand, she perused the table. "Look around you. Every one of these kids views you as family. They'll bend over backward to help you."

I believed her, but I wished one of them, a very specific one, saw me as more than a family member.

Mrs. Anderson narrowed her eyes. She nodded and patted my hand one final time before she left the table. Kate stood and followed her mom into the house. I remained seated, unsure of what had just transpired.

Chapter Seven

Pax

"Pax, come help me in the kitchen."

Without hesitation, I went to help my mom. I grabbed a couple of plates from the table and made my way to the kitchen, passing Kate on her way out. My curiosity piqued, and I wondered why Mom asked for help since she already had it. I shrugged my shoulders and decided it didn't matter. If Mom asked for help, I helped.

Entering through the sliding door, I put the dishes on the kitchen island.

"What did you need help with, Mom?"

Mom turned around with a steaming pie in each hand. I grabbed another set of oven mitts from the counter and took them from her. With a raised eyebrow, I asked where she wanted me to put them.

"On the cooling racks, please." I placed them on the dinged and well-worn racks and leaned in taking a whiff. The scent reminded me of the days I came home from school to find many baked treats on the counters.

"We'll let them cool for a few minutes before we take them outside. Help me with the dishes while we wait." I joined her at the sink and dunked my hands in the soapy water. I scrubbed and washed while she dried. In no time, the kitchen gleamed, and the pies cooled enough to serve. However, with a simple touch on my arm and a nod of her head, Mom directed me to join her at the island. She waited for me to sit with her on a stool beside her.

When our cousins came to live with us, Mom and Dad renovated the main living areas. They bumped the house toward the back, enlarged the kitchen and dining room, and added the massive island. Both spaces needed to accommodate ten people. They changed the cabinets to dark cherry wood and installed beige granite counter-tops throughout the space. They also replaced the small appliances with larger stainless steel ones.

The kitchen became the hub of our home. It was on those very stools my dad taught me how to treat a woman, where I filled out my college applications, and where I sat when I opened my acceptance letter to the fire academy. It was also the place where I finally internally admitted I had feelings for Susan on the night of her prom. She looked beautiful in a formal green dress. It was also the night Morgan was her date.

For all the good and bad memories I had in the room, they never surpassed the sense of home and peace I felt when I walked in. It was my favorite place to hang out when visiting my family.

I sat next to my mom and as best I could, I acted normally. She had an uncanny ability to read us.

"Pax, I'm proud of how you're always helping others especially those too proud to ask," she started, and I felt it in my gut. I feared the worst and jumped to conclusions, worried my dad or her were battling an illness. Maybe they needed my help in the house or Dad's business. Mom's hand on my bicep stopped my rampant imagination. "Stop freaking out. Your dad and I are fine."

I laughed as Mom cut through to the heart of my rampant thoughts.

"How about you tell me what you need then? Don't talk in riddles." She scooted closer. Placing her hand palm side up on the counter, she invited me to hold it. I took it and enjoyed the safety net it provided.

Mom smiled and winked at me. She mastered the art of riddles, especially when she wanted you to do something without coming right out and asking. "Very well. Susan needs you."

I gasped. I didn't mean to, but she caught me by surprise. My mind conjured all sorts of scenarios. Did she need me in the Biblical sense? Did she need me to help her move? Did she need me to take her to the hospital? Too fast for me to track, wayward ideas flashed across my mind.

When I didn't respond, Mom let go of my hand and smacked me on my arm. "Wherever your mind went, bring it back here young man."

I groaned. I didn't know what my mom read on my face, but I sure hoped she didn't see my blush. I didn't redden easily, but dirty thoughts of Susan brought it out in me. Choking back my visions, I waited for Mom to continue.

"She's outgrowing the shelter. She needs to expand and doesn't know how to go about raising the funds."

"I don't have the cash she'll need lying around, Mom," I responded too quickly, which resulted in another smack. I rubbed my arm working out the sting while I gave her my most innocent expression. Mom's petite stature did not diminish her heavy hand from inflicting pain. Something we all learned early on. She wasn't quick to use it, but when she did, a whack to our behinds set us straight.

"I'm not suggesting you pay for it. I'm simply asking for you to think of ways we can help her out," she said, and reached for my hand again. "She's overwhelmed right now, and she's drowning in worry over her shelter, her dad, and where she's going to live. I'm asking you to carry a part of her burden. Help her come up with the money and then building the extension at the shelter."

I sighed. Susan didn't ask me for help, and I didn't foresee getting one past her. Nevertheless, I couldn't deny my mom. "Sure, Mom. Let me sleep on it and see what I can come up with." I pushed back from the island and stood.

Mom's grip on my hand tightened indicating she wasn't done. Sitting back down, I waited for further instructions. I got none. Instead, I got a penetrating gaze.

"What? What am I missing here?" I asked and rolled my eyes.

"Don't you roll your eyes at me. I don't need to lay it out for you. You're a smart boy. Figure it out."

I laughed low and deep. Typical Mom. She didn't give answers; she made us figure shit out on our own. I took a few minutes considering my options on how to help Susan. Then it clicked. My mom knew the minute I'd figured it out, stood with the largest grin on her face, and patted me on the shoulder. Without another word, she walked out of the kitchen.

****

I sat on the stool and made plans. I needed to convince Susan to take the aid unknowingly. It meant I needed time with her. Alone time. My smile widened, and I ran out the door after my mom. I stepped out onto the deck to the guys and Kate arguing. I leaned back against the house and watched the mayhem unfold.

"It's not fair," Kate said. She stomped her foot like she always did when my brothers didn't listen to her. "Just because I'm the youngest I'm never allowed to be the team captain."

Caden pulled her into a hug and kissed the top of her head. His eyes twinkled with laughter as he leaned down and whispered in her ear. She smiled at him before punching him in the stomach. He doubled over pretending to be out of air. "Oh stop, you big lug. I barely touched you." Kate laughed.

Morgan shook his head in amusement at their display. Jesse, the most controlled of all of us, stepped up and gave everyone their instructions. The second youngest of the Andersons, at the age of twenty-five, Jesse commanded authority. Studying to be a pediatric surgeon, he often came off as gruff to his patients' families, but a true softy to the little humans. He loved children, especially sick ones.

He wanted to give them a better life. It might have had something to do with his rough start. As a premature baby, he'd spent months in the hospital as his body grew stronger. Over the years, he pushed his limits, which resulted in countless trips to the ER with broken bones. He'd grown into a strong man, honing his body to perfection. Ladies swooned over him, but he turned them away. He used medical school and his residency as an excuse.

"Susan, you're the team captain with Dustin, Parker, Kate, and Caden on your team. Since you're still on the mend, you will captain from the sidelines," he said, broaching no argument from anyone. Turning to me, he continued. "Glad to see you're joining us, Pax. You're the other captain, with, Foster, Morgan, and me as your team. If no one has any further objections, let the game begin." He walked away knowing we always fell in line.

"You all need to take your shirts off," Susan piped up, pointing to my team. I turned in time to see her blush. She covered her mouth with a hand, shaking her head as if she couldn't believe what she said. I grinned at her cuteness and happily complied.

Grabbing the back of my shirt, I pulled it off in one motion. She gasped, and it pleased me knowing I'd shocked her. I quirked my eyebrows at my brothers in challenge. They followed suit, and the four of us stood bare-chested in front of the other team.

"Ew. Cover up. I'm going blind," Kate shrieked, yelping when Susan smacked her.

"I'm enjoying the view. Shut up," Susan whispered to Kate, but not quietly enough. We laughed, making her flush.

Her gaze lingered on me for longer than the others, and I fought the urge to puff up my chest and show off my abs. Leaning close so only she heard me I goaded her, "Sure you can handle my glistening chest, Susan? Wouldn't want you to fall over and hurt yourself."

She huffed at me but couldn't hide her deepening blush. "I'm going to make you eat those words."

"I'd rather eat something else," I said, knowing I crossed a line, but for once, I didn't care.

At her stunned gulp, I walked to my dad standing by the deck. He waited for Susan and me to square off as team captains, and for Caden to hand him the special quarter. The coin belonged to Dad's friend, business partner, and brother-in-law, Dustin Sr., my cousins' father. It had been Dustin Sr.'s most prized possession. The very first quarter he earned as a kid when he ran errands for local store owners. Since his parent's death, Caden carried it in his pocket, and we always used it in the coin toss.

"Keep it clean. No tackling. Touch only. First team scoring five touchdowns wins. Losing team cleans up the picnic," he stated the rules, like he did every time we played.

Susan and I nodded our agreement. "Shake," Dad ordered, and we did.

"Ready to go down?" I taunted Susan.

She smirked in response.

****

Susan

We stood in a circle, arms over each other's shoulders, head bowed. I let Caden coach us on our next play. We were tied, four-four. He hoped it would be the last play giving us the win. "Dustin, get close to Susan on the sidelines, and we'll pass to you. I don't care how you get there, just do it," he said, turning to me. "Susan, once Dustin has the ball shake your booty or do whatever women do to distract men."

I laughed and nodded.

"Caden," Kate shrieked. She shoved him in the chest. "I can't believe you're using such a misogynistic ploy."

"If it works, why not?" Dustin added. He inched closer to Caden, either in team spirit or cowardice, and avoided Kate's flying fists. "Besides, we all know how Pax will lose his…" he said, stopping only when Caden hit him on the arm.

I wanted to ask him for clarification, but Kate piped up. "Parker, who are you siding with? Male bigotry or family solidarity?"

Parker shrugged and moved closer to his brothers. "Hey, you can't blame me. I want to win. If Susan shaking her booty distracts them, then I say shake it."

I bit my lip, holding back another laugh. As the only non-family member playing, it made sense using me as a distraction.

We huddled, chanted our team-cheer, and headed back to square off against Pax's team. Caden squatted and hiked the ball to Parker. With ball in hand, he stepped back and waited for Dustin. Dustin closed the distance between him and me. With ten feet separating us, Dustin plucked the ball from the air and ran toward me. Pax turned and focused his attention on Dustin.

Within seconds, Morgan and Pax ran toward Dustin. I danced and jiggled hoping to distract them. I stopped with a gasp. Pax's jaw-dropping body headed my way. The sight before me was glorious and I stumbled back and lost my footing.

One second I was airborne, and the next arms wrapped around my waist. I landed on top of a hard and unyielding body. I felt, rather than heard, the oomph of exhalation as our bodies hit the ground. I lay stunned and time slowed down. Turning my head, I caught a whiff of pure masculinity, sweat, and a woodsy aftershave. I didn't need any further information. I knew who was below me. With an internal grin, I moved my hands caressing the hard muscles beneath them. I took the few stolen moments and enjoyed the feel of him.

I enjoyed it too much and groaned. Mortified over the noise, I pushed against his chest, but he tightened his arms around me.

"Are you okay? Did I hurt you?" he asked, so close his warm breath moved my hair. I lay still, working hard at suppressing another groan. When I didn't respond, his hands massaged up and down my body. I couldn't have moved if I wanted. His hands felt wonderful, and I reveled in the way he caressed my arms, back and neck.

"Man. Are you two making out? Do we need to leave you alone?" Dustin asked from beside us.

At the intrusion, I jolted, kneeing Pax in the groin. He yelped, rolled to his side, and clutched his crotch.

"Oh my God, Pax. I'm so sorry." I knelt on the ground beside him and gripped his shoulder. His large frame made the position difficult, and I straddled him. "What can I do? Do you need ice?"

He grunted. "I'm okay. Give me a minute."

I didn't move. Instead, I leaned over and wiped the sweat from his brow. His eyes sprang open at my touch. His darkened gaze met mine, anchoring me to him. My hand hovered motionless mid-air. Shouting from behind us reminded me we weren't alone. I hoisted up and ran my hands down my body, pretending to clean off my clothes. I kept my head down hiding my blush.

Pax slowly stood bent at the waist supporting his hands on his knees. I wanted to reach out and check for injuries, but Morgan's sudden presence stopped me from acting foolishly.

"It's a no tackle game. What the hell were you thinking?" Morgan yelled at Pax, hitting him on the shoulder.

"I didn't tackle her. What do you take me for? I'm not an asshole. I know she's recovering, you jackass," Pax shouted back.

"Boys. Language," Mrs. Anderson yelled from the deck. "Susan, dear, come on up here so we can make sure you're okay."

I hesitated to leave them alone, not knowing if Pax's red face was from anger or pain. Pax and Morgan squaring off worried me. They rarely fought. The last time was when they were teenagers.

I didn't want to be the cause of a rift between them. I stepped in the middle and placed one hand on each chest. I pushed, unsuccessfully separating them. I swiveled my head back and forth keeping an eye on them. "Morgan, he didn't tackle me. I tripped, and he caught me before I hit the ground." Their dad approached, quickly closing the distance urging me to diffuse the situation. "Who's to say I didn't do it on purpose? You know we need to feed into Pax's hero ego at least once a day or else he'll feel useless," I joked. Relief coursed through my body when Pax's glare softened, and Morgan's shoulders relaxed.

Morgan stepped back and looked me over. Satisfied, he turned his attention to Pax. With a slap against his back, he smiled at both of us. "Not even a scratch."

Pax's gaze roamed up and down my body, much as Morgan had done, but I heated at his perusal. "I guess I met my hero quota for today. I'm good now." He exhaled on his fingernails and rubbed them on his chest.

I laughed and let out my held-in breath. I hated causing friction in the family. It was the biggest reason I stayed away from Pax.

"You better go see Mom and your dad," Pax said. "I'll come too. As a semi-trained medic, I can take care of your injuries."

Although he joked, his eyes told another story. I placed my palm against his chest. I yearned to explore every inch of his sculpted body, to lick every nook and cranny. However, with everyone watching, I forced my hand down, but not before I leaned in, kissed his cheek, and whispered, "Thanks for saving me. You are my hero. And I'm sorry I kneed you on the…in the…you know where."

He inhaled deeply and chuckled when I couldn't finish my sentence. Unable to stop acting like a girl with a crush, I pivoted and made my way to the deck where Mrs. Anderson waited to fret over me. I used every bit of my will power not to turn around.

Chapter Eight

Susan

"Are you okay, honey?" Dad asked. I stepped onto the back deck. Pax gently guided me, his hand on my lower back. Dad pulled me closer, and I immediately missed Pax's presence.

"Dad, I'm fine. Not a single scratch. Pax took the brunt of the fall and then I went off and kneed him in the...Never mind. I'm unharmed, thanks to Pax." I turned to thank him, only to twist awkwardly and miss-step. Pax reacted and wrapped his arms around my waist, stopping me from falling again.

The hair on my arms stood on end, and I shivered at his proximity. It wasn't all physical lust. Having him close fed my soul. I fell into the comfort of his arms as they wrapped me in warmth, and security. I wished it extended to love.

"Humor an old lady. Let's go inside and we can make sure," Mrs. Anderson said, as I melted in her son's grasp. "Pax, come with us."

I couldn't say no to Mrs. Anderson. I leaned down kissing her on the cheek as Pax kept a hold of my elbow. I thought of my mom and how she would have worried the same way as Mrs. Anderson.

"Emily, you are not an old lady," I said, smiling and placing her hand in the crook of my arm. I walked us through the backdoor with Pax and my dad following. "Most days, I have a hard time keeping up with you."

We sat on the couch in the living room, and I sunk into the soft, brown leather. The room's furnishings, three over-sized leather couches, a large coffee table adorned with magazines, several ottomans placed haphazardly throughout, and a large flat screen TV, made it feel homey.

Pax sat on the ottoman facing me. He laid his hand on my knee drawing my attention to where our bodies connected. The heat from his hand spread through my body, and I wanted to lean and feel his full lips on mine. Drawing my gaze from his hand, I made eye contact.

Big mistake.

Once there, I couldn't look away. He smiled; a dimple appeared on the right cheek. Both dimples only emerged when he laughed. Pax enjoyed life, and he didn't hold back from showing it. Those were my favorite times with him.

Reaching forward, Pax tucked escaped strands of hair from my ponytail behind my ear. His fingers stroked my cheek, cupping my face. "Did I hurt you? Maybe I grabbed you too hard?"

I wasn't listening, too mesmerized by the bluish-gray hue of his eyes and his caressing touch.

When I didn't answer, he grabbed my shirt and pulled it past my navel before I realized what he was doing. Heat pooled below as his hand grazed my abdomen. My breath hitched at the sensations his touch created and although I wanted more of it, I knew better.

I scooted farther back into the cushions, needing to regain balance. His hand against my skin perfect and the longer I sat the harder I worked at keeping a hold on my desires. "I'm the one who's sorry. I hurt you."

"Do I look like I'm hurt? You have nothing to apologize for. Now answer my question." At my quirked eyebrow, he quickly added, "Please," to the end of his demand.

"I'm okay," I responded, lowering the hem of my shirt. "Your body felt a hell of a lot better than the ground would have."

I blushed as what I said sunk in.

His smile deepened. "You like the way my body feels?"

My skin heated, spreading down from the tips of my ears, across my chest, and down to my toes. I felt like I was on fire. If people spontaneously combusted, I wasn't far from bursting into a tornado of flames.

Pax laughed, loud and heartily at my visible mortification. I shoved his shoulder, which only made him laugh harder.

His phone rang, silencing him. He leaned back and pulled it out of his pocket. With him distracted, I sat forward to leave the room. Pax jolted upright with a frown darkening his features. He stared as his phone for another second or two before silencing it. He walked away, but I spotted the furrow form between his eyebrows. He paced a few steps lost in thought. His shoulders tensed as the phone rang once again. My heart demanded I go and ease the worry away, but lucky for me my mind was in control. I turned looking for Mrs. Anderson and my dad only to find they weren't there.

During the period I fixated on Pax, they left. I had been alone with him.

"Where are you going?" Pax asked. I whirled around, surprised at finding him behind me, close enough to feel his breath on my face, and see the deepened frown lines. His plastered smile didn't hide the shadows playing across his eyes.

Nodding my head toward the silent phone, I asked, "Everything okay? I'll leave you to your call." I backed away from him, but he didn't give me the ability to get far.

He pocketed his phone, caught my wrist, and spun me to face him. "Everything's fine and we weren't done. I was going to ask you a favor. Come sit with me," he said, leading me back to the couch. This time he sat next to me. "I have to come up with a theme for the community outreach at the firehouse, and I need your creative mind. Can I buy you dinner?"

My heart stuttered. Was he asking me out on a date? Once the thought crossed my mind, I chastised myself. He wasn't asking me on a date. Simply a dinner between friends.

With an internal smack, I stammered out my response. "I…I don't feel so…"

"You said you felt fine. Are you sure you're okay…or are you making excuses? I understand…"

I placed my hand on his chest stopping him mid-sentence. "No, not at all. I'm just tired. I wasn't turning you down; I'm surprised you asked me."

His smile deepened, and I wondered if he guilt-tripped me into assisting him on purpose.

"Great. Come on. Let's tell everyone we're heading out." He linked our hands and pulled me up and toward the backyard. I dug my feet into the carpet using all my strength to keep me in place.

He turned, surprised at my abrupt stop, and cocked his eyebrow in question.

"I don't think it's a good idea. I'm still full. Can we go tomorrow? I hate walking out on your parents' picnic. Besides, how's my dad going to get home? You brought us here. We need a ride back first."

I rambled, much to my chagrin. Something about the way Pax eyed me made me want to explain. Yet keeping the truth hidden proved an arduous task. I needed more time to prepare for alone time with him. Thankfully, he didn't offer an argument.

****

Pax

Anxiety flitted across her face, and I stopped from pulling her to me. If I thought it would help I'd have kissed her concerns away. Her hand felt tiny in mine. I could shatter her bones if I squeezed too hard. She confused me. When I asked for her help she was eager, but then she backpedaled. I wanted to know why, but her look implored me to agree.

Truthfully, I didn't mind seeing her again, and without my family around. "Sure. Makes more sense anyway. I'll pick you up tomorrow at five and we can grab dinner."

Without a reason to continue holding her hand, I reluctantly let it go. At her look of disappointment, I stepped closer. Anticipation coursed through me as I closed the distance between us, my heart heady of its wants. I stood before her, our bodies aligned from head to toe, and tilted my head. My gaze fixed on her lips. A catch in her breath caught me off-guard, and I stumbled back.

I stopped a breath away from making the stupidest

mistake of my life. Kissing her in my family home with everyone, especially Morgan, close by could have destroyed what had been a perfect day. I cleared my throat, looked around seeing if anyone saw us, and avoided meeting her gaze.

"The picnic's winding down anyway, so when you're ready, we'll get your dad and head back to his place."

She hesitated, turned away from me, and wrapped her arms around her waist. Her stance worried me. I wanted to finish what I started. See if a kiss would finally rid her from my mind. Deep down I knew I was deluding myself, and I increased the distance between us letting her step away. I admit I was asshole enough to watch her hips sway as she walked ahead of me. Her luscious ass wreaked havoc in my mind. I wanted to grab her and do naughty things I fantasized about over the years. My growing erection was all the warning I needed to curb the trajectory of my thoughts. I buried my need for the woman back into the recesses of my body.

My mother smiled as we stepped onto the deck. "Everything all right?" she asked, her gaze focused on Susan. Knowing my mother, she noticed Susan's blush.

"Never better," I replied. I stepped away from them not wanting Mom reading too much into things. But if Mom's chuckle was any indication, I'd failed.

"I'm going to head out. Let's have drinks and dinner before you leave town again," I said when I neared Caden.

"Sounds good, especially if you bring a couple station flies with you," he replied, around his grin.

"Not this time, man. I want to spend time with

you," I said. When I first became a firefighter, I enjoyed my share of bunnies, but the novelty wore off quickly. There was no place in my life for a bump and dump ruining my reputation. Besides, I wanted to talk to him about his job and persuade him to consider returning home for good. I had a feeling he knew my angle, and Caden being who he was, would avoid talking about both topics.

After hugging each of my siblings and cousins, I shook hands with my dad. Mom stood last in the line of goodbyes. "Take care of her," she whispered.

Not understanding, I puzzled over what to say and settled with, "Who?" resulting in a cheek pinch.

Mom looked to the right, and I followed her line of sight. My heart hurt. Susan and Morgan holding each other in a tight embrace dug a hole in my soul. They stood chest to chest, leaving no room between them, Morgan whispering in her ear.

A fire burned inside of me and I ached to stalk over and pull them apart. Jealousy, possessiveness, and anger slammed me, but my mother's touch on my arm kept me grounded.

"Everything is not as it seems," she said. I leaned down and kissed her on the cheek before walking out the door. I didn't take a backward glance at the couple in love.

Susan and her dad piled into my truck seconds behind me, barely giving me enough time to get my emotions under control.

I drove them home, carried the casserole dish to their kitchen, and stood with Susan and her dad. Nobody spoke, and the silence turned awkward. I wasn't ready to leave but lingering any longer wasn't an option either. With a sigh, I shook hands with Mr. Hayes and kissed Susan's cheek.

"Tomorrow. I'll see you at five."

Susan's smile lit up her face.

Walking away unsettled, after seeing Susan with my brother earlier, I didn't know if the following day would bring me comfort or hardship. Yet I didn't let that stop me from making plans to keep her in my life for the foreseeable future. Whatever I decided, I hoped I kept my needy hands from getting me in trouble and my heart from breaking.

Chapter Nine

Pax

With my balls twisted up in knots, I spent the day at the fire station. I wasn't on the roster but staying home wasn't an option. I washed, waxed, and polished a truck burning off my nervous energy. Billy thought I was atoning for my misbehavior, and I didn't correct him. I hung out with the other firefighters and paramedics, shooting the shit, and playing a couple of rounds of basketball to keep my mind off Susan.

At home, after showering the day's stink away, I dressed in simple faded jeans and a red button down wanting to look good but casual for my date. I kicked myself for the hundredth time. It wasn't a date. It was simply friends getting together and discussing a project. Nothing more.

Besides, it didn't matter what I wanted. Morgan loved her and though they weren't a couple, they had the potential to be. I wasn't a dick, and I sure as hell would not step in his way. Especially since I had crossed the line the day before.

At her father's home, I stood by the stairs.

"Take a seat, Pax. She'll be down in a minute." Her father watched me with a bemused smirk. I fought the urge to sprint up the stairs to find her. Or run out of the house. Either option was easier than the anticipation grinding away at me.

I turned when he patted me on the shoulder. "I never thanked you for saving my baby girl. I can't express the gratitude I have for what you did for me."

"No need, sir."

Movement from peripheral vision caught my attention. I shifted and saw Susan coming down the stairs. My breath hitched. She wore the skinniest pair of black jeans I'd ever seen. They hugged her every curve as if painted on. Her teal top dipped low and showed off her cleavage. My mouth watered at the sight of her. It would take a flick of my fingers to expose her to my desperate eyes. With a low groan, I turned away, pocketed my hands, and adjusted my cock.

I thought of my crew. Baseball. My mom. Anything to help with the growing problem in my pants. I spotted a denim jacket on the back of the couch and grabbed it. Summer nights in Bellevue could be chilly, especially after a full day of sun exposure. I held it open for her. She stepped into it. Her hair caught on the inside of the collar.

On instinct, I pulled it out and the back of my hand brushed her skin. Goosebumps rose along the path, and I shifted hiding my hardening cock. The slope of her neck called to me. But with her dad watching, and Morgan always present in the back of my mind, I held off from acting on impulse. As her hair floated down her back, a hint of coconut escaped into the air surrounding us. I inhaled, taking it deep into my lungs.

Over the years, I deciphered her different scents. Apple during the summer meant she was troubled while in the fall it meant she was happy. Coconut indicated happy summer days. She wore flowery smells during the winter reminding her of spring, and vanilla on days she cooked and fed my crew, because it was the smell of home. I wasn't sure if anyone, including her, had picked up on this little nuance, and I didn't plan to reveal her tell. I held the knowledge close to my chest. My little secret.

"I won't be late, Dad. Don't wait up though." She stepped up on her tiptoes and kissed him on the cheek.

"You kids have fun. Take whatever time you need."

I helped her into the truck cab, holding the door open until she buckled in. In seconds, I climbed into the driver side and latched my seatbelt before putting the key in the ignition. Call me paranoid, or cautious, or whatever, but I've rescued too many people from car wrecks where seatbelts weren't used. Some walked away. The majority of them didn't.

Safety; I not only preached it, I practiced it.

Susan chuckled beside me. "I don't know how you handle Morgan's mode of transportation. You won't even start the car until everyone's buckled in."

She was right. It took years getting over my fears for my brother, and then Dustin's love for motorcycles. It took them both, and several discussions, to get me to trust them. Eventually, they convinced me to get on a bike.

I loved the exhilaration of a good ride, but it didn't deter me from keeping us safe. I made sure we were equipped with the best protective gear.

"Hey, I own a bike now."

"I know," she whispered. She turned toward the window, and although I couldn't see her expression, her tone was sad. "I've been hoping you would give me a ride someday."

My hands went rigid on the steering wheel imagining her on the back of my bike. Her legs and arms wrapped around me, the heat of her chest against my back, as we drove the open mountain roads. Images of the wind in her hair, she laughing in my ear as we leaned into corners assaulted me. I yearned for it, but it was a pipe dream.

"Remember the first time I went with Morgan? You were worse than my dad. Inspecting the helmet and lecturing him on safety and his responsibilities to me," she said.

Of course, I remembered. I sat on the front porch with my stomach in my throat waiting for her return. She hadn't known. The second the rumble of the bike approached the house, I ran back inside and hid behind the curtained window. My brother parked in the driveway and helped her off. Watching them convinced me to do nothing about my feelings for her. They were good at hiding it. Never kissing or holding hands in public, but the way they stared at one another told a different story.

"I'd started my training, and they showed us a crash video. It scared the shit out of me. I didn't like either of you getting on the bike."

She snorted and turned back to the window. "I don't think I ever thanked you."

"Thanked me? What for?"

"For looking out for me. It showed me another side of you. It showed me the man underneath all the gruffness. I was your brother's friend, and I irritated you. I didn't expect your protectiveness."

I looked over, although she avoided my gaze. I reached over, intertwined our fingers, and waited for her to turn my way. "You have never once irritated me. And you have always been more to me than simply Morgan's friend. You have always been my friend as well."

****

Susan

I looked down at our hands and reveled in the feel of the safety he provided without knowing. His words made my heart grow fonder, but they also told me we were only friends. Nothing more.

"Where are we going?"

When he didn't answer, I swept my gaze away from our hands to him. I barely contained my gasp. The look in his eyes held warmth and love. Pax always kept his focus on the road, but for a moment, he stared at me with an intensity I couldn't describe.

He turned away first and cleared his throat. He unfurled his fingers from mine and put them back on the steering wheel. "I thought we could pick something up and head back to my house. I need to pick your brain, and I don't think a loud restaurant is the right place."

I swallowed back my nerves. Alone in his house? I wasn't sure I'd survive but nodded my head anyway.

Pax bought his three-bedroom Tudor style home three years ago. He said it was a good investment although it was in shambles. With lots of hard labor and love, he'd transformed it to its original beauty.

The first floor's exterior boasted a decorative beige stone design, trimmed darker brown. The second level sported elaborate, exposed wood framework in between stucco walls. Attractive concrete steps led to the front door.

"Want a tour?"

I scanned the interior and nodded. "I'd love one."

He placed the bag of food on the kitchen counter, took my hand in his, and led me through the bottom level then the upper. He'd renovated the living room and kitchen. Decorated them in browns and blues. He'd also finished his bedroom and the master bath on the second floor, but the other two bedrooms, dining room, and basement were still in disarray.

"Last time I was here, you were still working on the living room. It looks great," I said, as we returned to the kitchen.

"Thanks. I work on it every spare minute I have. I hired out the plumbing and electrical, but everything else I've done myself, with a little help."

"Well, it looks fantastic. I love the blue walls. I thought it would be dark in here, but the color airs out the room. Nicely done."

"I can't take credit for the color scheme. Shannon was instrumental there," he said, while he surveyed the room in admiration.

A pang of jealousy hit me. I'd never heard of this Shannon person, but I already didn't like her. "Who's Shannon?" I asked, speaking before thinking.

"She's Beck's sister, and apparently she loves decorating. She took pity on me and we went shopping, where she made all the decisions. I can't tell you how relieved I was she chose colors I liked and kept the furniture to a minimum."

"That's good. You hate clutter."

"How'd you know?" His head jerked my way, and surprise laced his voice.

"You always ragged Morgan over his bike

paraphernalia. Tired of hearing you complain, he stored it in my dad's garage."

"I always wondered where his stuff disappeared to," he said, smiling at the memories.

"So is Shannon? Is she…Is she your…girlfriend?"

He looked bemused and shook his head in answer. "Nah. She visits Beck a lot at the station. I'm surprised you haven't met her yet. She heard Beck say one day I should date an interior designer and then dump her after she finished decorating the house. An enraged Shannon scolded me for listening to her 'dumb-ass brother'. She offered help, and I accepted. I ran out the door before she changed her mind and left her hitting Beck on the head."

Tension left my body in a rush. I too did my fair share of hanging out at the station, primarily to get my Pax fix.

"What did you need my help with?" I took my salad to the living room needing to focus on something other than the hot man before me. "Can I sit here and eat?" I asked, pointing to the soft beige couch.

At his nod, I plopped down. He sat by my feet on the floor and rested his back on the front of the couch. I concentrated on eating without choking since his arm rubbed my leg every time he moved.

We ate in comfortable silence for several minutes. He took a bite of his sub, and lettuce fell into his lap. He scooped the spilled food and laughed. "Yeah. I have to get the dining room done. I need a kitchen table. I'm tired of dropping food on my lap."

"I can help you with that," I said, my words registering a second later. Backtracking, I rambled on, "I mean, if you need it. I like working with my hands, and I can help you paint, or maybe you can teach me how to handle power tools. Maybe I can help you buy the furniture."

Pax placed his hand on my leg, igniting a quick burn through my body. "I'd love the help," he said. "Speaking of which, let me ask you something."

I slid to the floor and set my plate on the coffee table. Crossing my legs, I turned facing him, my knees butting against his thigh. I ignored the persistent butterflies in my stomach.

"Like I told you yesterday, I've been put in charge of the community outreach day at the firehouse."

Pax in charge made sense. Good with people, he dedicated his time to helping others. However, it still made me laugh, and I drew my hand to my mouth, hiding my reaction.

"What's so funny?"

"Nothing. Sorry. I don't mean to laugh. I…" I slowed, at a loss to explain.

"You better stop, or I'll give you a real reason to laugh," he said with mischief as he wiggled his fingers at me.

I scooted away and laughed harder. "You can't. You know how ticklish I am."

"Where do you think you're going?"

He grabbed my legs and pulled me back. I waited for him to remove his hands, but he left them resting on me and rubbed his thumbs on my thigh. I remained still. I didn't dare call his attention to his absent-minded strokes. I enjoyed the feel of his hand through the fabric and my skin tingled at the contact. I hoped my flushed face didn't make my desires obvious.

"Anyway. As I was saying, I have to come up with

an idea and a non-profit the firehouse can support," he said, continuing caressing my leg. "I've been thinking a lot about it and I'm stumped. Figured you might have a few ideas."

I sat back, thinking. "The foster kids could always use extra funds and volunteers."

"Nah. Already been done. My CO wants a different idea each year. I kind of hoped to go in Friday and blow his socks off, but…"

"But?"

"I don't know," he said, standing and pacing the length of the living room.

Bereft of his touch, I forced myself to stay seated. My mind wandered. I imagined us sitting on the couch, with his arm draped across my shoulders talking the night away. It would be comfortable. Familiar.

"The thing is, we like getting kids involved, and it makes for a fun-filled day. The station guys tell you they don't want kids, but they love whenever we host an event for them."

I half-listened as more images bombarded me. Pax holding a baby. Our baby. His muscular arms wrapped protectively around him.

A snap of fingers in front of my eyes drew me back to reality, away from an unattainable future. Pax squatted by me, his face close to mine. I struggled, but kept from leaning forward and taking his lips, like my body urged me to do. Losing myself in his gray-ringed sapphire eyes was not an option.

I focused on anything and everything other than his eyes, or lips, or the body heat rising between us at his proximity and came up with an idea. Yet I hesitated sharing.

"You thought of something. What?"

I didn't want to come across as self-serving and tapered my answer. "Kids like animals."

He waited quietly. I couldn't ask him outright. I wanted him coming to his own conclusions.

A grin spread across his face. "That's it. We can do an adoption day. We'll need a shelter willing to work with us. We can have a pet store on hand with supplies. And we can have games and a doggy obstacle course where the kids can try out the dogs. Brilliant idea," he beamed. "Do you know a shelter willing to help?"

My heart dropped, and disappointment flared. I diverted my gaze, hiding my feelings.

With a finger under my chin, he coaxed me to face him. "I was kidding. Of course, Kisses and Paws will be the shelter we sponsor," he said, looking me in the eyes. "Did you really think I would do this and not help your animals?"

"No...No..." I stammered. I closed my eyes against the forming tears, willed my body to relax, and enjoy the moment. Pax goofing around with me felt amazing. I knew he'd do everything in his power to help me if he knew the state of my business.

"Do you have enough cats and dogs? The event's in three weeks. I have a lot to do. First, I have to get the CO's approval, but I know he'll like the idea. What do you say? Want to work with me on this?"

I jumped into his arms. Happy couldn't begin describing my emotions. I rested my head on his chest and the warmth of his body enveloped me. He took a moment before wrapping his arms around me. Tightly.

"Thanks, Pax. You don't know how much this means to me," I whispered.

"By the strength of your hug, I think I do."

I tilted my head to see his face. He leaned down. His lips hovered over mine. We'd never been this close before. I held my breath. Hoped he closed the gap between us and kiss me. I licked my lips and his pupils dilated. His attention zeroed in on my mouth. I dared not breathe, anticipation flowing through me. For the first time I willingly accepted my desires for him. To take what he offered. To ignore my concerns. A heated moment passed between us and I grabbed a hold of it with all my strength. I would deal with the consequences later.

His hands kneaded my back as he tightened his hold and I groaned. His gaze shot to mine. I let my curiosity and desire flicker in my eyes the longer he studied me. I opened to him and hoped he saw my craving. His eyes widened, and my mouth parted in hope. He moved, gently placing his lips on mine.

We stood still, our lips and gazes locked. Impatient, I opened my mouth and brushed my tongue along the seam of his. It was all the permission he needed. Pax kissed me with an urgent hunger. His hand slid up my back until he gripped my neck, holding my head in place. With his other hand, he pulled my body flush to his.

My nipples hardened against his chest, and I wondered if he felt them. It didn't matter, because his lips, soft and full, teased me into oblivion. He kissed me with deliberate strokes of his tongue, leaving no part of my mouth unexplored. I moved my hands from around his neck and rubbed them along his shoulders and down his arms. I lifted my leg wrapping it around him bringing our bodies closer. Pax guided my other leg around him and rested his hand on my butt holding me close. Every point of our bodies cemented to each other.

His excitement grew against my core and I ground into him. He moaned, pulled away, and kissed his way along my jaw and down my neck. He then nibbled his way back to the sensitive spot behind my ear.

His hair tickled my neck, and I turned and buried my nose in it. I shook from the passion running unabated through my body. Holding him in my arms fed a part of my soul, a part that had been hungry for years.

I felt whole.

The living room around us faded away, and I lost myself in him. I stroked his chest and arms exploring the hills and valleys of his hard body. I closed my eyes in an attempt to store the abundance of information into my mind, wanting never to forget.

I nuzzled into the groove of his neck and took his scent deep into my lungs. His erection ground against me in time to a beat only heard by us. His muscles moved under my touch as I dragged my hand down his abs and back up under his shirt. I pinched his nipple and delighted in his escalating moans. His hips rocked harder. I met him thrust for thrust. I ached for him to fill me and by the feel of his firmness; I knew he wanted me just as much.

Chapter Ten

Pax

Shit. Susan's thighs gripped my hips. I held her, kissing her. My cock hardened, and I ground into her covered pussy. I wanted to carry her to my room, strip off her clothes, and indulge in her body for hours; explore all the ways to make her moan, whimper, and gasp. I wanted to discover what she liked and what made her crazy. But at the end of the day, what I wanted most was to hold her. Keep her by my side and play with her hair, stroke her back, feel her breath on my chest while we talked and laughed.

I wanted her to be my partner now and forever. To share my dreams and life with her. For her to tell me her dreams, and to be there when she achieved them.

Having her in my arms dug at my deepest secrets, and I kissed her with all the love and affection I had in me. Being with her felt like heaven and I never wanted to let go.

In the back of my mind, I knew I shouldn't, but I didn't care. Breaking my rules didn't seem important when I wanted to drown in the sounds she made. I chased her moans and strived to make her repeat them from her kiss-swollen lips.

I licked behind her ear, enjoying her wiggling against me. I felt her soft curves through the layers of fabric between us and it drove the animal in me. I wanted to claim her as mine.

I growled at the unexpected pinch of my nipple. I dragged my hand from her hair down her back where I hooked my fingers against her perfectly rounded ass. I tugged her up my body and rested her where I wanted. Where I needed her most.

She gasped into my mouth and rubbed against me. So good. My body threatened to finish before I was ready. A voice screamed for me to stop. To end it before we went any further. But I didn't listen.

Slipping a hand to her waist, I made quick work of the button of her jeans. Susan slid down my body and I knelt and tugged them off. I loved the sexy black panties she wore. I rubbed my knuckles against the fabric and my fingers lingered against her folds. Her hands trembled as she unbuttoned my shirt and in my desperation, I pushed her hands away and flung my shirt open. Buttons skittered across the room, pinging off the surfaces.

Grabbing the hem of her shirt, I pulled it over her head and groaned at the sight. Susan stood before me in nothing but matching black lingerie. I studied her, absorbed the image. A picture forever ingrained on my soul. Leaning forward, I took one of her breasts in my mouth and sucked through the lacy fabric of her bra. Her answering cry added fuel to the fire, and I reached into her panties, searching for her heat. Slipping a finger inside, I spread her wetness along her lips.

All thoughts of mistakes evaporated as I stared into her beautiful hazel eyes darkened by the throes of passion.

Susan shook in my arms. Making her whimper was no longer enough. I held her against me and lowered us to the floor, taking care not to crush her with my body. I kissed from jaw to ear, nipping at the tender skin, pressing my body against hers. My pants thwarted me, and I reached between us undoing them. I pushed them, along with my boxers, over my hips. I kicked them off the rest of the way and lay naked over her.

For a moment, I hesitated and considered my actions, but Susan's low growl killed any lingering doubts. She closed her eyes and took a deep breath before letting it out. It washed across my face, and I gave in to years of craving. I sealed my lips to hers.

I urged her mouth open with my tongue. Once she granted my silent request, there was no stopping me. I explored every inch of her, memorizing her reactions. I ignored the knock at the door, willing them to leave. They didn't give up, and I grumbled when Susan pulled away from me.

With a heavy sigh, I dropped my body against her and laid my head on her forehead.

"Pax?" Susan breathed out, her voice hesitant. I lifted onto my elbows, needing to see her eyes.

"Pax, love. Let me in," a muffled female voice said.

Susan placed her hands on my chest and pushed. I let her shove me away although I hated our separation.

"Sweetie?" said the voice.

I closed my eyes in denial. I knew who was at the door, and I didn't want to get up. If I wasn't already sick and tired of her, the fact she interrupted one of the best moments of my life drove me over the edge.

Angry, I pulled up, grabbed my jeans and shirt, and stepped back into my pants as Susan hurried to get her clothes back on.

"I have dinner. All your favorites. Let me in before it gets cold," the voice sing-songed.

"Are you going to let her in?" Susan asked.

"I...no...I don't...shit." I scrubbed my hands against my face.

Susan dressed, concealing her naked body from me. I rubbed my chest easing the ever-growing pinch. Realization dawned. I had screwed up. Took what wasn't mine. It didn't matter if she and Morgan weren't dating. She was his, and I had stepped over the line.

Emotions danced across my face, and Susan tilted her head in question. My body shook, and I turned and headed to the kitchen.

I braced against the sink and waited for the tremors to stop. I concentrated, taking slow breaths and willed my body to calm down. Once I was under control, I flicked on the tap and splashed cold water across my face and neck. Taking in a deep breath, I took stock of the situation.

It felt undeniably right to have Susan in my arms. Kissing her ignited a fire in me I never knew existed and now with the taste of her fresh on my lips, I wasn't sure I could let her go. Yet my relationship with my brother was too important to destroy. I couldn't break up our family. I had to leave her alone. No matter how much it hurt my heart Susan wasn't mine, nor would she ever be.

Her smell lingered on my shirt as I put it back on. I pulled it to my nose, inhaling her deeply into me one final time. Thinking I might have already done irrefutable damage, I knew what I had to do. Tell Morgan and take the blame for our actions. It was all on me, and I would do anything to save their relationship. I decided on a course of action, grabbed a beer from the fridge, and downed half before I bucked up the courage to face Susan.

I found her typing on her phone when I returned to the living room. Walking past her, I saw her contacting an Uber. Without thinking, I grabbed her device.

"What the hell?" She reached for the phone. I raised it high above my head. Anger radiated off her, but I ignored it.

"I don't like you taking an Uber. You have no idea who's driving you. I'll take you home. It's the least I can do."

"No. The least you can do is answer the door," Susan yelled.

Her anger stirred something in me. My softening cock stood to attention. I didn't react to angry women, but any emotion Susan showed turned me on. I wanted to yank her close and kiss her again. Kiss her until I made her forget.

She turned, and I reached around her. With my palm on the wall, I offered her the phone with the other. She took it and crossed her arms across her chest. The move pushed her breasts together, distracting me.

"My eyes are up here."

I jerked my head up. My gaze settled on her fuming one, and I shook my head dislodging my lust. "Give me a sec and I'll drive you home."

"No need. I have a ride coming." She turned, pulled the door open, and eyed the woman. "He's all yours," she told her, walking away. She held her head high and didn't turn back leaving me desperate on my stoop.

I wanted to stop her. Chase her and bring her back

inside. To talk or to finish what we started. I didn't much care. I hated seeing her leave. I ran a hand along my face and swallowed back my emotions.

With a scowl, I averted my gaze from the woman marching away to the one standing before me. Julie.

I didn't hate many people, but Julie and her relentless pursuit made me rethink my list. Convinced I was the love of her life even as she flaunted other men in front of me. I grew tired of her silly act. She called me at all hours of the day and night, hung around at the coffee house by the station, and waited for me to come and go. She likened herself as my girlfriend and told my engine brothers we were dating. Although she stood on my front steps, dressed in a tight leather skirt, a sequined tank top two sizes too small, and four-inch red heels I found nothing about her attractive. In fact, my cock shriveled.

Without invitation, Julie walked into my house. She made her way to the kitchen and placed the food bags on the counter, frowning at the empty containers before schooling her features. She made herself at home, opening drawers and cabinets, irritating me further.

"What do you want, Julie?"

She didn't answer; instead, she made her way back to where I stood. She snaked her arms around my neck and rose on her toes to kiss me. I grabbed her wrists and pushed her away. I used enough force sending her back without dumping her to the floor. Even with the increased space between us, Julie kept her hands on my chest.

With a few deep breaths, I centered myself once again. I needed to get rid of her and find Susan. As my gaze swept across the room, I stumbled. Susan stood in the threshold of the front door. My heart dropped. Tears dampened her eyes and her hand covered her mouth. I moved away from Julie, only for her to tug at my shirt. Susan tracked the movement and bit her bottom lip. Her stance screamed sadness, and it tore something inside me.

Susan's gaze darted away, and her fists clenched. "I forgot my purse," she said and grabbed it from by the door before taking off. I darted for her, but Julie wrapped her arms around me again.

"What are you doing here?" I asked, disentangling from her.

"Oh, baby, I saw you at work today even though it's your day off. I came by to make sure you were okay. You're so tense. Let me help you relax."

Julie dropped to her knees before me and reached for my undone pant button.

Shit.

I grabbed her arms, pulled her up, and ushered her to the door. "I don't need your help. What I need is for you to leave my house and leave me the hell alone. I've already told you I'm not interested." I knew I sounded harsh, but I needed her gone.

She grazed her hand along my naked chest under my ruined shirt, but when I paid her no heed, she turned to the door. Realization dawned, her face morphing before me. Anger spread across her features.

"Are you with *Her Skankiness*? Is that why you keep pushing me away? I can do so much more for you. She probably doesn't even know where her clit is."

Furious, I pushed her out of my house. "She's not a skank, and there is nothing you can do, or will ever do, to make me feel good. Get off my porch or I'm calling the cops," I yelled, before slamming my door.

"Fuck you," Julie yelled.

I stood by the front window and watched her walk to the end of my driveway, get in her car, and drive off. I breathed a sigh of relief before jumping into action.

Grabbing a new shirt from my room, I threw my ruined one on the bed. I hurried and dressed as I turned the house lights off, set the alarm, and climbed into my truck.

****

Susan

Humiliated, embarrassed, and exposed, I ran into my father's house and didn't stop until I closed my bedroom door. I listened carefully to sounds indicating I woke my dad. When none came, I relaxed against the door and rested my head against it.

I sat on the end of the bed and propped my head in my hands. I ran the last half hour back through my mind, and still couldn't come up with a reasonable explanation for what happened. Pax kissed me, and not only did I kiss him back, I threw myself at him. We almost had sex. I saw him naked. Oh, and what a glorious sight. I whimpered, remembering the feeling of his hands on my skin, the weight of his body over mine.

I shook my head ridding the images from my mind. I acted like a floozy and he had a girlfriend. I was a home wrecker. Of course he had a girlfriend. He was a great guy, and any woman would be lucky to be with him. God, how could I have been so stupid? How was I ever going to face him again?

I fought the tears all the way home. When the first tear dropped, I lost the will to fight and cried. I needed to get it out of my system and then figure out a way to move on. I wanted to talk to Morgan but didn't know what to say. I figured he would be angry with me for kissing Pax. Not because he was in love with me, but because he didn't like seeing me hurting or pining over anyone.

Pulling out of my pity party, I walked into the bathroom and washed my face. My dad installed an en suite for me when I was a teenager. He claimed I needed privacy as I grew into a woman.

Glad I could hide behind another closed door, I broke down again. I cried until I had no tears left to shed. I washed my face but refused to look in the mirror. I didn't need to see my swollen, tear-soaked eyes.

I jumped at the knock on my bedroom door. With a quick brush of my towel, I was ready to face my dad. I yelled for him to come in and kept my back to him. I hoped he wouldn't notice my puffy face. His silence forced me to turn and face him. Dad stood at my door arms crossed at his chest.

"Dad? What's wrong?"

He took a few seconds scanning my face before answering. "I don't know. Why don't you tell me? A grim Pax is in the living room. He said he's here to apologize. Now I find you holed up in your bathroom crying, and I suddenly feel the urge to kick his ass. What did he do to you?" The frown lines between his eyes grew deeper with each word.

"What? Pax is here?"

Dad stepped farther into the room and closed the door.

"What happened, baby girl?" He came closer and

wrapped me in his arms. Dad led me to my bed and urged me to sit down beside him.

"I'm…I'm not sure." I pulled back and studied my nails. I wanted someone to talk to, but I needed to swallow my pride. Dad lifted my chin and made me face him, and my bottom lip trembled.

Dad jerked to a stand. "I'm going down to have a word with that boy."

I jumped and grabbed his arm. "Dad, no. You can't. I'll tell you what happened."

His head swiveled back and forth between the door and me several times before he joined me. He pulled me into his arms again and I fell into his embrace. I needed to feel the safety he provided.

"We kissed," I said, after we sat on my bed again.

Having grown up without my mother, I relied on Dad to be both a dad and a mom. I talked to him about embarrassing and private topics. I trusted his advice, and he never judged me. He always guided me to make good decisions.

"Do you like him?"

I hesitated. I wasn't sure how to answer. I not only liked Pax, I was in love with him. However, could I tell my dad and not sound ridiculous? I settled on nodding.

"Does he like you?"

"I don't know? The worst part is I think he has a girlfriend. She showed up at his place right after he kissed me. But even before she arrived, he was backing away," I confessed. "I don't know if I can face him, Dad. Can you make him leave?"

Dad chuckled. "Baby girl, that isn't how I raised you. Go down there and face him. Explain your feelings and fight for what you want. Whatever his decision, you've done what you could, and you can live without regret. That's all you can do."

I kissed him on his cheek. "You're right, Daddy. Thank you."

"No need for thanks. I'm happiest when you're happy." He pulled me into another hug. "I'm going to my room to give you kids privacy." He kissed my forehead before he stood and left my room.

I braced for the worst and followed him out. I debated what I wanted to tell Pax. If I did as my dad said, I would reveal everything, but could I deal with his unreciprocated feelings? And what about his girlfriend? I couldn't believe he kissed me and cheated on his girlfriend. She had to be his girlfriend. She definitely was familiar with him and his home.

I slowly descended the stairs. I held onto the banister for support while I concentrated on breathing through each step. I stopped halfway and silently observed Pax. He paced the living room, mumbling; his chin pressed to his chest. He appeared nervous, and it made me smile. I'd never seen Pax unsure and seeing him vulnerable opened my heart to him more.

I choked back a sob, but it was too late. He twirled around. Our gazes collided and held. There was nowhere else I wanted to look. If eyes were windows of the soul, I hoped his revealed the answers I sought.

Chapter Eleven

Pax

Seeing her red-rimmed, puffy eyes killed me. I'd hurt her. I never wanted to upset her. Morgan was going to kill me, and he had every right to.

I'd rehearsed what I wanted to say on the drive over but watching her cross the room rendered me speechless. I wanted to pull her into a hug, but I also wanted to yell at her for kissing me. How could she kiss me when she was in love with my brother? Feelings of resentment, both at her and myself, warred in my head, neither one gaining a stronghold. I decided on not accusing her and giving her a moment to explain.

"How the hell did you get home? You better not have used Uber. It's not safe," I said through clenched teeth. Her anger erupted at my stupid remark. This wasn't the way I rehearsed my apology. Yet, I reasoned, no matter how I enjoyed the kiss and everything following it her safety was paramount.

"I made it back fine. No need for you to worry about me," she hissed.

I raised my arms and turned away before I gave in and did something rash. I wanted to hold her close, show her how her lack of regard for her safety pissed me off.

"You shouldn't have kissed me," she mumbled.

I stuttered. Even though she spoke the truth, she

couldn't deny she'd kissed me back. However, I wasn't the one cheating on Morgan. "What the hell does that mean? You shouldn't have kissed me," I said, tapping my chest for emphasis. "It was a mistake. One we can never repeat. I need to walk away. From you. From this. My brother…How could you? Shit."

Her face reddened the longer I spoke, but I couldn't contain my fury and I paced the living room.

"I don't know. Maybe if your tongue wasn't in my mouth or if you hadn't held me down on the floor, I'd have moved away. You're bigger than me, and…"

"Are you saying I forced myself on you? Do you even know me? I would never do anything to hurt you," I interrupted, spittle flying from my mouth. "Is that how little you think of me? What the fuck, Susan?"

"It's not like I had much of a choice. You took advantage of the moment. It was just a hug. And what about your girlfriend?"

"Girlfriend? What are you talking about? I don't have a girlfriend. I didn't cheat on anyone, unlike…"

"I saw it for myself. Hell, I was part of it. I've never felt dirty or cheap, but I do now, and I have you to thank for it," she interrupted.

Anger blasted through me. I wanted to pick up the furniture and throw it across the room. She accused me of using her. Forcing her. I couldn't process the shit she flung at me. I had to get out. Get to Morgan. Tell him what happened before she painted a fucked-up picture. There was no way I would let her drag my name through the mud.

Turning, I walked out of her house without saying another word. She called my name as I walked to my truck.

"Pax. I'm sorry," she yelled from the doorway. "I don't know what I'm saying. Please…"

The revving engine drowned her words. Putting the truck in gear, I skidded out of her driveway. My vision blurred as my blood pounded in my veins. My hands shook, and I held onto the steering wheel with enough force to bend it.

Knowing I wasn't fit to drive, I pulled over once I was out of her line of sight. I gained control of my emotions and centered my mind like I did when entering a burning building. I focused on regulating my breathing. Next, I willed my body to relax and loosened my hands on the steering wheel.

Once the red haze clouding my vision cleared, I put the truck back into drive and headed to Morgan's house. The sooner I got it over with the better. However, I wasn't an idiot. I called Caden and asked him to meet me there before I left the side of the road. I would not fight Morgan, but I couldn't guarantee I'd walk out of his house with our relationship intact.

****

I pulled into Morgan's driveway. Caden following close behind. He hopped out of his black Mustang smiling until he saw the anguish on my face.

"What's wrong? You look like someone died." He approached with open arms.

I backed away. "Nope. But I might be dead after this conversation."

"You're worrying me. What the hell happened?" Caden placed his hands on my shoulders. We stood close to the same height. Concern evident in his eyes. I turned away. I didn't want to see my screw up reflected in his gaze when I confessed.

I didn't want to tell him, but if I couldn't tell him, then I for sure couldn't face Morgan. Sounds of welding came from the garage Morgan used for his custom designs. Two years ago, he quit the shop he worked for and converted his garage and started a business. With a loan from our dad, he bought the needed equipment for designing images and decals for bikes, and his true passion of custom building. Although his company grew, he refused to move to a storefront. He preferred the solitude and quiet the house in a secluded wooded lot provided.

"I kissed Susan. I almost slept with her," I admitted. Focused on Caden, I didn't notice the noise coming from the garage stop.

Caden laughed, "It's about fucking time," he said, as Morgan growled from behind me.

Without warning, Morgan tackled me to the ground. He straddled my hips and shoved my face into the dirt. Caden laughed enjoying my predicament.

Tackling me wasn't an easy task considering my size. I stood at six foot four and weighed over two hundred fifty pounds of solid muscle. Morgan was three inches shorter with leaner muscle. He didn't have my bulk.

I let him keep me down and Caden retrieved his phone from his pocket. I closed my eyes as he circled us focused on Morgan's heavy breathing over the sound of the camera shutter.

"Just so I'm sure, say it again," Morgan demanded.

I shook my head, scrunching my eyes against the shame. I'd kissed my brother's girl, could have gone farther if she hadn't stopped me, and worse, I'd lusted after her for over fifteen years. I'm the worst kind of brother. "I can't. You heard me the first time. I'm sorry. It never should have happened."

"Is he for real?" Morgan asked. Not sure if he addressed me, I opened my eyes and studied him.

"I'm sorry," I said.

"No one ever said he was smart." Caden circled us.

"I said I was sorry. I'm so fucking sorry."

"Does he think we haven't known? He is an idiot." Morgan looked to Caden for an answer, ignoring me.

"I need to tell you…"

"Keep him down for as long as you can. This is the best video I'll ever record." Caden bent and held the camera close to my face. I wanted to swipe it away, but Morgan's knees locked my arms in place.

"He's not fighting me." Morgan loosened his hold.

He was right. I deserved to eat dirt. I blew out a breath and apologized again. I waited for Morgan's fist to connect with my jaw, but the hit never landed. Neither of them listened as I repeated my apologies. It took a while to note Morgan shaking above me. I registered his laughter, and I didn't know what to do. Morgan stood and toed me my ribs. I took the hint and turned over. I lay on my back and waited for the kick, and again, it never came.

I lifted my hand shielding my eyes from the sun to find Morgan and Caden standing on either side of me. Morgan with his fists clenched and Caden with his phone angled toward my face. "Tell us again what you did," Caden said with a smirk.

Morgan's booted foot landed square on my chest, quietly demanding me to stay on the ground. "Why do I need to say it again? You heard me the first time."

"We need it for posterity's sake. I didn't catch it on

video the first time."

"The only thing saving you is answering my questions on video. Besides, I need it for when they accuse me of assault. It'll justify my actions," Morgan said. "What did you do?"

I took a deep breath, faced the fire, and held my brother's stare. "I kissed Susan. There, are you happy now?"

Morgan shook his head. "Why? Why did you kiss her?"

I closed my eyes. I couldn't stand seeing the hurt my admission would inflict on him. "Because I wanted to."

"Again. Why?"

I shook my head, not understanding what he wanted from me. "I don't know. It was in the heat of the moment. We were talking, and one thing led to another. I didn't mean for it to happen."

"What? Why? Is she not good enough for you?"

"No man, she's too good for me. She isn't mine to kiss. It never should have happened."

"And how did she react?"

"Man. Don't make me tell you. This was my fault. I forced myself on her." I lied, but I didn't want to hurt him anymore. Susan and Morgan were meant for each other since childhood. I couldn't come between them. They needed to fix their relationship. I had already done enough damage.

Even though she apologized and recanted her words, I couldn't ignore them. Questioning and analyzing my actions ran on a continuous loop, and the deeper I dug the more her accusations rang true. I didn't give her a chance to get away from me. None of my brothers by blood, family, and station could take me down. She had nothing on me. Me the Hulk. I sucked in a breath.

I was to blame. My need for her so great I didn't think in the moment. I was a monster. I fought to get up. I needed to find her and apologize for what I did.

Chapter Twelve

Pax

Morgan lifted his booted foot and helped me stand. Unsteady on my feet, the world around me grew fuzzy. To make matters worse, the ground beneath me tilted on its axis. I reached out bracing for impact.

"Shit, man. I can't stop him if he falls." Morgan spoke as if from under water. Arms around my chest helped me stay upright while another set encircled me from the other side.

"Fuck. Let's get him inside," Caden said, his voice more muffled than Morgan's. They grunted as we moved, but I didn't have the energy or fortitude to help them.

"Put him on the couch."

I lost track of who said what. My head hit the back of the couch as they dropped me unceremoniously onto it. I didn't care what they did to me. I deserved it. Shame and guilt plagued my heart and mind.

Sweat beaded my forehead and ran down my back between my shoulder blades. I'd never had a panic attack, and I struggled to breathe. My heart thumped. I pressed my hand to my chest as someone forced my head down.

"He looks like he's going to faint." Fingers snapped in front of my face. "Shit, get him water."

"Pax. Snap out of it," a voice yelled in my ear.

It took all my effort to focus on my brothers' voices, and I fought to clear my head. A hard slap followed by another roused me. Anger rose to the surface faster than logic, and I lunged. I landed on the floor with another body beneath mine.

"He's back," Caden said, holding me off.

"Dumbass. Why the hell were you slapping me?" I asked angrily, climbing off him. My breathing still heavy.

My knees threatened to buckle, and I sat down on the couch. I worked to control my breathing as my fingertips tingled from lack of oxygen. Caden draped a cold cloth across the back of my neck. I welcomed the icy water dripping down my back. As I cooled off, I took in my surroundings. Logically, I knew they had brought me inside, but I didn't remember how. Nor could I tell how long I had been out of it. For all I knew hours had passed.

Caden pressed a cool glass of water in my hands and I gulped half the contents. The cotton feeling in my mouth dissipated. I finished, and Caden took it from my limp hand.

"What happened?" Caden asked, as he refilled the glass. "One minute we're screwing around, the next, you're white as a ghost and swaying on your feet."

"I'm calling Mom," Morgan said, as he pulled his phone from his pocket.

Raising my hand in protest, I grabbed for his phone, but my body laughed at my brain's demands. "Don't. I'm fine. Just give me a minute."

Caden settled in beside me on the couch while Morgan sat across from us on an ottoman. They looked worried, and I smiled to dispel their concern.

Then it all came roaring back. I told them about kissing Susan.

"He's looking green," Caden said, as he bolted for the kitchen. He returned seconds later with the garbage can. "If you're going to puke, do it in this."

I pushed his hand away. "I'm not throwing up."

I focused on Morgan desperately needing to read him. Like always, he kept his thoughts close to his chest. A man of few words and little emotion. Over the years, I learned to gauge his reactions, but in this situation, I hadn't a clue. In his living room, as I waited for his wrath, I couldn't put a finger on his emotions. "I'm sorry. It never should have happened. It was entirely my fault."

Morgan's eyes narrowed fractionally, and had I not been closely watching him, I'd have missed it. "No need to apologize," he hissed.

I silently asked Caden for help, but he sat back and gave me nothing. And if I wasn't mistaken, he was holding back a smile. "I kissed Susan. I've been fighting an att..." I started. I wasn't sure how much I wanted to reveal to either of them.

"Been fighting what, Pax?" Morgan asked. "An attraction? Don't you think I've known all along?"

I glared at him. I'd always thought I hid my feelings well. Caden's hand on my shoulder jarred me. Lost, I sifted through the years pinpointing when I revealed too much.

"We've all known. I think we all figured it out at different times though." When I looked at them in confusion, Caden laughed. "Mom overheard Parker and Dustin talking about you four years ago. She shut them up and then called a family meeting. You were at the store with Dad. She made it clear she didn't want us to interfere or joke about it. She asked us to leave you alone and give you the time you needed to figure your shit out."

"How the hell did I never find out about this? And why would I need to figure shit out? She's Morgan's girl," I yelled. I wasn't proud in that moment or for the last ten years if I was being honest. I lowered my voice and hung my head in shame. "I've screwed up. Haven't I?"

Morgan stood and headed to the window. I held my breath as his shoulders hunched and he put his hands in his pockets. He inhaled, kept his gaze out the window, and spoke.

"She's not my girlfriend. Never has been, nor will she ever be. We kissed once. It felt wrong. We were both disgusted, and knew we'd never be a couple." Lowering his head, he took several deep swallows. I waited for him to continue since it appeared he had more to say. Morgan only spoke when he had something important to contribute, and he'd already met his word quota for the day.

"The day I took her on the bike ride, I watched how you were with her. You waited by the window. I knew then you liked her, maybe even loved her. I was jealous. I didn't want to lose my best friend, even to my brother. I said nothing to you or Susan. I had a feeling she liked you too. I let you believe I loved her and wanted more. I knew you would never get between us."

He turned to me, his expression guarded. I should have been angry, but I wasn't. The guilt rolled off his shoulders. He lived with the knowledge and hid it from me for as long as I hid it from him. Whatever his reasons, I couldn't fault him.

"I'm sorry for being selfish," he said, when I didn't respond. I was still wrapping my head around hearing Morgan say so many words at once. "Shit," I mumbled under my breath.

"Damn. We all knew they weren't dating. Pax, how could you not have known?" Caden asked, his tone no longer amused. He misunderstood my reaction, but I didn't feel like correcting him.

"I...I don't know. I was too...blinded, maybe?" I directed my gaze at Morgan as he returned to the ottoman. "You know if something had happened between Susan and me, you would never have lost your best friend?"

"The younger me didn't know."

"How about now?"

"Now? Now you're an idiot for letting your misconceived ideas stop you from something great. Pax, you're an honorable man. I don't believe you forced yourself on her. Susan would never put up with that."

I leaped up. He was right. I was going after her, but Caden stopped me with a hand on my forearm.

"What the hell, man? I'm going to Susan and making her my girl."

"No, you're not," Morgan said.

I faltered. Had I made a mistake? Did he not give me the green light? My anger surfaced. "Why the hell not?"

Morgan and Caden shared a look then turned mischievous smiles my way. "We have an idea."

****

Susan

I called him, but he didn't answer. I texted him, but he didn't respond. I wanted to apologize. He didn't force himself on me, nor would he have cheated on his girlfriend.

Admittedly, my anger stemmed from him stopping. More humiliated than angry really. I thought he regretted it the minute he pulled away from me. I was wrong when I accused him of such vile behavior, and I'd never seen him so mad.

Frustrated I couldn't reach Pax, I went to Morgan's instead. I needed to talk to him and come clean about my feelings for his brother. I didn't want to hurt their relationship, and I didn't know what I would do if he asked me to not date Pax. Harboring a crush for over ten years had consumed me. It was time to decide and follow through with it.

I pulled into Morgan's driveway as Caden was leaving. He walked to me instead of his car and cranked his hand in a show to roll down my window. He greeted me with a roguish smile.

"Morgan seems to have a revolving door today."

"Huh? Why? Who else's been here?" I said, scrutinizing the area.

"He's in the workshop." He pointed toward the garage. "Hey, before I go, I want to say to take a gamble on him." Caden didn't say anything more, leaving me to decipher his cryptic message.

With a wink and a tap on the car roof, he headed to his. I didn't move until Caden peeled out of the driveway after revving his car's engine with a smile and fist pump in the air. I parked and followed the sounds of machines into the garage-turned-workshop and found Morgan hunched over a workbench. I stood by the door and enjoyed the play of the muscles in his back rippling with his every move. I wondered for the thousandth time why I wasn't attracted to him. Life would have been easier. Yet I loved him like a brother and nothing more. Pax held my heart.

Morgan straightened, wiped sweat off his forehead with a towel draped on his shoulder, and turned. He spotted me in the doorway and greeted me with the smile he reserved for me.

"Hey, Red. What's up?"

I walked to the workbench and leaned my hip against it. He bent over again and continued working. I spent many hours hanging out with him in the garage while he did his thing. I sat and read in the corner chair he put there for me or leaned against the bench talking with him.

I swallowed the bile in my throat. It was best I blurt out my confession while he was engrossed in his work. If he turned his eyes on me, eyes eerily similar to Pax's, I would lose my nerve. I crossed my arms over my chest and took a fortifying breath.

"I like Pax…I mean, I *like* like Pax." Covering my face, I hid the blooming blush. "God, I sound like I'm in middle school."

Morgan laughed. It wasn't the reaction I expected. Although he didn't laugh often, his displays of anger were far less. His hands tugged mine, pulling them away from my face.

"Open your eyes." I slowly opened them meeting his amused gaze. "It's about time."

Stunned, I concentrated on making a coherent sentence. "How did you know?"

"Just 'cause I'm a guy doesn't make me blind.

Question is, what're you going to do about it?"

I stuttered coming up with an appropriate answer. "I don't know. I've known for a long time how I feel about him." I paced. Feeling a headache coming on, I rubbed my thumbs on my temples.

Morgan followed and pulled me into a hug. I rested my head against his chest. "Want to know what I think?" I nodded my head against him and felt the vibrations of his chuckle. "Go for it. Own up to your feelings and go after what you want."

I shook my head. "I can't." His solution was too scary to contemplate. I couldn't put my heart out there for Pax to trample on, nor could I lose the Andersons.

"Stop overthinking."

"But I want it all."

"And you can have it." Morgan stroked my hair. He knew how it calmed me. "My parents love you. You're their daughter. You're my best friend. We aren't going anywhere."

I tightened my arms around his waist. "I'm scared."

Morgan pushed me back and looked me in the eye. To an observer, we seemed a couple in love with our foreheads touching and bodies aligned. Our go-to stance when either of us needed comforting.

"What fun is life if we don't face our fears? Time to step up, Red. Besides, he disobeyed orders to get to you. I think his actions speak loud and clear."

I sighed.

"Promise me you'll keep the details to yourself though," he said. His body shuddered against mine and I smiled.

Morgan knew all my crazy boyfriend stories. He

knew when I lost my virginity and the horrible experiences I'd had since then, like I knew about his. Having a boy for a best friend didn't deter me from talking about touchy subjects. In fact, I had an advantage. I often sought his advice on my bedroom prowess.

"Who am I going to share all the juicy details with then?" I asked, humor lacing my voice.

"On second thought, tell me how horrible he is so I have something to hold over his head."

Smacking his chest, I chuckled in relief. Having his blessing helped. Talking to Morgan gave me the confidence I needed. It was time for me to put my big girl panties on.

Chapter Thirteen

Pax

I didn't know if their idea would work, but I grew excited at the prospect of finally having Susan. Morgan explained how her deep-rooted fears made her hesitant to be with me, and it spurred me to prove her wrong.

Her anxieties were ridiculous, and I argued the point. After an hour of Morgan's incessant explanations, I finally understood. Over the years, Susan's desire to have a large family and a mother figure played a large role in molding her behaviors. Threatening her position in our family was not an option for her. Morgan believed she held her feelings close to her chest because losing what she had was a bigger risk than loving me. It was time for me to show her she stood to lose nothing, only gain.

Being honest and forthcoming with my feelings, proving to her how good it could be between us, had to work. I needed her to trust me to take care of her heart and understand my family was also hers no matter what. I had my work cut out for me, and I intended on winning her over.

I'd never had a hard time telling a woman what I wanted, but with Susan, I needed her to understand that, not only did I want to do things to her but also with her, to show her the permanency of my feelings.

I spent the rest of the evening researching online

and put together a budget for expanding Susan's shelter. With a few phone calls, the guys from the station promised to help with the construction. I printed out the city building request forms and prepared my 'To Do' list.

Often my mind wandered to Susan and the feel of her body against mine. Of how she responded to my touch. I wondered if the years we skirted around our feelings would help or hinder our relationship. Picturing her playing a significant role in my future settled a part of me. Knowing I was going to openly love her brought a sense of peace to my heart and mind.

My plan was two-fold. Easy in one aspect and difficult in the other. I needed Billy and the city approving my proposals for the shelter and the community outreach program. Then keep Susan by my side throughout the process, giving us the time I needed to make her see me as more than a friend.

****

The following day, I set off for the shelter and kept the skip in my step from showing. I could have gone to her house the night before, but I knew neither of us would make a scene if we were in public.

I walked in to the sounds of dogs barking and kids laughing. The front room, which resembled a living room, stood empty. With the two large couches, one brown and the other green, a light wood coffee table, and a few smaller tables spread throughout the room. It was comfortable and unobtrusive. Framed pictures dotted the cream-colored walls, exhibiting owners with their adopted pets.

Guided by the sounds of giggling children, I walked to the door leading to the back rooms and knocked. When no one responded, I carefully opened the door. The room beyond housed the animals ready for adoption. Open cage doors allowed the dogs to play throughout the space. Susan and an employee walked around the room filling food bowls, chatting and playing with the dogs as they went.

In one corner, a family of four played with a small, active puppy. The kids cackled as he jumped into their laps and licked their faces. The parents stood close, smiling and watching. I envied them. I wanted a family. I wanted the commitment and love my parents had, and I only wanted it with one person.

My gaze drifted to her as she bent down and opened a door. She reached in and held her hand out to a shy dog. He looked older and battle weary. I noticed Susan had a special place in her heart for him.

Susan plopped down, sitting cross-legged in front of the kennel gate. She petted him, speaking softly. He looked at her with an adoring gaze. With tepid steps, he crawled closer and laid his head in her lap. I suppressed a groan. Illogically, jealousy stirred within me.

I approached them, giving him time to take me in. He raised his gaze but kept his head in her lap. Deeming me a non-threat, he lay still and enjoyed the special attention bestowed upon him. His tail thudded against the floor while Susan delighted in him.

"What's his name?" I kept enough distance between us not to startle her.

She turned smiling for the briefest moment before her expression turned solemn. It killed something inside me, and I vowed to make up for my actions.

Sensing Susan's discomfort, the dog stood in front of her as she rose to her feet.

"Hi." She petted his back but kept her focus on my gradual approach. She didn't need to bend down to reach his back, and for the first time I took note of his size. He stood a few inches taller than her hips. He looked like he could take down a grown man. He seemed to puff out his chest as I studied his physique, and if I could decipher animal expressions, his told me to mind my step. I had competition in the 'protecting Susan' department.

"Hi. Can we talk?" I kept my voice low and extended my hand for him to sniff. He exposed his teeth, but I didn't change my stance. I was the alpha in the situation. The sooner he learned it the better.

Susan turned and nodded. "Sure. How about we take Darth for a walk?" She directed him to the door where they stopped while she leashed him. The other dogs barked louder.

"Is it always like this?" I asked as the chorus of barking reached a headache inducing pitch.

She laughed and walked through the door. "Only when they see another pup being leashed. I need a bigger fenced-in area, so I can let them all out at the same time. There are days I spend my entire time walking them." The light shining in her eyes belied the feelings behind her words.

"What happened to Darth? And who named him?" I took the leash from Susan's hand.

She sighed and petted Darth as he walked by my side. "He's a rescue dog, and he snarled at everyone. His new owner saw the good under the tough exterior. She named him Darth after one of her favorite movie characters. Unfortunately, she became ill soon after taking him in and passed away four months ago. Her brother's allergic. He knew I would keep him and brought him here. He's been here since. He's older and people usually want a puppy, so…"

She trailed off as tears shone in her eyes. Darth sensed her melancholy and wedged between us. His head butted my thigh making room. We walked in silence for a few more minutes before I directed us to one of the two benches inside the fenced grounds. Susan sat, and Darth settled by her feet, resting his chin on top of them.

For the first time our silence was stilted. It wasn't something I enjoyed. I needed to break the tension. "I'm sorry. I shouldn't have forced you…"

"Stop," Susan exclaimed, placing her hand on my thigh. She directed her gaze toward me. A smile graced her face, lighting up her features. "You forced nothing on me. I'm the one who needs to apologize. I never should have accused you. I'm sorry."

I shook my head and laughed. "I still feel like I should apologize for my actions."

She turned, facing me. Her knee rubbed along my thigh as she placed her foot under her butt. "We can both apologize 'til hell freezes over. We need to stop. I'm sorry, you're sorry. Let's drop it and move on as friends. Nothing happened. Just a moment. Agreed?"

I didn't agree, but I didn't object either. She took my silence as confirmation and stood. Darth darted to his feet and waited for her command. She stilled him with a hand gesture, and he sat down.

"Wow. That's impressive. I always wanted a dog."

"You should get one then. Darth here would be perfect for you."

I squatted and once again extended my hand in

invitation. Darth waited for Susan's okay and sniffed me. "He loves you. No way can I take him away from you."

"I love him too, but I don't have a place for him. If no one adopts him, he will always have a home here. Once I can get back on my own two feet, I'll take him home with me." Susan looked wistful. I wanted to pull her into a hug and give her platitudes. Something told me she wouldn't be receptive to it. I opted to silently help her get her life back together.

"Can you show me around and tell me what ideas you have for making the shelter bigger?"

"Sure."

I followed Susan around the courtyard. The smell of apples wrapped around me as we strolled through the yard. She pointed things out, and I listened to her vision for the place.

"That's it," she said when we circled around. "I have to get Darth water and take care of the other dogs." When I didn't follow, Darth yanked on the leash alerting her to the distance between us. "Aren't you coming in?"

Although I wanted to follow her in, take her into her office, and slowly kiss her until neither of us could breathe, I held back. I shook my head. "I'll be in shortly. I want to get a better lay of the land."

She retreated into the building. The door latched closed behind her, and I took my first real breath since I saw her sitting on the floor with Darth. All in good time, Susan would be mine, I reasoned.

I walked the grounds again and took measurements. I drew a rough sketch of the area. My mind drifted, and I struggled to focus on my task. Susan invaded my thoughts. I wanted Morgan's plan to work. I needed to expand on our stolen kiss. For her to see how good we were together, and by putting her faith in me, she would have everything she wanted. All she needed was to put a little trust in me and take a chance on us.

All in all, I had my work cut out for me.

****

Susan

He agreed to my ridiculous suggestion, and I hated my cowardice. I should have opened up to him. I should have taken the leap Morgan told me to. Although his smile brightened my day, I still feared the consequences of pursuing a relationship. The uncertainty was a bitch.

His family played an essential role in my life, and I didn't want to lose them. If he didn't feel the same way about me, it would make seeing his family awkward. On the other hand, if we did take a stab at being together and we failed, I could never see his family again. I'd never want to put them in a position where choosing sides was the grand finale.

Besides, I didn't have time for relationship woes. I needed to focus on the shelter, finding a new place to live, and picking up the pieces of my life after the fire.

I waited for him, completing tasks I had already finished. I stopped working several times and watched him through the windows. Every few minutes, he jotted down something on the pad he carried. I admit I stared far longer whenever he bent down. His ass was a work of perfection tantalizing me, distracting me from my job.

I scrambled to appear busy organizing the stock room when he came in. He didn't catch me ogling, but my red face probably gave me away. He didn't stay long after that, but somehow managed to extract a 'yes' from me to his dinner invitation. With a chaste kiss to my cheek and a wave, he was in his truck and rumbling down my drive before I reacted. He left me with a smile, wet panties, and more confusion than I started the day with.

****

Three hours later, I stood outside the shelter's doors, my hand on my cheek still feeling the burn of his lips against my skin. My heart skittered as he pulled into the parking lot. Throughout the day, the anticipation of the date hit me, but seeing him climbing out of his truck did me in. As he rounded the front and opened the door for me, seeing him in his tight shirt and well-fitted jeans, I knew the reality was far more dangerous to my health than the dream.

"Hope you don't mind, Rob and Beck are joining us tonight."

"Yeah? The more the merrier." I watched the passing buildings and hid the disappointment I was sure showed on my face.

I jumped when Pax put his arm across the bench in the truck and drove with one hand. He rubbed his thumb along my nape, and the feel of his calloused skin sent shivers through my body.

"Hey, are you okay?"

I nodded then realized he was focused on the road. "I'm good," I responded.

"I'm glad I got to spend time with you today. Your passion is infectious. I'm looking forward to do doing this with you."

"I feel the same way about you too."

For a second Pax turned a heated gaze my way and his fingers pressed into my neck. My core ignited at the small touch and I wiggled in my seat.

It didn't help.

"I could have met you guys. You didn't need to drive out of your way to come pick me up."

"Don't be ridiculous. I'd never ask you to drive yourself when I can pick you up."

"Always a gentleman," I said, and then whispered under my breath, "but I wish you weren't with me."

"What? I didn't quite catch that."

I flushed. "I didn't say anything."

I studied his profile. My gaze trailed along his strong jaw up to his eyes. My body responded to the proximity of his. Now I knew what it felt like cocooning in his arms, kissing him, and I craved more.

"If you don't quit staring, I'm pulling over to kiss you."

And we went from zero to sixty in less time than the fastest race car. Stunned by his admission, I snapped my head away, unable to come up with a response.

"Susan? Look at me."

I turned and shook at the look of desire darkening his eyes. "Pax," I moaned out.

"Stop. I can't do this now but later…later, I'm going to…"

My heart hammered in my chest. "You're going to what?"

"Anything and everything."

"What does that mean?"

"Means I want a repeat of the other night; this time without interruption. I want to take you out on a date, talk the night away, lose myself in you then talk some more as we hold each other in my bed."

He glanced at me, his eyes darkened. He shifted his hold and placed his large hand on my collarbone. His fingers rested dangerously close to my breast.

"Pax? What...what brought..." My heart leaped out of my chest envisioning us together. What he was implying went beyond any dreams I had over the years.

"It's you. I'm breaking my own rules. I can't, nor do I want to keep my hands off you," he said, understanding my unfinished question.

The drive ended far too soon, and we parked in the restaurant lot. Pax offered his hand and helped me out of the truck. As soon as my feet hit the ground, he pulled me into a hug. His hands spanned around my waist. He rested his forehead against mine and blew out a breath. It fanned across my face, and I inhaled. I wanted to hold onto his essence forever.

His gaze roamed my face and stopped on my lips. "I can hardly wait to kiss you again, and I want to explore every inch of your body with my hands and mouth. I want to be buried so deep in you and mark you like no one has ever done or will ever do." With a deep huff, he stepped back. He shook his head and looked to the darkening sky. I watched him in silence, curious to discover his thoughts.

"Okay. We better get inside before I do something stupid."

He took my hand in his and tugged me forward. I followed along lost in thought. I chalked off the kiss the other day as an in-the-moment kind of thing, but with his murmured words, I struggled to catch up. His declarations blind-sided me, and I was unsure of what I would have done if we stayed holding each other for much longer. Putting distance between us helped me regain control of my body, emotions, and thoughts. Pax held the door open and my arm brushed along his torso as I walked by. Electricity zipped through my veins at the slight touch.

Rob and Beck, sitting at a red-checkered table, waved as we approached them. A pitcher of ice tea and four glasses adorned the tabletop. Pax pulled out my seat and scooted me in before taking a seat beside me.

His friends were easy on the eyes, but Pax held all my attention. A fact I believe didn't go unnoticed as Beck's face crinkled in amusement.

"We've already ordered," Beck said. "Food should be out any minute."

No sooner had he spoken than two pizzas were placed on the table. I leaned forward and inhaled the delicious aroma of cheese and—I opened my eyes and scrunched at the offering.

"Ooh, disgusting. I hate olives."

"We know. Pax made sure we ordered a pepperoni pizza just for you."

"I can't eat all of it by myself." I beamed at Pax's thoughtfulness.

Pax grabbed two slices and placed one on my plate before he took a bite of the other. "You're sharing with me," he said after swallowing.

His Adams apple bobbed, and I fought the urge to straddle him and lick his neck. I turned red at Rob's snicker from across the table. Yet again, my ogling outed me, and I blushed at Pax's sly grin.

Chapter Fourteen

Susan

Throughout dinner, my skin tingled where Pax touched me whether deliberately or by accident. I spent most of the evening distracted watching him from the corner of my eye while he discussed plans with Beck and Rob.

By the end of the night, we decided on the size of the new structure and determined a budget for the building materials. The guys from the station had already promised their help with labor and the expertise of their construction-employed family members.

"Ready to get out of here?" Pax stood and pulled my chair out after I nodded. He put several twenties on the table, grabbed my hand, and led me out to his truck.

He took me home and kissed me goodnight. I was both relieved and disappointed when he didn't take the kiss further. There were two things I wanted most in life—a family and Pax. Could I have both? Or would one cancel out the other? Confused, I tucked into bed and replayed our kiss in my mind.

Pax's touches and small caresses left me needy. With the devil on one shoulder and an angel on the other, I debated throughout the night. Morning brought no clarity, and I was at a loss as to what to do. With Pax at the station for his shift for the next two days, I couldn't reach out to him. Whether he could give me answers remained to be seen.

The following day I woke tired and no closer to an answer, but a text turned the start of my day around.

Pax: *Morning beautiful*

I didn't want to text him back naked. Though he couldn't see me, my state of undress felt illicit. I took a quick shower, readied for work, prepared my breakfast, then sat at the island, and texted him back.

Me: *Hey yourself. How's work?*

Pax: *Boring*

Me: *Want to talk? I'm having my coffee, getting ready to go to the shelter.*

My phone rang.

"Hi."

"Hey, yourself. How'd you sleep?"

"A little restless. You?"

"A lot restless. I had too much on my mind."

"Yeah? What were you thinking about?" My voice turned sultry. The devil on my shoulder fed me my lines, and I smiled when Pax laughed from the other end.

"You. Our kiss. You. Our future kiss. You some more."

"Jeez, Pax. You aren't holding back," I said, my body heating.

"No need to anymore. I made so many mistakes. It's time for me to fix them. Besides, Morgan's given me his blessing, so…"

"Why would you need his blessing? He doesn't choose who I date," I said, quickly establishing my independence.

"So we're dating?"

I hesitated. Had I been wrong? Did I misinterpret

what he told me the night before?

"Hey. Stop whatever crazy thoughts are going through your head right now. I was kidding. I want to take you out on a date. Flowers, dinner, a walk in the park, star gazing. The whole nine yards."

Swallowing a few times, I waited until my voice didn't give away my excitement. "I'd like that."

"Want to come by today? Maybe bring those delicious lemon bars you make."

"What is with you and lemon? I swear you'd eat a whole tray of lemon bars or your mom's pie in one sitting if we let you."

"I like anything you make for me. But your lemon bars are my favorite."

I sighed. He didn't know I made the bars especially for him, knew he loved them. The first time I brought them to the station, he hugged me after having one. Ever since, I made them and received a similar response. In a way, he conditioned me. Lemon bars equaled hugs.

"I wish I could...but I can't. I have a family coming in to pick up a dog and the Pound called. They have three more dogs for me. I'm going to be super busy this morning. Maybe another day?" I asked hesitantly.

"Don't worry about it. Do what you need to do. How about I come by on Thursday night and you can make them for me then?"

"Sounds great. I'll see you then."

"'K, beautiful. I'll see you then."

I hung up, and even after running my hand across my face, I couldn't wipe away my smile. He called me beautiful. He wanted to see me, date me. However, in the back of my mind, I still feared a failed relationship. Not only would I lose him, but his family as well.

The smile greeting me in my mirror made my decision. I needed to live in the moment. Enjoy this for what it was, and I shoved my fears further back into the recesses of my brain.

****

I sat on the porch swing and waited for Pax. With one eye on the road and the other on the papers in my hands, I reviewed the 'To Do' list I created. His CO approved the plan, and we were ready to move forward. With the event only two weeks out, we had a lot to accomplish.

Pax pulled up in his truck, and I moaned, my gaze tracking his every move. He wore ripped, faded jeans, a simple black T-shirt, and worn leather boots. He looked good enough to lick, and I wet my lips. My skin heated with a flush, and I turned my attention back to the clipboard in my lap, using work to distract me from my wayward dirty thoughts.

"Now this is a sight I can get used to."

The butterflies in my belly fluttered to attention.

I wore white denim shorts and a simple ocean blue tank top combating the unseasonably high temperatures. Even as the sun descended, the heat didn't dissipate. He grasped my feet, pulling them off the bench, sat down, and cradled them in his lap. I shifted, and my foot rubbed against him. He hissed and tightened his hold on my ankles.

His heated gaze met mine as I sat motionless. "Sweetheart." He leaned toward me, "Shit..." Pax mumbled.

"Here you go, kids. It's hot out here," my dad said,

interrupting Pax.

Pax shifted and covered his obvious arousal with my feet. "Hey, Mr. Hayes." His voice was a pitch higher than normal.

"Hi, Pax." Dad placed a tray loaded with a pitcher of iced tea, glasses, and the lemon bars I made on the table by Pax. "I'm off to the bar with Ted," he said around a smile. "Don't wait up." He skipped down the porch steps, hopped into his vehicle, and was gone before I could blink.

"You made the bars. Thanks," Pax said, pressing his hands to my bare calf.

My blush deepened, and I leaned my head against the back of the swing. "Of course I made them. I also packed a box for you to take home."

Pax leaned over and crashed his lips against mine, surprising me. His fingers traced the outside of my leg as he deepened our connection. I yielded to him and wrapped my arms around his neck. The clipboard clattered to the ground, startling us. He pulled away, licking his lips, hovering over me.

"We should get through…"

"I want…" We spoke at the same time, and I laughed.

Leaning over my legs, Pax poured the drinks and handed me one. "Thanks."

"You're welcome." He turned away and took in the view. "I love the quiet of this neighborhood. When I first started searching for my own place, I wanted to buy a house here. It's funny now, but it was my mom who convinced me to look farther out of the city limits. I'm glad she did, but sometimes I wonder if I should have bought a place less secluded," he mused, staring off into the distance.

I didn't interrupt and quietly took in his profile. The Anderson boys had similar features with their strong brow and jawline, dark hair, and light eyes. They were all breathtaking, but Pax stood out among them. No stubble graced his face while he worked, but during his days off, he didn't shave. I wanted to reach out and rub my hand along his face, curious as to its coarseness.

"See something you like?"

I blushed and looked away. I hid behind my hair as I messed with the glass in my hand.

"Don't hide from me, baby," he said, lifting my chin with gentle fingers.

I didn't respond, but I didn't shy away from his touch either. He gave me the space I needed, and I regulated my breathing. His touch alone made my breath hitch each and every time.

"What you got there?" He picked up the clipboard from the floor and read the list. "It's a good starting point," he said. "I'm sure my family will help us get all this set up." He reached behind us and settled the board against the windowsill before returning his hand to my ankle. He rubbed circles into my skin, and I knew if I didn't find a distraction I would straddle his lap and finish what we started.

"I was thinking I can make calls, get the pet store to open a mini shop at the event. If you can make the fliers, get them to the schools, and hung up around the neighborhood, then I'll have enough time to get all the vendors in place. I already have a food truck on board. He'll sell ice cream and other sweet stuff. We'll get sixty percent of his profits. He adopted a dog from us three years ago after his son fell ill, and he said if it weren't for the dog, he doesn't think his son would have survived. Anyway, he wants to help, and…"

Pax placed a finger on my lips, his eyes sparkling with amusement. "You're adorable when you're nervous."

"I'm not nervous. Why would I be nervous? It's not like you and I haven't been friends forever."

"Baby, I already told you. I want you. This is going to happen, but we'll take it slow."

I swallowed, fighting a failing battle. Between his touch and his whispered words, I had a tenuous hold on my desires.

Chapter Fifteen

Pax

Content to sit all night on the swing, I got lost in the moment. Susan smiled and sighed the longer I caressed her ankle. Her eyelids drooped, and I craved carrying her to a bed and holding her while she slept.

"What are you doing tomorrow?"

"It's my paperwork day. I have a lot of volunteers coming in. I can sit in my office and get tedious stuff done."

"Can I take you out to dinner?"

She smiled and nodded. I rubbed my hand along the length of her calf. Goosebumps sprouted on her skin along the path I took. I ached to have her, but she wasn't ready. I took her feet off my lap. With a slight adjustment, I stood without giving her an eyeful.

I picked up the tray and walked inside, taking a moment in the kitchen as I willed my erection down. The more time I spent with her, the more I fought my need for her. In the end, however, I knew it wouldn't be in vain.

With my breathing and body under control, I stepped back out onto the porch. Susan was right where I left her, her head resting against the back of the swing, exposing the long curve of her neck. I bent and licked the column of skin.

She shuddered beneath my attention. Her hands

gripped my shirt and tugged me closer. I settled on my knees, and she turned, placing her feet on the floor. I scooted in between her open legs and molded my body to hers. "I should go," I said, between kisses. "I'll pick you up at seven."

"No."

I stopped mid-kiss, confused. She giggled and ran her fingers through my short hair. "How about you come here? My dad plays poker tomorrow. I can make us dinner. We can work on the program."

"We're not talking about the fundraiser. I want to take you out on a proper date. Do the whole getting to know each other thing."

"I'd like that too, and I like being with you. Let me do this for you. I'll make your favorite meal."

I smiled, stole a kiss, and closed my eyes holding onto the moment. "That's an offer I can't refuse, but I'll bring the wine. Pinot still your favorite?"

"Hmmm."

I rose to my feet but kept her tugged against me. She hooked her ankles together behind my back. "Baby, I can only keep myself reined in for so long. I should go."

She hummed against my neck. I kissed her slow and deep. I pulled back taking her lower lip between my teeth.

"I should go," I repeated.

"Okay," Susan said, as she unwound her legs.

"Tomorrow?"

"Tomorrow," she affirmed around a lazy smile.

****

I arrived at her house twenty minutes early. Curtailing my needs proved futile. After a day of fighting my instincts, I gave in. I was excited to see her and images of coming home to her bombarded me as I pulled into her driveway.

She greeted me at the door with a radiant smile. I wrapped my wine-laden arm around her waist and yanked her to me, planting a mouthwatering kiss on her sweet lips. She stepped back, eyes glazed with desire.

She looked radiant dressed in a light green sundress with spaghetti straps that refused to stay in place. She styled her hair in a messy bun and I imagined pulling the pins out while she straddled my lap. Her skin glowed and eyes sparkled. I stood just outside the door taking in the beauty before me until she took my hand and tugged me inside.

I kept the bottle of wine but handed her the bouquet I picked up on my way over.

"Thanks, Pax. These are beautiful." She turned, moving away, and giggled as I pulled her back to me. I kissed her senseless, leaving us both panting for breath. "I'm never going to get enough of that."

"Of what?" she asked me, as she studied my face in wonder.

"The feeling of you in my arms, and your lips against mine."

She sighed and tightened her one-arm hold on me. When I let her go, she took my hand in hers again, intertwined our fingers, and led me to the dining room. She grabbed a vase from the kitchen as I sat at the set table. The aroma of a home cooked meal wafted around me, and I imagined doing this every day with her for the rest of my life.

I waited for her to place the vase on the table before I snagged her wrist and pulled her onto my lap.

She giggled and wrapped her arms around my neck. She smiled, successfully making me weak in the knees. I knew I would live the rest of my life doing anything and everything to see her smile, to make her laugh. To make her feel cherished. I could sit and watch her all day and still never have my fill.

****

After dinner, we spent the evening swinging on the porch. I took every opportunity to touch her, from 'accidental' brushes to rubbing my hand along her thighs. We sat similar to the previous night, with her feet in my lap and sexual tension vibrated through the air. Every time her breath hitched, or she closed her eyes, I pressed on. I ran my fingertips along the inside of her thigh and stopped inches from the hem of her dress. She trembled under my touch.

The night sky kept us in the shadows, and with her dad out of the house, we had the privacy I needed to do what my fingers craved. I took the drink from her hands and placed it on the floor. I tugged her ankles and pulled her to me. I stopped just shy of putting her on my lap. Susan moaned as I caressed her cheek with the back of my hand.

She refused to look at me and scooted away.

"Hey, what's wrong?" I let her move.

She didn't answer but focused on a spot in the distance. She bit her bottom lip and continued avoiding me. The part of me that loved her, wanted her to open up. To trust I would hold her heart in the most secure place. The part of me that desired her wanted to take that bottom lip and bite it.

"You can tell me anything, baby."

She trembled under my hand, and I wanted to pull

her fully to me but held back. I was fine with waiting, and if there ever was a time for patience, it was now. I rubbed my hand along her thigh biding my time.

"I'm scared," she whispered, and studied her hands in her lap.

Cupping her chin, I lifted her face. I lowered my head looking into her eyes. "I know."

"How do you know? How can you possibly know how I'm feeling right now? I don't even know how to define what is going through my head."

A feisty Susan I could work with.

"Why don't you try explaining it to me then?"

She set her feet on the porch floorboards and set the swing in motion. "How can I explain something I don't understand? I've liked you for so long…" she stopped. I kept my gaze on her. She huffed. I didn't want to interrupt, but my heart thudded in my chest as I waited. "I guess I can't deny it anymore. Morgan and my dad told me to just tell you."

I made no attempt to take her hand in mine, although my need to protect her, even from herself, overwhelmed me.

"I like you," she said, around another puff of breath. "There, I said it."

"What's the problem then? You like me. I like you. We're adults. We can have a relationship."

"That's not the issue."

"Then what is?"

"What if we don't work out? I love your family. Morgan's my best friend. If we fail, then I lose everything."

I didn't hesitate. I pulled her onto my lap. At first, she wriggled in my grasp, but then snuggled, rubbing her face into my chest as I held her tight. I kissed the top of her head.

"Baby, you will lose nothing. My family loves you, and Morgan loves you more than he loves me. They will never choose sides. If anything, they will hate me for hurting you. Besides, how are we going to know if we will or won't work if we don't try? Please."

She lifted her head and cupped my cheeks in her hands.

"Give me a chance to show you how I feel about you. Take a gamble on us. If we go into this with either of us thinking the worst, it will never work. Do this with me. Be with me." I wasn't above pleading if it meant finally having her as my partner.

Her gaze never left mine, and with an imperceptible nod, she leaned in and kissed me slowly. Tentative turned to heated and then desperate. I shifted her on my lap, opening her legs wider. I slid my hand up her leg and played with the hem of her dress, pulling it up. She leaned into me deepening our kiss. I throbbed in my pants, but I held off my own needs. I wanted the night to be about her.

Lowering my mouth, I kissed along her jaw and neck. I stroked her stomach and rested my fingertips underneath her bra. With a flick of my thumb, I played with her nipple until her moans grew too loud for our public setting. I swallowed her whimpers with my mouth and kissed her as I explored her body. Taking her breast in one hand, I squeezed and kneaded her. She fit perfectly, and I enjoyed the feel of her soft skin against my palm.

"Pax," Susan pleaded, and her hips rocked forward begging for relief. My zipper threatened to burst from the force against it, but I ignored it. Susan coming apart in my arms was an image I wanted embedded in my memory forever.

"I got you, baby," I said. I licked and kissed her neck. Her taste burst against my tongue and it was all I could do not to leave my mark on her. Susan dug her fingertips into my scalp as I lapped at her collarbone.

With slow, purposeful movements, I moved my hand back down her stomach. My fingers tingled the closer I got to my destination. I ran my hand along her covered pussy. The heat of her desire penetrated through the layer of clothing. I rubbed my finger along her seam, and once again kissed her, muffling her moans.

"Please." Her voice spiked with yearning I couldn't deny.

I found the seam of her panties and pushed them aside. I slipped a finger along her outer lips and rubbed her wetness along her skin. Susan moved against my hand. Her scent rose between us and I inhaled. Her arousal intoxicating. Wanting more, needing more, I pushed a finger inside while my thumb stroked her clit.

Susan's chest heaved at the intrusion. She shut her eyes and laid her head back. I was lost in watching her. I added a second finger and pumped my hands against her grinding pelvis.

Her moans grew louder, and I knew she was close. I flicked her clit as my fingers inside found her sweet spot. She rocked faster against my hand. Wetness coated my fingers, and I pushed forward. My gaze homed in on her beautiful, bliss-filled face, and I reveled in her loss of control. Her mouth opened in a silent scream. I wanted to see her eyes, but I enjoyed the scrunched eyelids too much to ask her to look at me.

"Pax…feels so good. Don't stop."

"Wasn't planning on it, baby."

Her words spurred me, and I kept my pace, rubbing my palm against her. Susan held on tightly. Her mouth formed a silent 'O'. Knowing she was ready, I leaned down and pulled her covered nipple into my mouth. She came apart in my arms. I slowed the pace and let her ride out her orgasm.

Her chest rose and fell as she took several deep breaths. Slowly, she opened her eyes and our gazes connected. I knew then my patience to make her mine was threadbare. I wanted to see the look of bliss on her face over and over again.

Chapter Sixteen

Pax

With calls for three fires, two cat rescues from tree branches, and a car accident, the following two days of work kept me busy and Susan out of my mind for a few minutes of my day. But for the first time, I counted the minutes to the end of my shift. I wanted to see her and the longer I went without her the more obvious my Susan withdrawals became to the men. Although they joked, calling me love lost, I kept my budding relationship private. I wanted to enjoy the newness of us without the guys ruining it.

After she came off her high the night of our first date, we hung out for an hour. I didn't push for more and left soon after. I didn't want to scare her off by moving too quickly.

Although we ended the evening with a mind-blowing kiss, I wasn't sure if she was hungry for more or hesitant to move forward. I texted her first thing the next morning, and a few times throughout the day. Her continued responses with emojis worried me.

On my first day off, I met with two local news stations and made fliers. Several of my crew helped me hang them throughout town. Before long, I itched to see Susan. Pulling out my phone, I sent her a text.

The fifth one of the day.

Pax: *Hungry?*

The ellipses started and stopped three times before an answer came through.

Susan: *Starved*

Pax: *How about I come over and eat you?*

Susan: *...?*

I knew I shouldn't have, but who ever said a man in love was smart? I imagined her cheeks turning red, and I smiled. Currently my favorite look on Susan was the blissed out, red-faced, satisfied one.

Pax: *Oops. Meant to say, how about I come over and take you out to eat?*

She took a few moments before answering. Her response delighted me.

Susan: *I'm not sure I'll be very tasty*

Pax: *Beg to differ. You most definitely will taste as good as you look*

Susan: *Only one way to find out*

I gulped and checked no one was around before I adjusted my cock. My idea of fun was not sitting in the firehouse's parking lot, palming myself while I read and reread her texts.

Pax: *Food then fun*

Susan: *Promises. Promises*

Pax: *I'll be there in ten*

My need to see her spurred me on, and I put my phone in the cup holder instead of my glove box, where I usually kept it, and drove to Kisses and Paws.

Stepping into the cab of the truck, Susan noticed my phone immediately.

"Pax. You never leave your phone out. What's this?" She pointed at the cup holder, and I shrugged.

"Didn't want to miss any messages from you."

She blushed, and the knot in my chest unraveled.

Whatever reasons she had for her stilted responses over the past two days didn't seem to affect her now. "Why haven't you set up your Bluetooth? You can keep both hands safely on the wheel, just how you like."

"Don't know. Never had the need for it. Calls and texts can wait. Safe driving is important." I believed in what I said, and I never answered my phone while driving. A distracted driver ran a red light, hitting Aunt Karen and Uncle Dustin's car. At the age of eleven, the manner of their deaths made a lasting impression on me.

"But you have steering wheel controls. You can answer the phone with one push of your finger."

"I didn't know. Go ahead and set it up for me if you like." Making her happy satisfied me. And her awareness of my idiosyncrasies and lack of judgment further lifted my spirits.

She grabbed my phone. "What's your password?"

I kept my focus on the road because I didn't know how she would react. "Zero, three, two, six."

She gasped, and I held my breath and waited. "That's my birthday." I strained to hear her and snuck a peek. "You're breaking all your rules for me. Keep your eyes on the road," she admonished, when she caught me watching her.

I wanted to pull over and take her in my arms, reassure her of my feelings, but when she didn't shut down, I took it as a good sign.

"Pax…I don't know what to say. How long's it been your password? You know what? Never mind. I don't need to know."

I did what I always told others not to do. I took one hand off the wheel and placed it on her thigh. The warmth of her skin under my fingertips distracted me, but through sheer will, I focused on the road and not her skin.

"I'll tell you. I'm not ashamed of how I feel about you. It's been my password ever since I needed one."

"That was years ago." She pushed her hand under my hand on her thigh and threaded our fingers. She stared out of the widow and I left her to think. I drove us to the sandwich shop located on the way to the park and parked. I wanted to kiss her but held back and waited.

"I didn't know." Susan turned in her seat and tucked her left ankle under her. "How could I have not known?"

Mirroring her position, I turned and faced her. This time I reached out and moved my hand along her jaw. I trailed her skin until I rested my fingers on her neck. She didn't stop me, and I rubbed my thumb along her clavicle.

"I always thought you were Morgan's girlfriend. I hid how I felt because…" Lifting my other hand off the steering wheel, I ran it through my hair. "He's my brother. How could I move in on his girl?"

A smile formed on her luscious lips and I couldn't hold back any longer. Leaning over the center console, while tugging at the back of her neck, I brought her closer and kissed her. I pulled her lower lip in between my teeth. She sighed and responded with enthusiasm.

Kissing her grounded me, but when her hands landed on my chest, I almost lost it in my pants. I wanted her. I deepened our kiss, exploring her mouth with my tongue. My body roared with need, but I had enough sense to hold back from hauling her into my lap. I needed privacy for what I planned. A parking lot in front of a busy sandwich shop was not the place.

With enormous effort, I pulled away, but let my lips linger against hers. I took her ragged exhales deep into my lungs. Her eyes glazed over with lust and desire; no doubt, mine appeared the same. "It's always been you," I whispered, because any other volume would have shattered the moment.

I needn't have worried. My phone's ringtone blasted through my car speakers, and we jolted apart in surprise.

****

Susan

I pulled back, thankful for the reprieve and gathered my thoughts. Kissing him was like making love to a volcano setting my body to ignite.

For two days, doubts overwhelmed me. However, from the moment I stepped into the cab I knew I'd worried for nothing. His smile set me at ease. When he told me his password, I swear the earth quaked below my feet. Combine that with the whispered words from our date, the feel of his lips on mine, and his patience, I wanted to jump him in the cab of the truck regardless of any prying eyes.

His voice pulled me back to the present, and he looked at me apologetically. I stepped out of the cab giving him privacy. I rested against the grill of the truck and soaked in the afternoon sun only for a few minutes. If I didn't take care my freckles would deepen, and my skin burn. Besides, I figured Pax wouldn't take long on his call.

My thoughts centered on us and replayed the past week over in my head. I knew I loved him, but I never imagined my feelings were reciprocated. Pax dated the most beautiful girls in school. He was prom king and his girlfriend at the time was the queen. In college, he dated gorgeous, model-worthy girls. I had nothing on them.

Most days I wore cut-offs and a tank top, with my hair pulled up in a messy bun, and my face devoid of makeup. Usually covered in cat and dog fur, I probably smelled like a kennel. I stood no taller than five-foot-five and I carried a few extra pounds around my hips and stomach. Pax's huge and heavily muscled build towered a foot taller than me. Our personalities were different. Where I was quirky, he was quiet. I took risks, and he was the epitome of safety. Yet I couldn't deny the chemistry between us and the way my blood boiled when he touched me.

Pax's raised voice drew me away from my musings. I turned making sure he was okay. Anger filled his eyes, his body stiff. His mouth moved, but I couldn't hear his end of the conversation though the caller's voice came loud and clear through the car speakers.

"I love…How can you say…I can make you…But I can give you so much more than she can…"

I moved away from the vehicle to a nearby tree. Partially for shade but mostly to get away from the woman's pleading voice. I hated nothing more than a woman begging for a man's attention.

Believe me, I understood the power of yearning and desire, but I could never beg for a man's affections. I hoped, whoever she was, she found the strength to move on and find someone worthy of her. Pax obviously wasn't it.

Despondent, I schooled my features and hid the feelings crushing me. I loved Pax, and I knew he had feelings for me yet a part of me worried I wasn't enough. When an attraction went denied for so long a person built up the other in their mind. After all these years, I wondered if I could live up to Pax's vision of me.

"I don't know what happened in the two minutes you got out of the truck, but we're getting to the bottom of it," Pax said from behind me, startling me away from the tree.

I wanted him to pull me in his arms, reassure me I was all he ever wanted or needed. I wanted him to kiss me and make me forget my insecurities. "Nothing's wrong. Just thought of something and…Let's forget about it."

"No. You're sad, and it breaks my heart. Please talk to me." Pax pulled me into a hug and caressed my hair as I let out a deep sigh, secure in the comfort of his arms. Self-protection and doubts were ruining the moment. Whether the potential heartbreak or losing his family was the greater threat, I couldn't tell.

"Baby, look at me. You know me. Talk to me. Whatever you're thinking, we'll deal with it together. Please."

His vulnerability somehow comforted me. I burrowed farther into him and wrapped my arms around his waist. He held me tighter and rested his cheek on my head. I owed him an explanation. No matter how difficult, I needed to own my insecurities.

"How about we get our food and go over to the park? We can talk there," I mumbled into his chest. He nodded, let go, and followed me into the shop.

Chapter Seventeen

Pax

The turn of events frustrated me. Julie's call destroyed the ease and lightness of my time with Susan. I knew her curiosity sent her mind into overdrive. She didn't hide her sadness well, and I worried.

While I argued with Julie, my focus zeroed in on Susan through the windshield. My thoughts turned dirty at the sight. I imagined taking her on the hood. Claiming her. Making her mine. Susan brought out the caveman in me.

Unfortunately, Julie's shrill voice interrupted my daydreams. Her continued declarations of love grated on my nerves. I told her again to leave me alone, but it was like beating a dead horse. Her expectations grew wilder each day. She left packages of food or lacy underwear at my house. Her notes explained in great detail how she wanted me to use her to my satisfaction. I threw the food and gifts out but kept the letters, knowing the importance of saving them. I didn't want to involve the authorities, but if her obsession escalated, I would.

With Susan silent beside me, I ignored the gnawing inside my stomach and concentrated on her. After ordering our food, I insisted on paying. She huffed but relented when I didn't budge. Outside, I grabbed a blanket from the truck, and we walked in silence to the park two blocks away.

I found a shady spot under a big yew tree and spread the blanket underneath. Taking her hand in mine, I helped her sit before taking the spot beside her and unpacking the food bag. I lifted my face to the sun and enjoyed the warm breeze surrounding us. Summer rolled in and I loved the heat.

"What happened back there?" I asked after a few minutes of silence.

She ate a bite of her sandwich before lifting a bottle of water to her lips. The action drew my attention to her mouth and the fine lines of her neck. I fought the urge to lean in and taste her skin. I didn't hide my lust-filled gaze well and her skin reddened.

"I heard you on the phone with that woman." Confused, I waited for her to continue. "Car speakers' volume is sometimes loud enough to hear conversations outside the vehicle even with the doors closed. The things she said to you…"

"I'm not dating her. I wouldn't be pursuing you if…"

"I don't know what to think. Things she said made me…I don't know…question what we're doing here." She turned away, but not before I caught sight of a tear in the corner of her eye.

I cupped her jaw, turning her to face me. "I told you before, and I'll say it as many times as I need for you to believe me. You're the one I want. The only one I will ever want. I know the idea of us scares you but give me a chance to prove to you how much you mean to me."

"But what if I'm not enough?" Susan asked.

I pulled her into my lap and ran my hand up and

down her back. She didn't fight me, eventually molding against my chest. "You will always be enough. The reality is I'm worried I won't be enough for you. Every night I go to sleep and every morning I wake up with you in my thoughts. You make me want to be better. Your love and loyalty to Morgan, my family, your dad, and all your animals speaks volumes of the kind of woman you are. I hope you don't find me disappointing."

She rubbed her knuckles across my cheek. Her eyes brimmed with tears. I ran my thumbs along her cheeks and wiped them away. She wrapped her arms around my neck and pulled me to her. This time she crushed her lips against mine. I let her control the kiss, and she licked my lips. I granted her access and held back from taking over. She kissed me with ferocity, and I growled into her mouth.

She pushed away and giggled. "I like this kissing thing between us."

"Baby, you can kiss me anytime you like." I rubbed my hand along her back.

"Pax." She sighed. "You have to know. The very same qualities you said about me are also in you. They're what make you who you are. You can never disappoint me."

"The woman on the phone," I started, and Susan moved, but I held her tighter. "Let me finish, baby. The woman on the phone is someone I've never dated. Her dad's a retired firefighter. He's a mean son-of-a-bitch and one day she was at the firehouse crying. I sat with her and she gave me her entire life story. I listened and got her coffee. That's it. She's hung out at the station since then and believes I'm the guy for her. I'm not.

There's nothing about her I find attractive. I've told her, but she refuses to accept it. She's holding on to the misguided hope I'll change my mind. I won't."

Lifting her head from my shoulder, Susan gazed at me with concern. "Is she the same woman who came to your place the other day?"

"Unfortunately, she is," I affirmed. "She followed me home from work one day and ever since, she shows up unannounced…"

"What aren't you telling me?" she asked.

I took a moment to answer. I didn't want to tell her all the crazy stuff Julie did but with Susan being a part of my life now, I wanted her cautious and aware of the situation. I needed to tell her enough without worrying her.

"I came home one day and found her naked in my bed. I made her leave and installed an alarm system linked to an app on my phone. I get an alert and a live feed when anyone approaches my house. She shows up at the house whenever I'm on duty and leaves stuff for me. I throw it all out, except for the letters."

"Why keep those?"

"In case I need to go to the cops. I want something other than the videos to have as a record of her harassment."

Susan turned in my arms and straddled me. I groaned at the feel of her body against mine. I didn't need the distraction, the conversation too important to hold off. Suppressing my desire to kiss her, I continued. "When she didn't get my attention, she slept with one of the new recruits to make me jealous and when I didn't react, she started a fight with me in front of the station. I walked away before it got out of hand and the guys are weary of her. None of us want to be mean, but we ignore her when she comes around. I didn't invite her into my life, but I'm having a heck of a time getting her out of it."

"What does your family think?"

I shook my head. "I haven't told them. Mom would worry more than she already does. Dad would want to get the authorities involved. But I've already spoken to a buddy of mine on the force and he told me they can't do anything unless she harms me, my family, my friends, or my home. So for now I'm ignoring her. I don't know how she got my number and she constantly calls. I haven't had time to get my number changed."

"Oh, Pax." Susan fingered my eyebrows, smoothing them while her own furrowed. "Promise me, if she doesn't stop you will tell your brothers. They'll be upset if you don't let them help, especially Morgan and Caden. You always looked out for each other; they won't take it kindly if you don't tell them. Let me see your phone. I can block her number if you like."

God, the woman knew me well. The bond was tight between Morgan, Caden, and me, and even though Caden traveled a lot, I relied on him when I needed anything. "You're right, Caden's home for another two weeks. I'll call and talk to him about it." I handed her my phone and her face soured.

I grabbed it back. The screen lit up with several texts. Over the past hour, Julie had sent me love declarations, nude photos, and when I didn't respond, her texts turned nasty. I deleted the nudes, kept the texts, and handed the phone to Susan. After clicking a few icons, she gave it back with a small smile. "Done. She shouldn't be able to text or call you anymore."

The day's mood had soured and although I wanted nothing more than to wrap my arms around Susan and get lost in her, I needed to figure this shit out with Julie. I gave Susan a quick kiss before we headed to the truck. I drove her back to the shelter and then used the steering wheel controls and voice commands to call Caden. It was time to get help.

****

I pulled up in front of Caden's rental condo, parking my car twelve feet away from the fire hydrant. Thankfully, whatever Susan did worked. At least I hoped it had. I received no more calls or texts from Julie, but I didn't know for how long.

"Give up already?" Caden asked in lieu of hello as he opened the door. The smile on his face disappeared as he registered my somberness. "What the fuck happened?"

"Can I come in first, or are you keeping me out on the stoop all afternoon?"

He opened the door wider, silently inviting me in. Caden sparsely decorated the space since he wasn't home for long periods. Only a few framed family photos adorned the walls. I walked over to the black couch and plopped down. Caden retrieved two beers from the fridge and joined me.

"Here, you look like you need one of these. Maybe several." He opened the bottles and handed one to me.

I took a swallow and enjoyed the cool liquid coating my throat. After another long draw, I wiped my mouth with the back of my hand.

"Did Susan turn you down?" He stretched his legs, scooted down on the seat with a bottle against his stomach, and waited me out.

"She didn't. Things are going great between us. No, what's on my mind is something I haven't told you about. In fact, other than Susan and Simon, no one knows."

"Simon, the cop? What the hell? Are you in trouble?"

"Yes and no. I think I have a stalker." I waited for Caden to laugh at the absurdity of my statement, but he only straightened in his seat.

"Tell me everything."

Sighing, I told my story for the second time. I didn't skim over the details like I had with Susan.

"This chick Julie's fixated on having a relationship with me for about six months now. Her dad was a CO at another house. Had a problem with alcohol at the end of his career. Guys under his command said he turned mean toward the end, especially after losing his wife." I took a sip of my beer while I gathered my rambling thoughts. There was a lot of information to give, and my mind was a jumbled mess.

He waited silently, and after a few minutes, I laid out all the ugly problems with Julie to Caden.

"If I knew then what I know now, I would have called the department therapist and handed her off to him."

"I doubt that. You wouldn't have turned her away," Caden said.

Running my hand through my hair, I struggled to tell him the rest. "At times, when I'm home, I feel like someone's watching me. I close the blinds at night and sometimes during the day. I feel like I'm a prisoner in my own home. My closest neighbors are a mile away and I chose the house because of the privacy. Now I wonder if I made a mistake living in a secluded area."

Caden stood and paced. I tracked his movement before continuing. "A few times after I felt someone watching me I found footprints in the dirt out back. I haven't landscaped the yard yet and there's dirt everywhere. The odd thing though is the prints look like boots. Boots too small for a man. I think they're Julie's, but I've only ever seen her wear heels. I can't be sure."

I stood and walked in the other direction. Our shoulders rubbed as we passed each other.

Caden stopped, and I mirrored his action. We stood at opposite ends of the room both lost in thought. "Shit, Pax. This woman's off her rocker. Why didn't you come to me earlier? My place is yours. Stay here while we get more cameras on your house."

Typical Caden. He believed it was his duty to provide solutions to our problems.

"I appreciate the offer, but I don't think Julie's a threat. She's annoying. I hoped she'd grow tired of pursuing me if I ignored her. That she'd eventually move on. I don't know if I need any more security. I already have cameras on all the entry points."

"Why didn't you call the cops when she broke in?"

"I didn't want her to get in trouble. That was the first time she crossed the line. Until that point, she only hung out at the station trying to get my attention. I figured if I kept telling her no she'd get the hint and leave me alone."

"But she hasn't. Instead, she did more shit to get your attention. By the sound of it, she's unstable. He sat back down deep in thought.

Parched from talking, I grabbed two more beers from the fridge. Opened them, handed one to Caden, and downed half of mine in one swig.

"She told my crew she slept with me, gave them details of my bedroom. They believed her until I explained what happened." Taking another sip of my beer, I sat down across from Caden. "They stopped being nice to her. She's tried to win them back. Even slept with our newest recruit, Joel, and flaunted it in my face. I don't give a shit she slept with him, but I took him aside and warned him of her type of crazy."

"Does she still come by the station?"

"Yes. She shows up at least once during my shifts. She comes by my house on days I'm off. She knows my schedule."

"I don't know. I don't like the sound of this woman. Something's not right with her. I want you to stay with me, but it won't make a difference if she's following you. I think you need to give me all the letters for safekeeping and keep telling Simon about what's going on. Start an official record of her harassment. Maybe the cops can talk to her, scare her straight. Ask Simon what he thinks you should do?"

Caden took our empty bottles to the kitchen and returned with water.

"Thanks. I need to switch to water before driving home."

Caden nodded. "You can always stay here," he said, as he lifted his legs and rested his feet on the coffee table. He appeared relaxed, but the worry lines around his mouth deepened. He would think and plot until either the situation escalated, or Julie gave up and found another obsession.

"Thanks, but I've got shit to do at home before work tomorrow. I'll talk to Simon. I want to move on with my life, bring Susan into it, and go after the future I want with her."

"Then do it. Keep doing what you're doing. Stay away from Julie and she'll leave you alone when she realizes you're off the market."

"Yeah? I hope you're right." I reached for my drink, glad I spoke with him.

We sipped our waters in silence. I thought of how long I needed to stay at Caden's until the effects of the alcohol wore off, and if I had to guess, Caden planned to keep me safe.

"How's it going with Susan?" Caden smiled around the mouth of the bottle. I didn't have to say much. I let my smile do all the talking.

"That good, huh? When's the wedding?" He laughed as I grabbed the pillow from behind my back and hit him with it.

Chapter Eighteen

Pax

The next few days flew by between work and helping Susan get the final details completed for the charity event. We didn't have any alone time in the bedroom, but I kissed her every opportunity I got.

"Hey there good looking, come plant one on me." Susan laughed as she got into my truck, leaned over, and gave me her version of a kiss. She pulled away too soon, and I gripped her neck.

I licked the seam of her mouth. I wanted more, and she opened with a sigh. I could kiss her all day and still want more. I tangled my tongue with hers, and her hands explored her favorite place to touch, my chest. She ran her fingers through the dips of my muscles, and I trembled under her attention.

Her hands were small, yet they warmed my skin all over. The fact we were in my truck in front of her father's house was the only thing keeping me from hauling her into my lap or from lifting her shirt and taking in the sight of her naked body. Although my body ached for her, I willed myself off the ledge and pulled back from our kiss. I grinned when she looked at me with glazed eyes. She looked as desperate for me as I was for her.

I couldn't resist and pulled her in for another kiss. I caressed her thighs with the barest of touches until I reached the hem of her skirt. I bunched the fabric in my hands. My fingers grazed the inside of her thigh and she moaned into my mouth.

Susan shifted in her seat giving me access to her heated flesh. The temperature inside the truck soared. Sweat trickled down my neck, but it didn't stop me from going further. I slid a finger across her panties and she bucked against my hand.

"God, I want you," I whispered against her mouth.

"My dad's home," she said between panting breaths.

My excitement deflated at the mention of her father, and I pulled away. When I was with Susan the world melted away, and all I saw, wanted, tasted, and held was her. She made me forget. She made me break the rules I lived by. She made me happy. With a regulating breath, I started the truck and edged out onto the road. "I forbid you to wear a skirt until I make love to you," I grumbled, my body keyed up.

"Forbid me? Yeah, good one. Why can't I wear a skirt?"

"Because I want you, and you wearing a skirt is way too tempting. I'm giving us time but seeing you like this is testing my patience." I risked a peek at Susan and smiled at her red face, her eyes gleaming with undeniable lust.

"Shit, woman. Don't look at me like that. If we didn't have this meeting with my CO, I'd take you home and explore every part of your body like I've wanted to since I was a teenager with raging hormones."

"Seriously? Now we have to go back so I can change my underwear."

I white-knuckled the steering wheel as images of her in wet panties assaulted me. "Damn, now I have to meet my boss with this." I pointed down to my lap. "Quick, tell me something unsexy. Take my mind off your delectable body."

"Okay." The sound of cheekiness in her voice raised a warning flag. "I can help with that," she said, pointing at my crotch. "Keep your hands on the wheel and your eyes on the road and by the time we get to the firehouse, blue will only be a color."

I groaned at the image, but no way would I allow her to do something dangerous while I drove. "You made it worse. And you're crazy."

Susan laughed as she eyed the undeniable bulge in my pants and when her hand petted my thigh, I winced.

"Pax, you flinched. Do you really think I'd distract you while you're driving? I mean you won't even look away from the road for a second."

I relaxed, and she giggled. I smiled at the ease with which she joked with me, and it warmed my heart. Over the years, although friendly, Susan treated me with distance. She kidded with Morgan and others of my family but held back with me.

I finally understood aloofness was her armor, protecting her feelings. I couldn't fault her because I did the same thing. Usually laid back, unless it came to road and fire safety, I didn't behave normally around her. I was always aware of her proximity, keeping my distance. I liked the intimacy and familiarity growing between us.

"It's stupid, I know. I like being careful."

She touched my cheek and stroked the day-old stubble covering my face. "Oh, there's nothing stupid about how safety conscious you are. Your aunt and uncle's accident happened when you were so young. Of course, you'd ensure everyone's safety on the road. I admire you, you know?"

Although my family liked teasing the way I drove, had they known the reasons, they would have left me alone. It cracked my heart open to know Susan understood my need for safety without explanation, question, or judgement.

"Woman, you're too good for me.

****

Susan

Pax thought I jested about relieving him, but my desire to please him ran deep in my veins. I was willing to do anything to bring out his dimpled smile.

He was loosening up around me, but I didn't want to change him. I liked the sparkle in his eye when we joked. I used to watch him and envied his ease with his family and friends. His walls were coming down, and I wanted to shatter them altogether. And on the heels of those thoughts always came the fear of him leaving me.

However, as he concentrated on driving, I fell more in love with his innate nature to keep us safe. He made me happy. Even though he kept our contact to kissing, his body betrayed him when we hugged. Each time, I ached to reach out and grab his erection in my hand.

Initially, I thought it would be weird to get physical with him, but the first time we kissed, I knew we fit together. The more he touched me the more I wanted. Being in his arms, feeling his weight on me as he pumped into me, was all I thought about on most days. My body hummed in anticipation. As soon as the fundraiser was over, I planned to convince him to take the next step with me.

"Hey, baby. We're here."

I pushed away my desire and realized not only were we parked at the firehouse, but Pax had turned off the engine.

"Don't be nervous. Everything's set up. Billy wants to touch base with us. Besides, you know he's all bark and no bite." Pax rubbed my leg reassuring me. He didn't realize the feel of his hand played more havoc with my mental state than the meeting with his boss. My desire for him to lift the hem of my skirt and have his way with me was what made me fidget.

My body was on fire, and only one fireman had the tools to put it out.

I snickered at my visual and he stared at me. His lust-filled gaze focused on me, and my desire ratcheted up several notches. By his look alone, he not only pushed me to the edge but close to going over. I groaned at the idea of climaxing without him touching me and shifted in my seat to get relief. It didn't help and the throbbing between my legs intensified.

"If you keep touching me, I might be the one doing the biting."

He growled, and his hand tightened on my leg. His fingers dug into my muscle. "Shit, now I'm hard again. God, woman, you are a vixen and it's turning me on. I need a minute to get myself together. Wouldn't want my CO to think his ugly mug did this to me."

He adjusted the bulge in his pants and my panties dampened. I leaned over the console and his hand on my leg traveled higher. I held back by sheer will and kissed his cheek. But it wasn't enough, and I trailed my mouth down his cheek and along his jaw until I reached his ear. I licked him, and his ragged breath caressed my skin. Little fireworks erupted all over my body as his hands gripped me to him. I ignored the console digging into my side and touched him over his clothes.

He hissed, and his groin rocked into my hand. I rubbed his length, and he reached under my skirt. Calloused fingers played with the hem of my underwear. I hovered at the brink, anticipation driving me more than his explorations.

I jumped at the rapping on the driver's side window. Pax sat back, fighting to control his reaction before opening the door. Billy stood outside, a smirk on his face.

"I am thankful the foggy windows kept your make out session from my view. Unless you want to be cited for public indecency, I suggest you kids get in my office in the next two minutes." He turned and headed toward the building.

Pax turned to me, and I laughed at the craziness of the situation. It took a second, but he joined in and laughed. Once we had ourselves under control, we exited the truck and followed his CO.

Pax took my hand and intertwined our fingers as we walked to the building.

"Well, thank fuck he showed up when he did. He proved to be an effective erection killer."

"I'm going to have to take a picture of him and hold it up whenever you get carried away."

Pax moaned, his eyebrows furrowing in mock horror. "You are a cruel, cruel woman."

He pulled me closer, wrapped his arm around my waist, and burrowed our clasped hands into the elastic band of my skirt, trapping my arm behind me.

Chapter Nineteen

Susan

Five hours before the event, I pulled into the parking lot and smiled at the commotion greeting me. With a sunny sky and seventy-degree weather, it was the perfect day for the community outreach.

My staff constructed the obstacle course before unloading the dogs and cats from the rented vans into the fenced-in area the station crew assembled. The sheer number of volunteers both overwhelmed me and filled me with gratitude.

Pax's family helped where they could. His parents set up the dunk tank, splashing and laughing like kids. I envied their love after all their years together. Caden and Morgan helped haul the animals into the constructed shaded shelter. Foster couldn't lift due to his back injury, but he reassured the frightened animals. Parker and Dustin, ever the flirts, made moves on my female staff, but claimed they were helping carry bags of food. Jesse directed the chaos. Kate bounced around, helping Jesse with his delegated tasks, all the while unaware of the firemen watching her.

I loved them all and my heart grew seeing them help make the day run smoothly. Too occupied with the activity before me, I didn't hear Pax's approach until his arms wrapped around my waist. He pulled me back to his chest and kissed the top of my head.

"You smell so good. Let's skip out and make our own kind of fun. I want to take you into the bunk room and have my way with you."

His body heat combined with his whispered words affected me. I swayed on my feet. His hold on me the only thing keeping me upright. His large hand skimmed across my abdomen, fingers splayed open encompassing my stomach and grazing the underside of my breast. I held my breath as his fingers caressed my bra.

"Behave," I admonished him, even though if he asked again I would have given in.

"It's about time. Stop hogging the lady and let's get to work, young man," Mrs. Anderson said from beside us. I was so focused on his caresses I startled when she spoke. I turned and found several amused grins aimed our way. I burrowed my face in Pax's chest, hiding the rising blush.

"We're getting to know each other, Ma."

"Oh, psht." Mrs. Anderson waved her hand in dismissal. "You've practically grown up together. Stop wasting time getting to know each other." She winked and walked away, missing my mortified look.

"Did she give us permission to have sex?"

"In her own way, I believe so, yes." Pax laughed, watching his mother's back. "I think it best we appease the woman. Have any ideas?"

I leaned my head back to better see his face. "It's all I've thought about. I have lots of ideas of how we can take her up on her suggestion."

Pax's hold tightened, and his erection grew against my stomach. "Shit, I need a cold shower."

"Well, it's good you're first in the dunk tank then."

Pax leaned back. "I never signed up."

"I volunteered you." Humor laced Morgan's voice as he walked up and stood behind us.

"In that case, you'd better have volunteered yourself." Pax let go of me, grabbing his brother in a chokehold. I stood by, laughing. Morgan's approval eased a knot in my heart. I wasn't losing my best friend as Pax and I explored our relationship.

"Stop being a dick. Muscles and sheer brawn do not make you a man."

Suddenly, all ribbing stopped as Morgan's attention moved away from his brother. I followed his line of sight and clapped my hands in glee. Ann Marie strutted toward us, her petite frame belying the strong woman underneath.

Wearing vibrant purple leggings with a white sleeveless shirt tied in a knot at her belly button, showing off a sliver of skin and the shiny glint of jewelry, she looked carefree. Her long, untamed, dark curls blew in the slight breeze, and her lips were lined to perfection with her signature red lip-gloss. She knew the attention she garnered, but never paid it any heed. Comfortable in her own skin, she didn't give other people's opinions much thought. Her one-track mind made her successful in building her business from the bottom up. Ruthless in her endeavors, but always with a smile, she dominated the marketing world.

Morgan scrutinized her approach.

Reaching our group, she pulled me into a fierce hug. "Bitch, I missed you."

"I didn't think you were going to make it." I hugged her tightly as we spoke. "I'm so glad you're here."

She pulled back and waved her hand in dismissal. "What kind of cousin would I be if I didn't come and support my bestie?"

"Ann Marie?" Morgan asked, as he stood beside Pax watching our exchange. The first time he'd met her, we were kids. He hadn't seen her in years.

Caught in my excitement, I forgot the guys behind me. Ann Marie turned to Morgan, raised one eyebrow, and inspected him from head to toe. Undeniable appreciation filled her eyes.

"Stop eye fucking Morgan, you wench. You're spoken for."

"Just 'cause I'm sleeping with a man doesn't mean I can't appreciate eye candy when it's available." Her gaze skimmed over Morgan again before she diverted her attention to Pax. "Shit, woman. You weren't kidding when you said he was big."

I stifled a giggle when Pax smiled and puffed out his chest. "Oh, she did, did she?"

He extended his hand, and she took it pulling him into a hug. I laughed at his surprise as he stumbled into Ann Marie's embrace. She whispered something in his ear and his gaze locked with mine as he nodded.

If I knew my cousin, which I did, she warned him not to hurt me. She pulled back and appreciated Morgan again. "And who might you be?"

"You remember Morgan? You guys met the summer you stayed with me," I reminded her.

"Oh my. You sure have grown. Filled out nicely."

"Nice of you to notice." Morgan huffed and walked away.

"What crawled up his butt and died?"

I shrugged.

"Don't mind him," Pax spoke. "He's always moody."

"Well, that's no way to live. Come on, cuz. Show me what you need me to do. Pax, nice meeting you." I winked at Pax in apology as she hauled me away. He laughed, and I was thankful he didn't put up a fuss. I thought of ways to show him my appreciation later.

I wanted him, and I was done waiting.

****

Pax

Susan turned the corner out of my sight, and I took a deep breath and forced my gaze from the building. My parents' laughter came from my right, and I turned. Mom had the hose, spraying Dad as he wrestled it away from her. Laughing at their antics, I headed to the firehouse for the towels.

I whistled as I rummaged through the supply closet. The space gave me ideas and I wondered if I could convince Susan to sneak a few minutes away with me. I couldn't wait to have her and grew hard as images of her naked body raided my mind. I closed my eyes and stepped out of the closet. A scent lingered in the air. To my dismay, it wasn't Susan's sweet aroma I smelled, but another I was all too familiar with.

Julie stood inside the firehouse. She stared at me, her eyes wild. I halted as her gaze raked over me. A predator stalking his prey, and I was the prey.

"How could you? Is she the reason you've been so mean to me? I love you. I'm the woman for you. Not her," she cried and gestured to the door behind her.

A crying woman was the worst thing; it made me want to comfort her. I stayed rooted and mustered my strongest voice without sounding like an asshole.

"You don't love me, Julie. You love the idea of me. This needs to end. Find someone who will love you. It isn't me."

She wrapped her arms around me and reached up for a kiss. I turned my face and grabbed her shoulders. I pushed her away but not quickly enough.

Susan walked through the station doors and my body revolted. She gasped, and every fiber of my being screamed. I put distance between us and reached for Susan.

To my surprise, Susan didn't direct her angry gaze at me. No, she leveled it at Julie.

Her face softened when she flicked her gaze toward me. I sighed in relief. I stepped back and watched my girl in action. Susan was headstrong and loved with all her heart. I'd seen it many times over the years as she rehabilitated hurt animals back to health, or when the kid picked on Morgan when they were younger, or when people said mean things to my cousins. That fierce Susan stopped before Julie.

Julie held onto my arm, as a lover would, rubbing her side against mine. She wiped her mouth with the back of her free hand. "I'm sorry you had to see that," she said, with an evil glare. "Pax and I were catching up."

Disgusted, I moved her hand off me and stepped to the side. I itched to lash out at her, but Susan's glare stopped me. Once again, I stood back and admired her.

"You are a pathetic woman if you think I believe for one minute Pax kissed you. He doesn't want you. It's women like you who give us a bad name. You prey on men, with your tits and ass, thinking all you need to do is shake them and get a man's attention. It's sad you have so little respect for yourself. How do I say this simply enough for you to understand? He is not interested in you. Grow up and leave him alone."

God, a riled Susan was sexy. I loved she defended me. Not falling for the shit show Julie created. Susan trusted me, and it turned me on beyond belief. I wanted to haul her against my body and rub my hands along her curves. I wanted to kiss her neck to the juncture of her legs to her ankles and back up again. I wanted to indulge my every desire and give her more of me along the way.

However, as their stare off heated I grew concerned. This was Susan's day, and I didn't want her enjoying it with a black eye.

Julie's cocked fist spurred me into action. I stepped between them, positioning Susan behind me.

"If you hit her, I will end you," I bellowed. Julie ignored my warning and stepped to the side. I shielded Susan, grabbing Julie's raised arm, stopping her from landing a hit on either Susan or me. Julie grunted in my hold, but I didn't let go.

I pulled Julie's arm and hauled her toward the door.

"You're hurting me," Julie yelled. "I'm calling the cops, and then I'm calling the fire chief. You can't hit me and get away with it."

I yanked her arm, refusing to listen to her bullshit any more. Billy walked out of his office. His hand on my shoulder stopped me from throwing Julie out the door.

"I'd like to say something," he said, addressing me but staring at Julie.

Julie straightened, smirked at us, and waited for my

reprimand. I knew better. Billy treated the firefighters with respect and he trusted us to act appropriately. He didn't take threats against the station or us lightly.

"Miss, I knew your parents, and I'm sorry life took a turn for you and your dad when your mom passed. For the past few months, you have treated my crew as your personal harem. Have some respect for both yourself and your father and walk out of here with your head held high."

Julie shifted on her feet, indignation plastered on her face. She opened her mouth to speak but Billy's raised hand stilled her. "But hear this," he warned, his voice thick with barely restrained anger. "Leave. Do not come back. Pax is one of the most honorable men I know, and if he thought you were about to hurt his girl, he would defend her without hesitation. A man does not run into a burning building against orders for a woman if his heart belongs elsewhere. You make whatever call you think is necessary, but in the end, you will stand alone with your lies. You are no longer welcome here, and I will have you removed if I ever see you again."

"You can't. This is public property."

"I can, and I will. My crew is important to me. This is their home as much as it is mine. I will defend them and ensure their safety when they are here. Mess with me and you will feel the wrath of the entire fire department and police force. It's time for you to leave."

He stood his ground, arms across his chest. Julie stepped toward me and he sidestepped, blocking her advance. She looked at each of us, sadness written on her face, but when her gaze settled on Susan, it morphed into anger.

Susan watched Julie, her own ire visible. She

shuddered, and I wrapped her in my arms. My protective instincts surfaced, and I moved us to the kitchen and away from the standoff. Seconds later, the door clicked shut, and I breathed again. I wasn't sorry for any actions that ensured Susan's safety. Adrenaline coursed through me, my heart pumping double time. I ran my hands along Susan's arms and body, needing to assure she was unharmed. Susan allowed my mauling and relented to my careful inspection. Once satisfied, my gaze met hers and my fear for her safety morphed into desire.

I hauled her to my chest and kissed her with the pent-up energy I had in me. I moved us backwards until her back hit the wall behind the kitchen door.

Her moans and adventurous hands urged me on, and I pulled her tank top up exposing her bra. I splayed my hands against her bare skin loving the warmth under my fingertips.

Easing my hands up, I gave her a chance to stop me, but when she dug her nails into my back, I took the silent invite and cupped her breasts. Her chest heaved, and I pulled the bra cups down and squeezed. Her nipples hardened against my palms and I tweaked them. I trailed my tongue down her throat, loving the taste of her skin. I explored her breasts and yearned to tug her shirt off and feel her breasts against my tongue.

I moved my hands away and stepped back taking in the beauty before me. My gaze roamed her exposed skin and naked chest. She breathed heavily, and I took in my fill. Without warning, I leaned forward and took a nipple into my mouth.

Her head fell back and a low whoosh of air escaped her parted lips as I continued my relentless teasing. I bit down on one nipple and pinched the other. She buried her fingers in my short hair and I welcomed the sting of pain. Her ferocity only intensified my need for her.

"Pax," she moaned. "I'm close. God, I can't…"

With a final lick, I pulled away from her. She lifted her head from the wall and her unfocused gaze delighted me.

"Need…you…inside…"

"Hang on, baby. I got you." I reached around and picked her up with ease. She wrapped her arms around my neck. Her red, swollen lips tempted me to stop and have her right there in the kitchen.

With the last remnants of coherent thought, I yanked open the door and headed to a more private location. I wanted to get lost in her. Forget the events of the past ten minutes and shower her with as many orgasms as needed for her to forget as well.

Chapter Twenty

Susan

I shuddered. His wild and wanton look of desire heated me from the inside out. I didn't care about my partial nudity. How fast we made it to his bunkroom my only concern. I marveled at his ability to continue kissing me as we passed the fire trucks parked in the bay.

Reaching the stairs, he pulled his mouth from mine and silently asked for permission. I nodded. I flung my head back and laughed when he ran up the steps two at a time.

I loved it. I loved him. I had unleashed the beast.

He made it to the bunkroom in record time, showing no signs of exertion. He opened the door, and I sighed in relief seeing it empty. Everyone outside continued setting up for the fundraiser, and even though I needed to be out there with them I wanted to be inside with Pax far more.

Kicking the door closed behind us, he turned and propped me against his leg while he locked the door. His gaze skimmed my body and stopped at my breasts. My skin heated at his continued perusal.

Gripping his head, I pulled until his lips met mine. I kissed him hungrily. He met me stroke for stroke and it scorched me to the bone. Our movements became frantic with need. Without preamble, he moved us and dropped me on one of the beds.

Noticing the cot, I laughed. "How do you sleep? Your body barely fits." I sprawled out demonstrating my thoughts.

My laughter died at his heated gaze. His eyes darkened as he took in my exposed flesh. I took in a sharp breath as my body responded to him. Eager to feel him on top of me, I sat up and reached for the buttons of his jeans.

He stilled my hands.

"It isn't easy, and I believe I'm going to make it even more difficult. Now every time I lie down I'm going to think of being deep inside of you. Licking and kissing your wonderful tits as I make you climax, over and over again."

"God, Pax. Just listening to you is going to make me c…"

"Yeah? Not gonna happen. I want to be inside you first. Feel you tightening around me. Hear you scream my name. Feel your nails digging into my back. I want all that, and then I want it again and again and again."

"Hurry up then. The anticipation is killing me." Pax laughed from deep in his abdomen, warming me all over.

"Stop rushing me, woman. I'm taking my time with you." Reaching back, he tugged his shirt off one-handed. I catalogued the sexy move, filing it away for future play in my head.

I wanted him to take his time, but I also wanted to feel him inside me. My body clenched in anticipation. "Someone's going to come searching for us, and I don't think I can handle waiting. Please Pax. Take me. Make me yours."

He growled low in his throat and lowered himself onto me. He covered my body with his and the bed shifted. I prayed the frame held our combined weight.

Pax kissed me along my collarbone, moving lower kissing and licking with his tongue and lips. Everywhere he touched ignited. I climbed higher and closer to climax. He reached the waistband of my shorts and undid the button. Gripping both my shorts and underwear, he tugged them off. His gaze traveled the length of my body before he grabbed my thighs and pushed them apart. I watched him as he took in my bareness.

"Just a taste." His voice low, I barely registered his words before his mouth descended on me with a long swipe of his tongue.

He lifted my ass off the bed with his hands and held me closer to his mouth. His tongue danced over me and circled my opening. I screamed. I felt his smile as he buried his tongue into me. With relentless licks and kisses, he brought me closer and closer to completion. My hips moved on their own accord, but his strong hold gave me no wiggle room.

I breathed through my mouth and focused on a spot on the top of his head. When he raised his gaze, eyed me with mischief, and bit down, I lost the battle. My body disconnected from my mind lost in the sea of the sensations he inflicted on me.

He moaned and placed open mouth kisses on my clit. The vibrations spread through the length of my body. I curled my toes into the sheets and dug my nails into his scalp. I wasn't sure if I wanted to push him away or keep him rooted.

"I'm...so...close," I panted.

Doubling his efforts, he ran a finger along my seam and continued flicking his tongue. My hips bucked, and he gave me room to move. I rocked my hips, taking what I needed most from him in that moment.

He explored my body with his hands. After a quick squeeze of my breasts, he rested one hand across my belly, pinning me down once again. With his free hand, he opened my lips and penetrated me. He crooked his finger and rubbed my g-spot. With pressure from both inside and outside, I had no alternative. My breath quickened, and my muscles tightened as my orgasm loomed closer. Pax bit my clit and I screamed at the sensation. Yet I still fought to hold on.

"Let go, baby. Let me see you lose control," Pax spoke softly against me. The coolness of his breath against my heated flesh along with his words sent me careening. My hands flew up grappling for something to grip to keep me grounded. Pax continued guiding me through the strongest orgasm I ever had. Rendered senseless, I lay on the bed waiting for my body to come back on-line. Pax shifted off me and I didn't have the strength to argue.

"I love how responsive you are. You are so sexy, lost in your bliss." My insides clenched, ready to go again. "Open your legs, baby."

I hadn't realized I shut them. He stood before me and I took in the beautiful sight. Pax, naked, sheathed, and ready. He ran his hand along his length watching me watch him.

****

Pax

I couldn't get inside her fast enough. Her wide-eyed gaze settled on the hand holding my erection and she opened her legs wide in silent invitation.

"You are a dirty, dirty girl."

In that moment, I didn't care if the world burned down around us. I needed to have her, to claim her as mine. Positioning my legs inside of hers, I hovered over her holding my weight on my elbows. I used my knees opening her wider and rubbed along her seam. I coated my shaft with her wetness and positioned myself at her entrance.

I inched my way in. I groaned and willed my body to savor the feel of her closing around just the tip. I struggled but gave her time to adjust. With slow, shallow thrusts I drove us both frantic with need. I prayed the incredible sensations would ebb. I didn't want our first time together to end before it began. "Baby, you feel so good. So good."

Sweat pooled on my forehead and across my shoulders as I fought my instincts. Susan moved under me, shifting her hips. I slid farther into her body. I growled at the sensations. I restrained my need to bury my cock in her, slamming into her over and over again until I was spent.

She didn't make it easy. Susan swiveled her hips, her body sucking me in. I threw my head back and moaned. Buried deeply, I held steady and gazed into her eyes.

She looked as needy as I felt.

"Move, Pax. You're killing me."

Who was I to deny her? I moved.

I pulled all the way out and pushed back in, making her take me to the hilt. Her walls pulsed around me, sucking me in deeper me with each thrust. Her hips rocked, and she met my demanding pace with her own.

She swung her head back and forth across my pillow. Her hands scratched at the sheets. Sweat trickled along her neck and I bend forward licking away the drops. I inhaled her sweet scent and nuzzled her neck all the while pumping into her.

Susan grabbed my face. She directed my mouth to hers. I kissed her with desperation, dipping my tongue, tangling with hers until my air-depleted lungs screamed for relief.

"Baby, I'm not going to last. You feel too good," I said and rested my forehead on hers. I didn't care that the bed bumped the wall with every rock of my hips, nor did I care that my legs and hips burned from the exertion. My focus centered on one thing. Making her fly.

"Are you close?"

"Yes!" Susan panted, and I concentrated on not crushing her with my body. "Don't stop."

"Not planning on it." I barely got my words out through gritted teeth before Susan dug her heels into the bed and lifted her ass high. The new position forced me deeper, and she took all of me with several loud moans. Needing more, I grabbed her ankles and placed them on my shoulders, pushing forward.

"So deep. Shit, Pax you're so deep."

I rocked into her body, not giving her a chance to breathe. She tightened around me, and I moaned around the resulting jolt of pain, but I wouldn't have it any other way. I reached between us and pinched her clit, sending her into orgasm. She yelled my name and gripped my arms.

Watching her, hearing her chant my name, and feeling her come apart was my undoing. With a growl, I buried my cock as deep as I could and let go. Her walls milked every drop out of me.

My arms shook from effort, and I collapsed, turning my body so I didn't crush her. My biceps were on fire, but I couldn't move them to work out the soreness. I had never climaxed as hard in my life, and it only confirmed what I already knew.

She was my one. She was my soul mate.

Rolling off, I lay beside her on the cramped mattress. I removed and tied the condom before dropping it on the floor. I pulled her closer, and she rested her head on my chest. She squeezed her leg between mine, and I loved being entangled with her. Having her in my arms, our bodies entwined, and too exhausted to move was my idea of heaven. She was my home, and I closed my eyes absorbing the feeling of fullness in my heart.

The sound of the door shutting downstairs reminded me I couldn't spend the day wrapped in her like my heart and body wanted. Reality called. "We better get back outside before they send the cavalry after us."

Susan giggled as I stood and struggled to balance on jelly-like legs.

"Be careful there, big boy. Don't want you falling and getting a concussion. I don't think I can move you if you pass out."

"Think you can do better?"

"No. That's why I'm still in bed." She licked her lips, peeking at me from under her lashes.

The sound of footsteps outside the bunkroom kept me from pouncing on her again. A knock on the door, followed by Ann Marie yelling out, pulled us apart.

"Pax? Susan? I know you're in there. The troops are growing restless, so I volunteered to come and get you. Now stop having fun, get dressed, and get your sweet asses downstairs so we can get this show on the road."

Susan laughed at her cousin but was unable to speak.

"We'll be right down," I yelled. I couldn't keep my gaze off Susan's flushed appearance.

Ann Marie's footsteps echoed down the hall as she retreated.

Bending down, I hauled her to my shoulders and carried her in a fireman's hold to the bathroom. I slid my hand up her leg, tempted to sink my fingers in her but settled on swatting her ass.

She yelped and pinched my ass in return. I jumped and jostled her. "Be careful, woman. I might drop you."

"I doubt that," she said, and pinched me again.

"Get cleaned up before the guys pound down the door." I set her on her feet.

She squealed and gave me a quick kiss on my cheek. I gathered her clothes and placed them on my cot awaiting her return. I dressed quickly, and before long, Susan sauntered out of the bathroom toward me. In a matter of seconds, I was ready to take her again.

I shook my head and dislodged my insatiable lust for her. I wasn't successful.

"Pax, you ripped my shirt. I need one of yours." She stood with her hands on her hips dressed in her black lace panties, bra, and nothing else.

"My locker's right there. Pick out whatever you want," I said, turning away before I gave in to my yearning.

She stood on her toes reaching for my locker. She

rummaged through the clothes I left at the station, oblivious to the damn near perfect sight she presented me. Now, if she were naked, it would have been perfect.

Hearing me groan she turned her head and amusement sparkled in her eyes. "Get your mind out of the gutter, big boy. We need to get back down there."

"Then hurry up and cover yourself because I'm about to jump you again."

Seeing her wearing one of my work shirts stirred my blood. I loved seeing her in my clothes and I imagined her naked with only my shirt covering her delectable body as she made pancakes. I wouldn't keep my hands from reaching under the hem feeling her smooth skin before taking her on the kitchen counter.

"I said out of the gutter."

I adjusted myself, and her gaze tracked my movements. She licked her lips and another image of her down on her knees assailed me. I groaned in frustration, and with a plea to a higher power for strength, I reached out and enveloped her into my arms.

"When we're done here, you're mine. I'm off until tomorrow, and I have every intention of making you forget everything but me. Every time you sit down, you're going to think of me. Remember me and what I did to your body. For the next two days, your body will heat up with every step you take because of the needy ache between your legs."

She shook in my arms as I whispered in her ear all the things I wanted to do to her. Her nipples hardened against my chest. I licked her ear and placed small kisses along her neck down to her chest. She shivered with every pass of my tongue and lips.

I rubbed my hands along her ribs and waist. Susan squirmed in my hold. I smiled at my discovery and ran my fingers along her sensitive skin. She wiggled as I tickled her, covering her mouth with her hands. I continued until she laughed out loud, only then giving her a reprieve.

"I love your laugh. Promise to always laugh like that for me." Susan beamed as I played with her hair. "And if we don't get out of here right now, we might never leave. Let's go."

Chapter Twenty-One

Susan

We walked out hand in hand. While we were otherwise occupied my father arrived, and I went over and gave him a hug, but Pax didn't let go of my hand. *The* sentiment mutual, I never wanted to let go of him either.

"Susan. Pax. There you are. Everything's ready. We were waiting on you two to open the gates." Mrs. Anderson said with a knowing smile on her face. Yet I didn't feel embarrassed. I wasn't ruining the moment with regrets because there were none. "Pax, you're first in the dunk tank. Why didn't you change while you were inside?"

"Because he was too busy doing other things," Dustin said, as he winked at me. "And who could blame him?" Dustin wore one of his many funny shirts, *Pet me for a lick or two,* making me laugh, but Mrs. Anderson grumbled under her breath when she saw it.

"Yeah, if I had a woman like Susan in my arms I'd forget all sorts of stuff," Parker said, coming to stand by his brother.

"Hey, when you tire of Godzilla here, I'll be available. You don't want Parker. Everything he knows he's learned from me," Dustin smirked.

Parker and Dustin spent most of their time together and loved owning a bar in Lincoln Square, the hub of

Bellevue. With dark-brown hair and green eyes, they were often mistaken for twins, and they were definitely easy on the eyes, which attracted a large female clientele.

Pax pulled me to his side, growling low at his cousins. "When the two of you grow up, you might be lucky enough to have a woman like Susan give you a second look. The bar isn't earning you the greatest reputations."

"Depends on how you look at it," Parker shot back, elbowing Dustin in the ribs.

"Damn straight."

"Boys. I don't need to hear about your escapades. It hurts my ears," Mrs. Anderson said, chastising her nephews.

"Sorry," they quickly replied, but as soon as she turned her back, they smiled like kids with ice cream cones.

"I forgot the towels. I'm going inside to change and grab them. Want to come with me?"

Parker yanked on my arm and drew me away from Pax. "If she does, we might not see either of you again for the rest of the day."

Dustin poked his brother and added, "Or maybe the rest of the week."

"Or the rest of the year," Parker piped in.

"But then again, Pax is an old man. He's probably tired after only one time. He needs at least a week to recover. Let me show you how it is to be with a young, virile man," Parker continued, directing his smile at me.

"When you find such a man let me know." I laughed as Dustin and Pax high-fived.

"She got you," Pax said, pulling me in for a

scorching kiss. It didn't matter we had an audience; the minute his lips touched mine I wanted to climb him. His hands on my ass told me I had done exactly that. Laughing, I pulled away and placed my feet back on the ground.

"Did Pax just have a PDA moment? This is too good to be true," Caden said, approaching us. "I'll never let you live this down."

"Don't give a shit. Nothing you say will stop me from kissing her." Pax beamed. "Come with me, baby. These hooligans will never leave you alone."

"I got her," Morgan said, walking up beside me. Smiling, as the Anderson and Jackson men surrounded me, I counted my blessings. All of them gorgeous in their own right, but Pax was the most beautiful of them all.

"Shit. I've died and gone to heaven. Lord, please forgive me for I plan on sinning," Ann Marie exclaimed, joining us. Morgan stiffened beside me.

He eyed her from head to toe while she chatted with his brother and cousins. If I didn't know better, I'd say he was jealous. However, Morgan liked his women tough, and they usually wore leather and rode a bike.

Ann Marie might be tough on the inside, but she personified female charm on the outside. I catalogued his look and resolved to talk to him about it when we were alone.

****

Pax

I left Susan with Morgan and headed back inside. As soon as I entered through the door, images of Julie lifting her fist to hit Susan came to mind. My heart rate sped at all the possible outcomes. Anger rose inside me the longer I thought of Julie's integration in my life. I hoped what happened earlier would be a wake-up call for her, and she'd walk away. If she didn't, I had limited options left.

Clearing my head, I let the negative feelings go. I needed to get back outside. Peering through the window, I grinned seeing the number of people and families with young kids filtering in. Children ran around taking in the games and activities or dragged their parents to the animal shelters.

I hustled back to my bunk, grabbed my board shorts, and dropped my trousers. I didn't care if someone walked in. My only concern was getting back to Susan. Grabbing the towels from Billy's office, I headed back outside. The people gathered around the tank cheered as I neared.

Beck, Rob, and several of my family members clutched dollar bills in their fists, eagerly waiting to dunk me. I was disappointed to see Susan wasn't with them. My body already missed her touch. I wanted her close for purely selfish reasons.

****

"Stop looking like your better half is gone forever. She went to speak with a family adopting a dog," Caden said from next to me. "Besides, I'm ready to dunk you." He shoved me forward. I climbed onto the small board and dipped my feet in the cold water.

The hot sun warmed me, and before long, I hoped someone succeeded in hitting the target. I heckled my brothers and egged them on, using family friendly name-calling and jokes antagonizing them. Caden stepped up, wound his arm, and threw the ball. He hit the board dead center, which released the lever beneath me. With a rush, I fell in and swore my balls shriveled from the frigid water.

I surfaced to the sounds of laughter and various family members arguing. They all wanted to be next. I wiped water from my eyes and climbed back onto the narrow piece of wood. I ignored them and surveyed the area for the one person I wanted to see.

I spotted her across the field talking to a little boy petting a small dog. She held onto Darth's leash, who sat by her feet watching me. He looked as if the surrounding shenanigans amused him.

Seeing Susan interact with the young boy opened my mind to the possibilities. I imagined her playing with our son. Watching her fortified what I always wanted but believed impossible to have. Until now.

I wanted to ask her to move in with me but knew it would scare her off. Instead, I settled on convincing her to stay the night with me whenever I was off duty.

The sounds of my brothers bickering penetrated, and I turned away from her. In due time, I would have everything I ever dreamed of.

"Just pick already. It's not as if anyone else can dunk me."

To my surprise, my mother stepped around them and handed the attendant her money. A dollar a ball, and she handed the girl a wad.

Fear gripped me as Mom gleefully handed out the balls. She gave one each to Morgan, Parker, Dustin, and Foster. The last two, she held onto. Stepping up she raised her hand. I wanted to heckle her, but she was my mother, and I knew it was wise not to. She threw with surety, and color me surprised when she hit the target plunging me back in.

That was only the beginning. Each of them landed a hit including Kate when she joined in on the fun. After missing several times, they gave her a break, and moved her three feet closer. She dunked me four times. Frozen solid by the end of my allotted time, I wanted out. The sun's warmth no longer penetrated my soaked clothes since I spent more time in the water than on the board. The smiles on my family's faces throughout the ordeal kept me from quitting. Their happiness meant everything to me.

Susan didn't get the chance to dunk me, and I was disappointed when she didn't make an appearance. I forgave her absence since she was busy talking with potential adoptees, Darth a quiet sentinel by her side. Catching glimpses of the success of the day written on her beautiful face, I couldn't hold onto my frustration.

"Pax, your time's up. Dustin, it's your turn," the attendant said. Dustin whooped and quickly shed his shirt. The attendant offered me a towel as I climbed out of the tank and down the steps. I smiled at her but didn't accept the offer.

Hearing Susan, I turned and found her a few feet away with her back to me. I crept toward her, and before she registered my presence, I pulled her to me. I wrapped her in my arms and rubbed my body against her. My own personal warm towel. Her shrieks turned to giggles the more I soaked her. Darth stood by but didn't interfere as I feared he might. Instead, I swore he smiled.

"Pax, cut it out. I'm all wet."

Leaning down, I whispered in her ear. "Good to hear, because I'm always ready for you, baby." I nipped the skin at the base of her neck before licking away the sting. She shuddered in my arms. Feeling her response turned me on. I held her tighter. "My trunks are very unforgiving. Don't move."

She gasped as I pushed my hips into her back. Tilting her head up, she gave me a wicked smile and rubbed against my erection. "This is a family friendly event."

"It is, and if you'll stop rubbing your body against me, I'll calm down, literally. But for now, you need to walk in front of me until we get back inside." I moved with her so her back covered my front. Parker and Dustin laughed, enjoying my predicament. Scratching my eyebrow with my middle finger only resulted in them laughing louder, and I smiled at their ridiculous response.

My plan backfired. There was no harmless fun when it came to Susan. Her proximity elicited a visceral reaction, and I wasn't ashamed. My body wanted what it wanted. And lucky for me, she wanted me, too. Contentment flowed, hearing my family's laughter around us. I waved at them and used Susan as a shield. Best of all, my dad's laughter rang through the air as he held my mom in a loving embrace. They were my role models, and if Susan and I had half of what they had, life would be grand.

Chapter Twenty-Two

Susan

Riding a high, I thanked the volunteers. Seven dogs, four cats, and one rabbit adopted made the day a success. Between the carnival games and food, we raised enough money for the building supplies needed for the outdoor kennels and fence in the exercise yard. Several families donated money and their generosity would help expand the shelter building as well.

Although the day started out on a shaky note, I pushed Julie from my mind. Pax's constant presence by my side gave me the fortitude to continue with the day as planned. Between the unbelievable sex, adoptions, and money raised, exhaustion dug its claws deep into my bones.

Pax's family helped clean up. My excitement bubbled through my waning energy and reached a pinnacle when Pax asked me to stay with him at his place for the night. We left my car at the station, and I planned on driving in with him when he went to work in the morning.

I sat in the truck, leaning against the window. Outside, Pax spoke with his CO. A few minutes later, he climbed in and leaned over. He brought the belt across my lap and chest and secured me in after stealing a kiss. Although chaste and sweet, it kindled a spark. I was hungry for him all over again. To say I couldn't get enough of him was an understatement.

"Do you want to stop at your dad's? Get your clothes?"

I shook my head. I learned my lesson years ago. I always had a packed bag in my car. Animals were unpredictable when moved or placed in a stressful situation. The first time a dog threw up on me, I discovered the importance of having a change of clothes handy.

"No. I have a bag in my car." I moved to undo my belt, but Pax's hand stayed me.

"I've got it. Give me your keys."

I handed them over. Our fingers touched. My breath hitched at the contact and he leaned in and kissed my collarbone. "Baby, if Billy wasn't right outside and firefighters roaming the grounds, I'd pull down these ridiculously small shorts you have tormented me with all day," he said, fingering the hem, "make you straddle my lap and ride me right here in the front seat of my truck."

I fought to form a sentence, any sentence, but in the end, lost. I moaned, and my body yearned for Pax's touch. No longer tired, I fidgeted in my seat seeking relief-giving friction. His words heated me, and I closed my eyes against the onslaught of images of him taking me in the truck.

"I see I've made you speechless. That's good, baby, because the only thing you need to say tonight is my name, preferably so loud my neighbors can hear you."

"Pax," His name came out breathy, not at all what I intended. "Keep talking like that, and I will straddle you and make you keep your promise."

His sharp intake made me smile, glad I wasn't the only one affected. He rested his hand on my thigh, dangerously close to where I wanted his touch most, but he made no move to get closer. Instead, he squeezed my leg, and fought to gain control.

"How fast can you get us home?"

Happy I succeeded in keeping my voice even, I rubbed my hand along my leg, inching it upward. His gaze tracked my hand's journey until I cupped my breast. Without hesitation, Pax bolted out of the truck, ran to my car, and grabbed my bag. He was back in the cab and buckled with the ignition running before I could blink.

I laughed at his eagerness, enjoying seeing him heady with desire. Reaching over the console, I placed my hand on his thigh careful not to get too close to his crotch. If he thought my move distracted him from driving, he didn't say anything.

"Are you driving over the speed limit?" Landmarks passed by faster than usual. I leaned over viewing the dashboard, but Pax moved his arm and blocked the speedometer from my sight. "You *are* driving faster. Who'd have thought I'd see the day Pax broke the law?"

His forehead crinkled in amusement, but he didn't turn my way. There was only so many dangerous things he would do at one time.

"See, here's the thing. I'm so freaking hard, I need to get us to a bed. If we get in an accident, I might break in half."

"You know that makes no sense? You'd need to drive slower to avoid any accidents. I think by driving faster you're actually putting your dick in harm's way."

"Woman, you cannot say dick. I'm already hard enough."

"What? Does my talking dirty turn you on?" I loved watching as his Adam's apple bopped. "So if I said things like suck dick, I want to fuck you, or cunnilingus, will you blow in your pants?"

Pax surprised me as his boisterous laugh drew the attention of the people in the car next to us at the stop light. "You have no idea. But instead, I'd say eating pussy. I like the sound of that so much more. My mouth is salivating at the idea. And, baby, I'm saving myself for you. There is no way I will come in my pants tonight like a horny teenager. No. When I do, I will be buried so deep inside you we might as well be one body."

I crossed my ankles, not sure if I wanted to stave off my need for him or ease the ache between my legs.

****

Pax

Yes, I broke a few traffic laws getting us home faster, but I didn't care. All I wanted was Susan beside me in my bed writhing under me once again. My lust for her not satiated from our time at the station.

She awoke a hunger in me not easily satisfied. Nor would weeks of sleeping with her guarantee a decrease in my need. Sweet, sexy Susan was finally mine. She might not believe it yet, but I knew. I craved no one else, and I intended on showing her how much I loved her. I wanted to take my time exploring her, and with every touch learn what she liked. I planned to catalog her every whimper, moan, and groan and pull them from her until we were boneless.

I pulled into my driveway and immediately knew

something was wrong. I left the engine running and glanced around. The front porch lights were out. I set the timer keeping the lights on from six in the evening until midnight. It was seven.

I reached over and grabbed Susan's arm stopping her from opening the door. "Stay here, get in the driver's seat, and lock the doors after I get out. Have nine-one-one ready on your phone, and if I'm not back in five minutes, call them and get out of here." I failed to keep the edge out of my voice.

Her red cheeks turned ashen. I pulled her across the console and kissed her. "I'll be fine and back in five."

I stepped out of the truck and waited for her to settle in my seat. Once she locked the doors, I pulled out a flashlight from the toolbox in the bed of the truck. I hesitated for a second before grabbing the tire iron. I hedged my way to the front of the house. The truck's headlights illuminated a partial path, and I used the flashlight for a focused beam.

I slowly stepped onto the porch and cringed when my boots crunched broken glass. I directed the beam down confirming what I already knew although the security app on my phone had not alerted me of any disturbances. I shoved the thoughts to the back of my mind and focused on my surroundings.

I ensured Susan was safely tucked inside the truck. The faint light of her phone showed the worry evident on her face as she watched me through the windshield. It gutted me I had to leave her alone. It was the better of two evils. Releasing a deep sigh, I followed the porch to the side of the house.

A sound from the back of the property alerted me to movement. I rounded the corner holding the tire iron down by my side. I turned off the flashlight and waited as my eyes adjusted to the darkness. Soon the moon illuminated my way, and I crept along the porch and down the steps leading to the lawn.

The lights I installed in the back were motion sensor triggered but stayed dark when I moved into their path. I side-stepped the broken glass and landed quietly onto the grass. I crouched and listened for any indication the intruder was still lurking nearby. Hearing nothing, I worried the prowler was out front.

I turned and fell forward as something hard hit the back of my head. I had no time to react before the culprit ran toward the woods bordering the back of my land. Bursts of light, much like fireworks, exploded in my eyes making it difficult to see. By the size and stance, I was sure it was a woman.

Taking several careful steps, I struggled to keep upright, making my way to Susan. She flung her door open and ran toward me as I rounded the corner. I faltered. She put her arms around my waist but couldn't support my weight. I fought to stay conscious, knowing if I didn't, it would leave Susan vulnerable to the intruder.

I climbed into the truck and regulated my breathing. The fog in my head didn't dissipate, but I did register when Susan got in beside me. She muttered but I couldn't decipher her words. Darkness pulled at the edges of my vision. I couldn't keep my eyes open. I leaned my head against the window and surrendered to the sweet pull of oblivion.

****

Susan

I struggled to adjust the seat in the mammoth truck.

Driving it made me nervous, but I didn't have a choice. Pax passed out in the passenger seat spurred me on. I reached around him, pulled his seatbelt across his body, and buckled him in.

I dug his phone from his front pocket and silently cheered when I had it in hand. I dialed Morgan's number from memory and placed the phone between my ear and shoulder. In my haste, I forgot the phone was connected to the vehicle and swerved, narrowly missing the fence, when it rang through the speakers.

"Hey. Don't tell me she already ran off on your sorry ass," Morgan's voice sounded loud and clear.

"Morgan," I yelled while maneuvering the truck down the road. "Someone hit Pax. He's bleeding. I need help."

"Red! Where are you?"

"We're…we were at his house. I think…I think someone broke in and waited for him. He's bleeding, Morgan."

"Get to the hospital, I'm right behind you."

"Don't hang up," I pleaded. "I don't know if I can do this. His truck is so big. I can barely see over the hood."

"Red, you can do it. Pax needs you."

"I know. I know, but what if something's wrong? Morgan, what if…what if…" I couldn't finish my sentence through my sobbing.

"He's going to be fine. Concentrate on driving. Okay?"

"I'm almost there. Can you call the hospital and have them waiting outside for us? I can't carry him through the doors."

"No, I'm on the phone with you. All you need to

do is pull up in front of the ER. Leave the truck. I'll move it when I get there. You got this, Red. He'll be fine. Pax is too stubborn to go anywhere."

Within minutes, I spotted the lights of the hospital, and for the first time since Pax came stumbling toward me I took in a deep breath. Although Pax stirred during the drive, he never awakened. I wanted to shake him but didn't dare take my hands off the steering wheel.

I pulled up to the hospital doors, shut down the engine, and unbuckled my seatbelt. I forgot about Morgan and made a mad dash through the automatic sliding doors as they whooshed open.

"Help," I yelled, waving my arms. At the stares, I calmed down my crazy. A man in nursing scrubs approached. "Please. Pax is in the truck. He's bleeding. He's unconscious. Please help."

The man turned to another nurse signaling for her assistance. She turned away, but quickly reappeared with a doctor, another nurse, and a stretcher. I led them to the truck and opened the passenger door. The seatbelt kept Pax from toppling out. The first nurse turned to me as the doctor reached in with gloved hands to check for a pulse.

"Did he fall? How did he hurt his head?"

"I don't know. We got home, and something was wrong. He made me stay in the truck. I don't know."

"How did you find him?"

"I didn't. He walked back to me. Once I got him in the truck he passed out."

"Okay, good. We're going to take him out carefully and brace him. We want to make sure we don't aggravate any neck injuries if there are any."

"I want to help."

A third nurse appeared by my side and took me by the shoulders. "They have this. We need to check you out. Are you injured?"

For the first time since Pax rounded the corner of the house, I paid attention to myself. My hands and clothes were covered in blood. His blood. My knees wobbled, and I freaked out again. The woman's hands wrapped tighter around me and held me up. She walked us inside to a small partitioned room and directed me to the bed.

I hesitated. I didn't want to lie down. I wanted to be with Pax.

"I promise you once the doctor checks him over, and he's in stable condition, you'll see him," she said, and placed a hand on my elbow nudging me forward. "Now let's take care of you." She took my temperature, checked my pulse, and blood pressure. She ran her hands along my arms and legs but didn't find any injuries. Done with the exam she swung the stethoscope around her neck and studied me.

"Okay. So, head traumas bleed a lot. I don't think any of this blood is yours. I'm getting you orange juice and spare scrubs. I know Pax'll be upset if you're not taken care of."

The ugly green monster surfaced, and I scrunched my eyebrows.

She giggled. "Sorry. Don't mean to laugh," she said when I braced my arms against the mattress. "Let me reassure you, I've never slept with him. My brother and Pax are on the same crew. He's come by the hospital with Robby a few times. Besides, I see a lot of firefighters in my line of work."

"I'm sorry. I didn't mean…"

She waved her hand. "Don't you worry about it. I need to take care of you if not for your sake then his. I'll bring in the paperwork for him when I come back."

"Wait." I grabbed her wrist as she turned to walk away. "I don't have his insurance information."

"That's okay. We have it on file. I need you to fill out what you do know and what you saw."

The second she left, I sat up, desperate to wash my hands. The sight of the darkening blood made me woozy. I stood and struggled to keep my balance as the privacy curtain flung back, and Morgan sprinted toward me. He pulled me to his chest, but I pushed away from his hold.

"I'm all bloody."

He stepped back but held onto my shoulders. His gaze traveled along my body and face. "I'm not hurt. It's Pax's blo..." Tears welled in my eyes. I couldn't continue. I gave in to the second hug and cried into Morgan's chest while he nuzzled my hair. He held me, and I appreciated the gesture. Morgan wasn't a hugger, but I always found comfort in his arms when he offered.

"Phone." Morgan handed me Pax's phone when I pulled back and sniffled into my shirt.

"Shit, I left you on the phone, didn't I?"

"Yeah, but I figured you made it to the hospital."

The nurse returned with soap, towels, scrubs, and orange juice. Morgan stayed by my side and I drank the juice. He then helped me to the bathroom at the end of the hall. I washed, watching Pax's blood disappear down the drain. I started crying all over again.

Morgan wrapped his arms around me from behind. "Come on, Red. Let's get you dressed then you can go see my lug of a brother."

"Okay," I said, my voice rough with emotion.

Morgan pulled my shirt off and helped me put on a clean one. Being nearly naked didn't embarrass me. I didn't have it in me to care. I needed to get to Pax and if it meant Morgan helping me, then so be it.

Once I was dressed and clean, Morgan led me to the waiting room to, well, to do just that.

Wait.

Chapter Twenty-Three

Susan

We sat in the waiting room for hours and before long family members trickled in; first, Parker and Dustin, followed by Mr. and Mrs. Anderson with Kate. Foster and Caden came in right behind them. Jesse was the last to arrive, dressed in scrubs.

Jesse checked in on Pax. His position at the hospital benefited us. Absorbed in watching the doors Jesse disappeared through, I didn't notice the two police officers standing near the emergency doors.

Kate nudged me in the side, and I turned facing the direction she indicated. They approached Mr. Anderson and spoke in hushed tones. I shifted on my feet and folded my arms across my chest when their heads swiveled in my direction.

"Miss Hayes, we'd like to ask you a few questions. Can you please come with us?" one of them asked, when they made it to my side of the room.

Panic rose and my gaze ping-ponged between them and the door. "I'm not leaving. Pax is in there." I pointed in the general direction of the ER as if they didn't already know. "I can't leave him."

"We understand, but it's vital we speak to you while the incident is still fresh in your mind."

I wanted to stay in the waiting room. Anger filled me. Morgan pulled me to his side and addressed the officers. "There's a table and chairs over there," he said, pointing to a secluded area of the waiting room. "She can answer your questions while we wait."

The officers nodded, and I breathed a sigh of relief. They led us to the table. Morgan followed and stood behind my chair, a quiet sentinel, while the officers questioned me.

"I'm Officer Cage, and this is my partner Officer Howe. Can you tell us what happened tonight? No detail is too small or insignificant. What you may see as unrelated may aid our investigation." One sat, and the other stood, mirroring Morgan and me.

I took a moment calming my mind. I relayed my story to the officers. They gave me time and space and I told them the details I remembered. Morgan placed his hand on my shoulder, providing comfort and support as I grew more distraught. I appreciated it, but I yearned for Pax's arms instead. In the short while we'd been together, his presence grounded me. When things got chaotic or overwhelming, Pax's smile centered me.

"Did you see anyone other than Pax come around the corner of the house? Even a small glimpse?"

Sitting Officer's question didn't register, being lost in worry over Pax. After Morgan nudged me, I shook my head. "No. I saw no one else."

"We found items on the master bed. Do you mind looking at them?"

I nodded, and Morgan's hand squeezed my shoulder in support. "Yeah. Sure. Okay."

Standing Officer lifted a large brown paper bag from the floor. I shook in my seat, worried. The officer pulled two transparent evidence bags and placed them in front of me. I noted the information on the stickers before he turned the bags, their contents clear. One contained a red lace thong, the other a matching lace bra.

My fingertips hovered on the edge of the bra bag, but I didn't touch it. "Those aren't mine," I said and clasped my hands together under the table. "You found them on his bed?" The logical part of my brain knew there was an explanation for the lingerie, but the self-doubting part created scenarios of other women with Pax. I stopped from descending into the past and concentrated on the here and now.

"What do those have to do with the investigation?" Morgan asked from behind me.

"We can't tell you but trust us when we say they raised our suspicions."

Before the officers asked any more questions, Jesse came through the doors and over to me. "He's awake, ornery, and asking for you."

I stood on shaky legs. "Are we done? I need to see Pax." I wiped away my tears and schooled my face. The officers and I followed Jesse through the doors after he filled his family in. He led us back to a makeshift room behind a curtain. When the cops requested I hold back, Morgan and Jesse fought on my behalf and convinced the officers to let me see him first.

Pax reached his hand out and smiled as I entered. No matter how strongly I held my emotions in, seeing Pax vulnerable in the hospital bed broke me. I cried, relief coursing through my body.

He was alive. Pallid and weak, but alive.

"Baby, come here. I'm fine. Just a bump on the head." I hurried to him and grabbed his hand before sitting on his bed.

"I was so scared." I kissed the knuckles of his hand and caressed his cheek. I couldn't stop touching him. I needed to feel his vibrancy through my fingertips. Feel his heartbeat.

"You drove my truck?"

"I'm sorry. I didn't know how else to get you here. I didn't even think to call for an ambulance. You were bleeding. I panicked."

"Hey, hey, hey. Stop that. I'm not mad." Pax pulled his hand from mine and reached for my nape. He drew me closer and kissed me. A kiss not filled with sensuality, but with love and tenderness. When we separated his love for me was clear in his eyes, and my tears ran once again. "Baby, it's okay. It would take a hell of a lot more to take me down. I'm here."

"I never want anything bad to happen to you again. I don't know what I would…" I faltered to finish.

"I'm not going anywhere." He wrapped me in his arms and encouraged me to lie down beside him. I rested my head on his chest and listened to his steady heartbeat, feeling his warmth seep into me.

An officer cleared his throat, and I jolted in Pax's arm, forgetting they were in the room with us. I only had eyes for Pax. I sat up, moving away giving them a chance to question Pax. He grabbed my leg and kept me seated by his side. "Stay with me. I need your protection," he said, making me giggle.

Satisfied, he turned to the officers and nodded. "I'm ready."

****

Pax

It hurt seeing Susan cry. I wanted to take her in my arms and reassure her but moving made the pain in the back of my head worse. I refused the pain meds the doctor offered, but having Susan next to me was medicine enough.

The two cops stepped closer and introduced themselves. I recognized one of them but never had any interaction with him. They looked questioningly at Susan but didn't ask her to leave. The officer I didn't recognize told me they had already spoken with Susan and were hoping I could fill in the blanks from her statement.

Although tired, I answered their questions as best I could. My blood boiled when they showed me the panties and bra. Susan stiffened beside me and avoided my gaze. "I've never seen those before. You found them on my bed?"

"We did, along with a note."

"What? Did you read it?" Susan blushed, and for a moment, I believed the lingerie belonged to her. Thinking they read a letter Susan meant for my eyes only made me angry and I glared at the officers. However, pain lanced through my skull and with it came clarity. The fundraiser kept her busy. There was no way she had time to leave the items on my bed.

Then it dawned on me. I knew who had.

The officers handed me a third bag and Susan sucked in a breath.

"You didn't show me that," she said.

"No, ma'am."

Susan leaned in and read the note with me. I tilted it giving her a better view. I didn't need to read it, already guessing what it said.

I love you

Three simple words but in those three words I

knew I would never get rid of Julie unless I took drastic measures.

"What about the lights?" I asked while handing the note back to them.

"As far as we can tell, someone shattered them after they clipped your electrical wires. Your security company had already put a call into dispatch when the silent alarm triggered. You got home before a unit arrived."

"Mr. Anderson, if you have any idea who did this, even if it's far-fetched, it's important you tell us."

"I do have an idea and I've already spoken to Detective Simon." When the two officers shared a look, I elaborated. "He's a friend from college."

"Okay. So tell us what you told him. Let us follow up on your suspicions. No detail is too small."

I heaved a sigh. Repeating the story, yet again, proved maddening. Susan squeezed my hand in support, and I delved into my problems with Julie. I told them about my experience with her over the past several months. Susan remained quiet throughout our back and forth. I answered their questions quickly, wanting the officers to leave.

Closing my eyes against the harsh lights, my headache worsened the longer I spoke. The officers took their cue and left after, promising to look into Julie and to speak with Simon. We also arranged for them to retrieve the letters from Caden's.

As soon as the coast was clear, my family filtered into my room two-by-two. Thankfully, Caden filled them in on my situation with Julie, and although they weren't happy, no one pressed the issue. Once reassured of my well-being they left Susan and me alone. The last to leave were my parents and on her way out, mom enveloped Susan in a hug.

"You take care of my boy. He may be a hulk, but inside he is all heart," Mom said to her. She wiped the tears from Susan's face and squeezed her cheeks. I think my mother's affections turned Susan more into a puddle than seeing me in the hospital bed. Mom left the room holding Dad's hand. Their love showed as she laid her head on his shoulder and Dad patted her arm.

"My mom loves you, you know," I said to Susan's back. She refused to sit on the bed while my family visited. "She never would have left if she didn't trust you."

Susan muffled her sobs with her hand, but she couldn't hide her shaking shoulders. I wanted to go to her. Hold her. Love her. But the monitors kept me from moving.

I jumped at the bit to get out of the hospital. Being hit on the back of the head resulted in ten stitches and a concussion, I desperately wanted to break free from my curtained cell. Returning home was out of the question, and Caden insisted I stay with him. I agreed but hoped Susan would stay the night with me as well.

"Baby, come here. Please."

Susan wiped her cheeks on her sleeve and turned. Her red, swollen, tear-filled eyes broke my heart. I opened my arms for her, and she ran into them. We cuddled, closed off the noises of the ER, and lived in the moment.

Eventually, the nurse came in, and I signed the discharge papers. Susan flitted around, gathering my things. Watching her from the corner of my eye, I grew wary. The assault unnerved her, but whether she was afraid for herself or me, I wasn't sure.

Chapter Twenty-Four

Pax

It seemed as if hours passed before I was discharged. I fought using the wheelchair. However, seeing Susan happy, I relented in the end.

She drove Caden's Mustang while he drove my truck back to his place. I rode with Susan. She talked the whole way about frivolous things, and I kept quiet, enjoying the sound of her voice.

"We have to call your CO. You can't work tomorrow, and I'm calling out as well. Your mom said she'd bring breakfast in the morning, and Morgan is coming by with lunch. It looks like all I'm going to have to do is help you shower and get you into bed."

Even in pain, my body reacted to her innocent words. "You can help me shower anytime."

Susan blushed. "That's not what I meant."

"You can mean it any way you like. All I'll hear is shower, naked, you, me, and my answer is absolutely."

"You have a concussion and stitches. How are you horny?"

Reaching over the console, I played with her hair, relishing in its silkiness. "Baby, haven't you realized when it's anything involving you, I'll be the first in line? Better yet, I better be the only one in line from here on out."

She gasped. My words struck a chord. I

begrudgingly removed my hand from her hair knowing it distracted her.

"Susan. It's always been you. It will always be you. Now that I have you, I will never let you go."

Shifting in my seat, I faced her. If the night's events proved anything, it was life was too short not to grab it by the horns.

"I was going to wait until you were more comfortable with the idea of us, but I don't want to anymore. Move in with me. Forget finding an apartment. Your home is by my side. I want to go to sleep and wake up with you every day. I can't think of anything I want more."

Susan teared up the longer I spoke. I shut up and waited for her response, nervous she would turn me down. No matter. I would show her taking a chance on me, on us, was worth it.

"That won't work," she finally said. My heart pounded against my chest, disappointment clouded my thoughts. "I refuse to sleep at the firehouse with you."

I broke out in a laugh, hurting my head when I threw it back. "Is that a yes? Because any other answer won't work."

"Pax, I don't know. It seems kind of fast."

I itched to reach out and hold her but didn't want to distract her from driving. "We've spent over ten years denying our feelings. I'm done being stupid. Tonight convinced me to go after what I want. I want you. Move in with me." Her knuckles turned white on the steering wheel and I hated I caused her discomfort. "Baby, talk to me. Tell me what's on your mind."

"I'm scared. What if you decide my crazy hours at work are too much for you? Or what if you realize all my hair products clutter your counter? What if you decide you can't stand my cooking or house cleaning skills? Or if I snore and it annoys you?"

"First off, that's a lot of what ifs. I work crazy hours as well, and your stuff will never feel like clutter. It will only remind me of the beautiful woman I get to call mine. If I wanted a perfect dinner or a clean house, I'd hire a cook and housekeeper. And if you snore, I'll think it's adorable. I don't care about any of it. I care about you. I want you and I want to live my life with you."

Indecision wavered in her eyes and she struggled to answer. "Baby, my family loves you. No matter what happens between us, you will always be a part of the family. But I promise, you and I are meant to be. There is nothing you can do to dissuade me from wanting this."

Susan veered, and the car skidded into a nearby lot. She slammed on the brakes coming to a full stop before shifting into park. She took a fortifying breath and turned to me. "You sure about this?"

Regardless whether she questioned my decision or my family loving her, it didn't matter. Either way I answered the same way. "Yes."

A smile spread across her face. "Okay. I'll move in with you."

I rushed forward, but the seatbelt pulled me back. My brain rattled in my head. "Shit. Baby, I'm so happy right now. But I can't move. You better get us to Caden's because I need to hold you and show you how happy you make me."

"No sex."

"Why do you have to go killing my fantasy? Get us

to a bed, woman."

****

Susan

My exhaustion evaporated as desire flared in Pax's eyes. I shocked myself when I agreed to move in with him but seeing him smile bolstered my confidence.

He was right, life was too short, and I wanted to enjoy it with him by my side. If we broke up, I would deal with the aftermath. It would be hard to lose his family, but I'd survive. What I wouldn't survive was regret. I didn't want to regret not moving forward with our relationship.

I drove faster than he liked, but since he didn't ask me to slow down, I took it as affirmation. We needed a more private location. Getting there was paramount. Not that I intended getting in his pants while at Caden's. I simply wanted to hold him, feel his heart beneath my cheek, revel in his aliveness.

By the time we reached Caden's, early morning light graced the sky. I took a moment enjoying the tranquility of the dawning day. Caden and I would keep Pax awake for four hours before we allowed him sleep in two-hour shifts.

For the first time since I knew him, Pax needed help. No matter how tired or scared I was, Pax was my priority. He always insured the safety of others. It was my turn to do for him what he did all the time. Caden beat us home and waited in the driveway of his waterfront condo.

"Thought you got lost." He leaned down and extended his hand to Pax.

"Nope. Just convincing Susan to move in with me."

"Halle-fucking-lujah."

I giggled. Contentment filled my every pore.

We helped Pax out of the car, surprised he didn't protest. He leaned on his cousin, and they walked through the front door and up the steps to the guest bedroom.

Caden helped Pax lie down. I knelt at the end of the bed and took off his shoes.

"I'll do just about anything for you, brother, but I'm not helping you bathe."

"That job's reserved for my lovely lady," Pax said as I blushed. "Now get your grubby hands off of me. Once I'm clean, you can stay up with me and Susan can sleep."

"No. I can stay up with you. Caden can sleep. I want first shift."

Pax and Caden shared a look and with a wink directed my way Caden laughed. "Far be it from me to deny the lady's wishes. If you guys are all set, then I'm going to bed. Susan, wake me up in two hours and I'll take over. By then we'll have a rotating door of help, anyway. Towels are in the bathroom closet."

I helped Pax out of the clothes Jesse provided at the hospital. They were a size too small and fit snugly across his sculpted chest and butt. My hands shook as I undid each button of his burrowed shirt.

"Nervous?" Pax grabbed my wrists. He pulled them to his mouth and kissed along my knuckles.

"No."

"Then why're your hands shaking?"

I didn't want to admit it. Seeing him vulnerable frightened me. Pax was invincible. A big, badass firefighter. Seeing him in the hospital bed rattled me.

He could have died, and it devastated me imagining a life without him. My nerves were not because of what I wanted to happen in a bed, but because I loved him so much it hurt.

"Baby, sit down." Letting go of my wrists, he tapped the bed beside him. I sat, and like at the hospital, he put a calming hand on my thigh. "I have a thick skull. I'm fine."

I heard him. I really did, but I couldn't ignore the little voice in my head. Pax was human. Vulnerable. Just like the rest of us.

"Do you really think Julie did this to you? Why would she?" By his raised eyebrow, my shift in subject did not go unnoticed, but he obliged me.

"I don't know what to think. Maybe she wanted to surprise me again, and when we interrupted her, she freaked out. That's the best explanation I have. She might be crazy, but I really don't think she'd resort to violence."

"If it was her, you have to be careful. Who knows how far she'll go now. I'm scared for you."

"Baby, please, don't worry. She's probably afraid now and will leave me alone. Let's not concern ourselves with the what ifs and what could happen. I need to wash, and I can't think of a better shower buddy than you. What do you say? Want to rub your hands all over my body?" Pax's words light and suffused with airiness helped ease the tension between my shoulders.

I finished undressing him, planting a quick kiss on each inch of skin revealed.

"Baby, you're killing me."

"Sorry. I'll stop," I said but gave him a nip under his jaw before actually following through.

His groan made me smile. "Shower, then it's payback."

He swung his legs off the bed, tugged his underwear down his legs, and slowly headed to the door. I walked behind him admiring the naked view. Legs as thick as tree trunks led to the most perfect bubble butt. I wanted to run my tongue along the two dimples where his back met his ass. I licked my lips lost in thoughts of Pax's body when he stopped. I slammed into his back, and he reached behind steadying me.

"I can hear you panting, woman."

"Can't help myself." With his back to my front, I wrapped my arms around his waist and rubbed my palms down his chest, stopping shy of his happy trail.

"Shit, woman, keep doing that and Caden's not going to get any sleep."

I giggled and rested my cheek on the hard planes of his back. He stood silently in my arms, permitting me unimpeded exploration of his wide torso. Unable to link my fingers in the front I fluttered them along his skin. I memorized every dip and valley of his chest, storing the information in the part of my mind belonging to Pax.

"You okay?" he asked after an unidentified length of time.

"Yeah? Come on, big guy; let's get you cleaned up and comfortable." I reluctantly disengaged and immediately missed him. "Let me get the shower started, and then I can figure out how to protect the stitches."

"There's a plastic bandage in the bag I got at the hospital. I'll start the water while you grab what we need." Pax nodded toward the bedroom.

"Okay."

I turned to leave but Pax pulled me against him once more. He gazed into my eyes. His own turned a darker shade of blue and filled with desire. "And when you get back, I want you naked."

Chapter Twenty-Five

Pax

She walked out of the bathroom and my body heated at the sight of her swaying hips. The pain in my head forgotten.

Lusty thoughts invaded my mind, and I grew harder. I reached for the shower handles and adjusted the knobs. Ice cold for a solo shower, but tonight called for a steamy one. Satisfied with the water temperature, I took towels out of the closet and placed them on the vanity counter.

"I found them," Susan announced, holding the package of plastic bandages as she walked back into the bathroom. She reached for me with a frown. "You're too tall. Sit on the toilet."

"Wow. Already bossing me around."

"Pax." She slapped my arm, groaning out her frustration, but she hid a smile with a lowered head. "It's not what I meant, and you know it. Sit down, you big oaf, so I can take care of my man."

She stopped, stunned at what she'd said, and I beamed inside. I loved the sound of it. *Her man*. Words I thought she would never say. After endless years of yearning and suppressing my desires, I had excelled at shutting down thoughts of a future with her. However, hearing Susan say "my man" made me virtually beat my chest in victory.

I took the seat she suggested not because she needed to reach my head, but because I became dizzy with happiness. And from too much movement.

When she didn't approach, I dared a glance. I hoped to see the same happiness. Instead, shock filled her face. Refusing to let her fears ruin the moment, I hauled her onto my lap. She wrapped her arms around my neck, wary of the stitches.

"I love how that sounds. *Your man.* Truer words have never been spoken. Say it again."

She giggled, and our gazes locked. The knot in my belly loosened. I needed to hear her say it again.

"My man."

"Damn, right I am. Now I get to make the same claim. You are my woman."

She blushed, and tears coated her beautiful hazel eyes. I wiped her cheek. "Baby? What's wrong?"

"Nothing…nothing." She wiped the remaining tears with the back of her hand. "I've always been your woman. You might not have known it. Hell, I denied it most of the time, but I'm yours, Pax. Always will be."

She whispered at the end and I strained to hear her over the running water. But I did, and my heart no longer belonged to me. She held it in her hands. It was hers for safekeeping.

Standing, she nudged me and reached for the back of my head. Her hands shook as she tended to my injuries, and in my gut, I knew her admission rattled her.

"Come on, baby. Time for my sponge bath." I pulled on the hem of her shirt and tugged it over her head. She raised her arms and smacked my hand away when I reached for the button of her shorts.

"I can do that. Besides, remember, no sex."

I growled my disapproval. "I know. But you never said no touching. Besides, you haven't kept your hands off me all night." I leaned in and nipped her earlobe before whispering. "I want to undress you because I want to feel you shudder as my hands rub along your naked flesh. I want to see your eyes heat up with desire for me. But most of all, I want to hear your little whimpers."

I loved her immediate response. She dropped her hands from the button of her shorts and regarded me. I took my time unbuttoning them and rubbed the back of my hand inside the waistband. Her belly trembled beneath my touch, and I leaned down and inhaled the scent of her arousal. I didn't register the pain at the back of my head. Regardless, it wouldn't have stopped me.

I tasted and licked her shoulder and neck. Her whimpers encouraged me on. She clutched my shoulders, digging her nails into my skin. I grasped her hip and helped keep her balance as my tongue danced over her skin.

"I wish I could be on my knees for you."

"No. Your head," she panted out.

I slipped my hands down her hips and lowered her shorts and lace panties in one move. As she stepped out of them, I concentrated on keeping my balance. Between the heady scent of her and my already throbbing head, I risked the chance of passing out.

I sat up to keep the contents of my stomach down, although I didn't hide my nausea well.

Susan grasped my biceps and held me steady. "Damn it, Pax. You're hurt. This can wait. Shower and then bed, big guy. No more arguments." Once the queasiness subsided, I stood and followed Susan into the shower. I held onto the wall as I stepped in. The space wasn't big, but you didn't hear me complain. With barely enough maneuvering room, I savored the feel of our bodies continually touching.

Susan lathered her hands with soap and rubbed them along my back. She took her time and washed me with care. The contrast between the pinprick sensation of the water hitting my chest and the softness of her hands on my back had me ready and eager before long. I stopped fighting my physical enjoyment of her touch and let the feelings rise in me.

"Turn around, big guy. But keep your head out of the spray." I did as instructed and laughed when she took in my erection. Her eyes widened and no matter how much she diverted her gaze it kept returning to it.

"Baby, I can't help it. This is what you do to me."

She gulped and reached out, grabbing me. I groaned at the feel of her small hand wrapping around me. Her fingertips didn't touch. Susan stroked me with a strong, sure hold. My skin broke out in sweat, the water washing it away. My climax neared, and I fought it. She ran her thumb along the tip. I groaned and thrust my hips as her grip tightened. Her hand hit the base of my shaft before moving up again. I stumbled back when she ran a fingertip along the vein on the underside.

Tingling in my lower back was all the warning I needed. I wanted to be inside her when I came. I pulled away, reached the back of her neck bringing her closer, and smashed my lips to hers.

****

Susan

The tight quarters didn't leave much room, but I did my best in the small space. If he was normal size, the stall would have been perfect for two people, but they didn't call him the Hulk for no reason.

Pax spent hours training in the gym and at the firehouse and it showed in his sculpted perfection. He wasn't a gym rat but trained in order to fight fires and rescue people. I loved the intensity with which he worked, and over the years, I fell more in love with him as he grew into a fierce fireman.

He kissed me with vigor, and I responded. His unrestrained reaction to my hands on him made me heady, but the feel of him rubbing against me set my libido on fire. He licked the seam of my lips, and I opened for him. Water rained down over our heated bodies not dampening my need for him. We kissed until I needed air. A couple deep breaths and with oxygen flowing back to my brain I regained coherent thought.

I pulled back. "Let's finish and get to bed," I said. I reluctantly let go of him, and he growled his disapproval.

"I'm open to going to bed," he said around a smirk, eyes flashing with delight. I ignored him, took the bar of soap, and ran it along his front. I avoided the 'V' of his abdomen, knowing it would lead us into dangerous territory.

Biting my lower lip, I fought my desires and focused on washing. However, I promised to revisit shower sex with him once he healed. Every chance we got. Conservation of water being at the top of the list of reasons. I giggled at my ludicrous reasoning.

"Something funny?" Pax asked through gritted

teeth.

"I was thinking how we should always shower together. Conserve water."

Pulling me into his arms, he kissed the crook of my neck. The warm water cascading over us had nothing on his heated breath against my skin. "I like how your mind works. I agree wholeheartedly. Showering together for the sake of the Earth is a great idea. But right now I have a better one."

He reached behind him and shut off the water before pulling open the shower door. I shivered as cool air hit my wet skin. He grabbed a towel from by the sink, draped it across my shoulders, and rubbed his hands up and down my arms. He wrapped a towel around his waist and led us out of the bathroom holding my hand.

He was lighter on his feet, yet exhaustion pulled at me. Between the weeks of prep, the fundraiser, and the attack, I was spent. How he stayed upright and healing so quickly was beyond me. Once he closed the bedroom door, he dropped his towel, casual in his nakedness.

He sat on the bed. Scooting backward, he adjusted the pillows, so his back rested against the headboard before turning his scorching gaze on me.

"What do you want to do to stay awake?" I said, proud I kept my voice level, but deep down every cell in my body flared to life. He was beautiful with his tanned skin against the white sheets. I regretted not having my phone. I wanted to capture a picture of him in the moment; his hair damp from the shower and eyes darkened with desire.

"I have some thoughts."

"Yeah? So do I. Let me find the remote. We can

watch a movie."

"I have a better idea."

"You do?" I gulped and fidgeted, anxious for his answer.

"Yep. It involves your sweet body on top of mine. I think two hours is not nearly enough time for me to do what I want with you."

The air in my lungs whooshed out. I didn't catch a breath as he continued describing what he wanted to do to my body. I grew needier with each suggestion. My legs felt like lead. I couldn't take a step closer or a step away. My core pulsed. Willing, ready, and able.

"Come here and ride me, baby."

Pax splayed his arms out and rested his hands on the sheets.

"What about your head? Won't it hurt?"

"I promise to sit back and let you do all the work today. But, tomorrow, tomorrow I will do all those things to you and more."

I could come from his words alone. I climbed onto his lap, took him in hand, and aligned him to my opening. I rubbed my lips along his length while he held my hips for balance. Pax moaned beneath me and let me control the pace. Pushing up onto my knees, I bent at the torso and brought my mouth to his.

I slipped my tongue out caressing his parted lips. He opened wider for me and I took the invitation. I pushed my tongue into his mouth. I explored him, taking my time, learning and discovering what he liked.

I savored every second we were together. Pulling back, I rested my forehead on his chest and ground my hips against him. "We have to be quiet."

"As long as you promise to keep that sexy mouth

close to my ear, so I can hear you."

"God, I want you inside me."

"He's not here, but I'm happy to oblige."

I laughed. My eyes crinkled in amusement and love. Pax dug his fingers into my hips, stilling my motion. "Condom."

Reaching across him, I opened the nightstand drawer hoping Caden kept a supply in the room. As luck would have it, he did. I pulled out a sleeve, ripped one off, and left the rest on the bed.

"High expectations," Pax said, with a quirked eyebrow. I followed his gaze to the condoms. "Anything for my woman."

"Not today, big guy. This is only happening once and then you're sleeping."

"As long as you're in my arms, I'll do whatever you ask."

Ripping the packet open, I pulled the condom out and rolled it onto Pax, feeling along the length of him. Pax stilled my hands, a light sheen of sweat dotting his forehead as he held his eyes shut.

Jumping off him, I knelt by his side. "Are you okay? Did I hurt you?"

Pax opened his dark-as-night eyes. "Fuck no, woman. I was close. Your hands are amazing. Now get back up here and ride me." He pulled me back, and I straddled him again.

Reaching between my legs, I positioned him at my entrance. Pax gripped my hips and guided me down. He stretched me the farther he pushed in and I flung my head back in ecstasy. My walls pulsed around him sucking him deeper. Sweat beaded across my body and I fought to contain my scream. I lowered until I fully seated him within me, enjoying the groans escaping his parted lips.

"You're so deep."

"I know, baby. You feel fucking amazing."

I moved, and Pax gripped me harder, sheathed deep inside me. "We need to figure a way to live our lives with me inside you. I never want to let you go."

I couldn't stay still any longer. His words stoked the fire. Bracing my hands against his chest, I rolled my hips making him move within me. He closed his eyes in bliss, loosened his hold, and I pressed my advantage, moving faster. I rocked with gusto, riding him like a bucking bull. The harder I rocked, the louder his moans. I wanted him to scream, no longer caring about our lack of privacy.

He pinched my nipples between his fingers and sent a shock of pain straight to my core. My movements became erratic, and I rode the crest. I held back my orgasm. I wanted Pax there with me.

Pax sat up and took one of my breasts into his mouth. He took as much of it as he could and sucked hard. His tongue lapped at my nipple and my blood scorched me from the inside out. I held onto his shoulders and pumped my hips up and down. The burning in my thighs didn't slow me down. All that mattered was how good he felt.

"Let go, baby. Do it for me."

Reaching between us, he fingered me and rubbed my clit in circles. I lost all ability to move and Pax took over. With his mouth sucking on my breast, his hands expertly playing me as he pistoned into me, my climax hit me like a freight train. I screamed, my orgasm enveloping me. My walls pulsated against his hardness making him pulse inside me. Pax roared and let go. Our cries drowned each other out.

Pax was my world, regardless of what lay beyond the walls and the bed we snuggled in. Had I known those moments were the calm before the storm, I would never have left the room.

Chapter Twenty-Six

Susan

The next few days flew by. Between Pax's family and me, we took care of him until the doctor cleared his return to work. He had no lingering effects from the concussion. I returned to work two days after the attack and Pax insisted on driving me. He worried about my well-being and I worried about his. No matter how much I argued he take another week off, he didn't.

Pax contacted the security company monitoring the house and added services. He wouldn't let me move in until he secured the place as tight as Fort Knox. A week passed. With my packed meager belongings, I waited for him to pick me up from the shelter.

I hung out inside where the air conditioning kept me cool. The firefighters Pax sent over to help excavate my land had gone home for the night. With the ground ready for building, they planned on starting early the following day to beat the heat.

The dogs barked in the backroom, and I checked on them, walking through the kennels again before heading out for the night. I didn't want to leave them agitated for the night staff.

I had a great setup with two college students as overnight employees. They liked to study in the quiet of the shelter. Each had their own key and alarm codes and let themselves in after I shut down. They alternated nights and slept in a small room outfitted with a bed and a desk. Neither of them needed many amenities, and since I had a shower installed in the staff bathroom, they used the space to clean up in the morning before heading to class.

The animals settled and with nothing amiss, I shut off the lights and returned to the reception area. An envelope was stuck under the front door. I called out for Max, my employee for the night, and when he didn't respond, I tugged at the door. Still locked, it didn't budge. I was alone in the building and glanced outside. It was too dark for me to see anything but my reflection in the window.

I pulled the envelope free and inspected it. I didn't recognize the handwriting across the back. I opened it. Fear dug its jagged claws into me as I read the letter. I stepped closer to the reception desk and used the light from the lamp to confirm what was scrawled across the paper.

Stay away. He's mine and always will be.

I spun on my heels looking for the person responsible for freaking me out. Needing to act, I stepped to the door once again looking for the deliverer. Anyone. Julie.

Even without a signature I knew exactly who left the letter, and she was too close for comfort.

My legs shook, and I made it to a couch before they buckled from under me. I jumped when a knock sounded at the front door. Pax stood with his hands cupped at the glass to see inside. His smile faltered when he spotted me and pounded on the glass.

I rose and disarmed the alarm with shaky fingers. He pushed through as soon as the lock clicked open and hugged me to him. With my head buried in his chest, he swiveled us back and forth. After several minutes of calming me, he sighed and pulled back, resting his hands on my shoulders.

"What's wrong? What happened?"

From between us, I produced the letter and held it up for him. He took it from me and stiffened as he read it. His hold on me tightened.

"Pax...Can't breathe..." I panted.

He loosened his arms but didn't give me space to move. "Shit, baby, sorry. Come on, we need to get out of here." He pulled back enough letting me reset the alarm and lock the door.

He secured me in the truck and ran back to the door and tugged. He looked around the doorframe and up and down the street before getting in the driver's side.

"Where are we going?" Pax drove holding my hand, and I was thankful for the physical contact.

"To see Simon," he said through clenched teeth. "If she wants to fuck with me, that's one thing, but she will not mess with you." It was rare for Pax to lose control, but in that moment, his anger and concern were palpable. I stayed quiet as he drove recklessly—for Pax—through the streets of Bellevue. He pulled into the police station and raced out of the car before I undid my seatbelt. Helping me out, he wrapped me in his arms again and led me up the steps.

"Hi, I'm Pax Anderson and I need to see Detective Simon," Pax said to the woman sitting behind a glass window. Bright fluorescent lights lit the space. Behind us, a row of blue stadium-like seats lined all the available wall space. Closed, and I assumed locked, doors stood on either side of the reception area. They had key scan locks and signs displaying "Police Personnel Only".

"What's this regarding?" the woman asked Pax.

"Does it matter? I need to see Simon." I felt his anger pulsing below the surface and tugged on his arm until he paid me attention. I silently asked him to calm down. We didn't need to get kicked out or arrested. He nodded in understanding and took a deep breath.

"Can you text him?"

He fished his phone out and typed a quick text. The woman kept a keen eye on him, and I turned him, so she only saw his back. Figured it was his least imposing feature.

"Simon'll be out in a second," he said, after reading the incoming text. He turned back to the receptionist and inclined his head to acknowledge his less than polite manner. She nodded in return. "He said we'll need visitor badges. Can we get those now, please? It is a matter of some urgency."

The woman slid a ledger over to Pax and showed him where to sign. She handed me two badges identifying us as visitors. She reviewed the ledgers and then ignored us as she returned her attention to her computer.

We stood in awkward silence until Simon came through the door on the right. He approached with a smile. His lips thinned out the closer he got, undoubtedly noticing Pax's scowl.

"Seeing your grumpy ass tells me your visit isn't for the sake of shooting the shit." He slapped Pax on the back and eyed me. "You must be Susan. Why don't we go on back and you can tell me what brought you into my neck of the woods?"

He led us through the same door from where he'd come. We followed him, and I took in our surroundings curious to see the inner workings of a police station. Desks sat two-by-two and back-to-back throughout the cavernous room. The room buzzed with activity as we walked past them to a hallway interspersed with many doors. At the end of the hall, Simon gestured to a small room with several couches and chairs. Bulletin boards with menus, flyers, and various other bits of colorful information adorned the walls.

We sat, and he fixed several cups of coffee in the small kitchen area. Handing one to me and one to Pax, he sat across from us with his own cup.

"What's up?"

"Susan found…" Pax stopped mid-sentence with the letter in hand. "Where did you get this?" he asked me.

"I found it under the door at my shelter." I took it from Pax and handed it to Simon.

"Place it on the table, please."

I did as he asked. Simon drew a pen from his pocket and maneuvered the letter to face him. "I don't have gloves and the fewer prints the better. I'm assuming only the author, possibly the deliverer, and the two of you have handled the letter."

We nodded. "Okay. I'm going to bag this and hand it to the officers working your case. I'm also going to invite them to sit in while you tell me what happened tonight. Sit tight, I'll be right back."

He returned with an evidence bag and Officers Howe and Cage behind him. We exchanged pleasantries as they sat down on either side of Pax and me.

"Take it from the top. Tell us what happened and how this came into your possession."

I told them my story as Pax fumed beside me.

"Is this your normal routine?" Simon asked.

"No. Usually I set the alarm, lock up, and then leave." Pax reached for my hand and placed it in his lap. "Tonight, I was waiting for Pax since we agreed I wouldn't hang outside by myself. The dogs began barking, and I went to check on them one last time before he got there."

The officers and Simon shared a look I couldn't decipher.

"When you locked up for the night did you notice anyone? They might not have been suspicious looking, but simply hanging around, maybe looking out of place."

I thought back and shook my head. "I didn't really look. My only concern was the dogs. Sorry."

"No need to apologize. And if I'm not mistaken, you believe the sender is Julie?" Simon turned to Pax.

"Yes. Who else could it be?"

The officers shared another look, but Simon spoke first.

"We believe it's her. Unfortunately, we have no hard evidence she was the one at the house. Unless there is a street camera by the shelter catching an image of her slipping the letter under the door, there isn't much we can do. She's made no physical threats to either of you." He held up his hand to stop Pax when he made to interrupt. "Let me finish. Even though we can't prove it's her, doesn't mean we're ruling her out as a suspect. The department therapist is reviewing the letters you saved and will determine the degree of danger she poses. What we need from the two of you is to keep bringing us any letters or items, preferably touched as little as possible, and call us if you see her. We can pursue restraining orders, but they take time. In the meantime, keep your eyes open and go nowhere alone."

Pax absent-mindedly circled his thumb across my knuckles. "Can't we lure her in or something? I need to ensure Susan's safety."

"No. We don't want to bait her. She's angry. She'll make a mistake. And when she does, we'll catch her. Stay vigilant and have us on speed dial." Simon rose to his feet, and we followed suit. He walked us out to the truck before shaking Pax's hand.

Once away from the security of the police station, fear dug in. I shoved it back. Pax had enough on his mind. I didn't want to add to his burden. As long as we stood strong and united, we would be the victors. Julie wasn't going to get what she wanted.

****

Pax

I fumed all the way home. I felt out of control and helpless. When Julie targeted me, I took precautions. I didn't feel the need to change my life other than to install security cameras. From the moment Susan showed me the letter, my gut clenched. I wanted to protect her. Hide her in my house.

When Simon confirmed my greatest fear, I wanted to race out of the station and find Julie. To get to her and end this crazy rollercoaster we were on. The police failed in finding her after she put me in the hospital. They said she was running scared, but I didn't accept their explanation. I believed she was biding her time.

The message she left for Susan only solidified my beliefs.

Finally, in the newly fortified safety of my home, I perched on the couch, my head braced in my hands. Susan sat beside me and placed her hand on my thigh. Warmth seeped through my chilled bones from the slight touch. I covered her hand and took the strength she offered to calm me down.

"I don't want you to go to work until this is over."

"Pax. Don't be ridiculous. People'll surround me all day. She won't be able to get to me."

"I hate I can't protect you." I kissed the top of her head and wrapped my arms around her waist.

"I promise I'll be careful. She won't do anything stupid. You and I both believe she reacted without thinking when we got to your place and surprised her. I doubt she'll do either of us any further harm. Once she sees we're serious about each other, she'll leave us alone."

I didn't hold out much hope.

"I still hate she has her sights on you. I'll drive you to and from work the days I'm off. The days I'm on, maybe you can stay with Morgan. I don't want you here by yourself." I needed her to agree, but if she didn't I wondered how many days I could take off without the department heads getting pissed.

She opened and closed her mouth a couple of times as if changing her mind. She closed her eyes and gave me a curt nod, surprising me when she relented without argument. "If it'll make you feel better, then I will."

"Okay, now that's settled, how about I call in delivery?"

"Sounds good. But Pax, we also have something

else to talk about." I sat quietly, fear clutching my insides. I calmed when she reached for my hand and smiled. "Whatever you're thinking, you're wrong. I wanted to talk about your birthday next weekend."

Smacking my forehead, I realized with all that happened I had forgotten about it. "What? Want to spend it in our birthday suits?"

She giggled and scooted closer. "Although the idea is tempting, your mother called me earlier today. She's having everyone over and wanted to make sure you'd be okay with it."

"And so it begins. My mother scheming with my girlfriend. Couldn't wait another couple of months before you ganged up on me?" I joked and let the smile on my face take the sting out of my words.

"She knows how much you hate being fussed over. She figured I could convince you to let her." Susan shrugged, and the motion exposed her tantalizing shoulder.

"I can think of a couple of ways for you to convince me."

She smacked my chest and laughed. "Oh, I'm sure you can. Would getting on my knees to beg help my cause?" The sassy minx winked, knowing full well she had painted quite the picture in my head. Laughing, she scurried away from me. I pounced and pinned her beneath me only then realizing my mistake. She wiggled and with every brush of her breasts on my chest, or her hips against my erection, my need for her intensified.

"You are so fucking sexy right now. I think it's time we christened all the flat surfaces, and then all the not so flat ones." I loved seeing her eyes glaze over with desire as she cataloged all the available spaces around the room. "Then when we're done with the horizontal, we'll hit all the sitting ones and then we can tackle the vertical ones."

"That's a lot of surfaces. Do you plan on doing this methodically with a formal list, or haphazardly?" Susan asked huskily. Her voice turned me on even more.

Leaning down, I nipped her lower lip before running my tongue along the inside. She moaned, and I moved my hand up her torso until it rested on her breast. I pinched her nipple through her clothes and bra. "I assure you there will be nothing haphazard about this, but I will take you everywhere I can, and then I'll invent places."

Susan shifted under me rubbing her core against my thigh. Her skin flushed and if it weren't for her rumbling stomach, I would have stripped us both and made good on my promise.

"Come on, baby. Your growling stomach is going to scare the neighbors. I need to feed you." I sat up, pulling her with me. Her messy hair, a result of our little tussle, and her skewed skirt didn't help me with my predicament. With a silent resolute promise to finish what we started, I hauled her to the kitchen to decide on dinner.

Chapter Twenty-Seven

Susan

The following day Pax headed to the station after dropping me off at the shelter. The next two nights I'd spend at Morgan's. I hated being away from Pax, but while Julie roamed free, it was for the best. I adjusted my schedule to bring Pax lunch at the station the days we were apart.

The busy morning pulled me in a thousand directions, and I forgot my phone in my purse. Between the adoptions, barking dogs, and ringing phones I was ready to explode.

Finally, I found a moment of reprieve and locked myself in my office. I sat at the desk and propped my feet as my phone dinged. I pulled it from my bag, surprised to see the number of missed texts, calls, and voice-mails. I tended to the texts from my dad, Ann Marie, and Pax first. He canceled our lunch plans because a fire called his crew out. I worried for him, but I knew I didn't have to. He would take the necessary precautions to ensure his crew's, any civilians', and his safety.

I turned my attention to the voicemails. I didn't recognize the number but listened to them, anyway. I hit play and turned on the speakerphone and sat back to enjoy my much-needed cup of coffee.

I spluttered and dropped the cup. Coffee splashed

across the desk, flowing off the side to the floor. I didn't care. My only concern the messages playing.

What's it going to take to make you leave him alone? I already told you he's mine.

I love him, and he loves me. He's just humoring you since you're a family friend. He will never love you the way he does me. If you know what's good for you, break it off with him.

Here's the thing, bitch. If I can't have him, then no one can. One way or another Pax will be mine. Break it off with him and stay the fuck away from his family, or I swear I'll make him pay for hurting me.

He needs to feel the same pain I feel when I see him with you. You're nothing special, you know. Strutting around. All he sees are your fucking tits and ass. He's a tit man. Told me he loves mine especially when I'm playing with them for him.

Where the fuck are you? Why won't you answer the phone? Are you scared, bitch? Go ahead and keep ignoring me.

You know what? If you keep ignoring me, maybe the next fire he responds to won't be as small as the one he's at right now.

****

I should have stopped listening after the first one and called the police, but I didn't. Fear for Pax's safety pushed me forward. I had to make her leave him alone. With trembling hands, I dialed her number.

"Well, took you long enough," she answered. My heart pounded against my ribs probably bruising the bones.

"Julie?" I wanted to yell but knew it wouldn't accomplish anything if I put her on the defense.

Thinking on my feet, I treated her like a growling dog. And like a dog, her aggression was most likely a reaction from fear rather than malice.

"Bitch, you know it's me. You lied to the cops. Now they're crawling all over my place. I haven't been able to go home."

"I'm sorry. Maybe if we talk to the police together we can clear things up."

"Are you fucking kidding me? I'm not talking to the cops. Pax deserved what he got. He shouldn't have brought you to the house. He was fixing the place up for me, and you shoved your way in. I'm sick and tired of his playing hard to get bullshit."

"Maybe he isn't playing. Maybe he likes you as a friend. Pax doesn't mean to hurt you." I hoped reason would win out but worried her delusions were too far gone.

"He loves me. You've messed with his mind. He'll never be happy with you. He'd be better off dead."

I worked to keep my breathing steady and my voice level, but inside my gut churned with abject terror. "You don't mean that. You won't hurt Pax. You love him. Why'd you want to see him dead?"

"Because I won't be far behind. We can be together, and my dad can finally feel what it's like to be alone. Or maybe he'll be sorry he was such an asshole. I don't care. My place is by Pax's side, alive or dead."

I gasped at her conviction. No matter what I said, she believed in her intended path. Eyes closed, I asked the question I already knew the answer to. "What do you want, Julie?"

She laughed. She played to win, and in the end, she was the victor. "Leave him alone. Break up with him.

Move out and stay away from him. If you don't, I'll take Pax and make him mine. Is that clear enough for you, bitch?"

I swallowed the rising bile and nodded though she couldn't see me. Tears pooled in the corner of my eyes, and I fought to hold them back. I didn't respond, but I wanted to reach through the phone and strangle her. Her brand of crazy was taking away the only thing I ever wanted.

"No one's safe as long as you're with him. Pax, you, his family, your dad. No one. Walk away and Pax'll live a long and happy life with me beside him. And you better make sure he doesn't come after you."

"How am I supposed to make him leave me alone?" Clearly asking for her advice was not one of my brightest ideas, but rational thought eluded me.

"I don't give a shit. Figure it out."

For better or worse, she hung up before I had a chance to ask anything else. I lost my battle and cried, holding my phone in a death grip. My head swam with nonsensical thoughts and I lost track of time. I stayed in my office until I gained control over my emotions. I loved Pax, and I wanted to protect him. It was simple.

My old fears were now inconsequential. His family loved me, and I knew I would never lose their affections if Pax and I didn't work out. What was important was Pax's safety. He sacrificed for his family, his job, and his community. It was time for someone to do the same for him. If walking away from him and his family meant their safety, then I would.

I hardened my heart and resolved to fix this for him. It should have been the most difficult decision of my life, but, in the end, it was the easiest. I denied my feelings for him before, and I would do it again. Even though we finally found each other, I'd rather have a broken heart because of our break up than because of his death.

I methodically readied to leave the shelter for the evening. I didn't want to wait for Morgan to pick me up. I needed to find Pax, break up with him, and get as far away from Bellevue as I could before he got off shift. I needed a few days away and visiting Ann Marie in Seattle sounded like a good idea.

Using the shelter's rescue van, I drove to the fire station while practicing my speech. Crying was out of the question and I prepared for the thundering heartbreak I was about to inflict on both of us.

I arrived and sat in my parked van. My legs refused to listen to my command to move. I was weighed down, and for a hot minute, I contemplated leaving town like a coward. Tempting, but stupid. I knew he wouldn't stop searching for me or calling.

No. Julie's instructions were clear.

I exited the van and trudged through what felt like quick sand to get inside. With a bolstering breath, I pulled the door open and came face to face with the man I wasn't ready to see.

"Hey, baby. We just got back. Did you come to make sure I was okay?" Pax greeted. "I'd hug you, but I'm covered in soot. How 'bout a kiss?"

With our bodies a few inches apart, he bent down to kiss me. I turned my head at the last second. If our lips touched, my resolve to leave him would break. Leaving him guaranteed his life. I had no other choice.

He stepped back and eyed me with trepidation. I made eye contact and delivered my practiced lines.

"I'm breaking up with you."

As if I slapped him, he took another step back. He didn't say anything. His focus unyielding.

"We aren't going to work out. I thought I was in love with you, but it was a stupid childhood crush." I hated every word I uttered. I held my breath thankful Pax remained silent. If he spoke, I would cave. "I'm glad I realized this now rather than later. We can both move on with our lives. I'm heading to your place and getting my stuff. We're through. Please don't call me." I spoke quickly, needing to get it all out before I took it back.

I moved to leave, but Pax turned me around and smashed his chest to mine. "What the fuck has gotten into you?"

My hands rested on his chest, and I wanted to rub them along the ridges. Instead, I pushed back. "Absolutely nothing. I realize what we have isn't the real thing. I can't waste my time on you."

"Waste your time on me?" Pax yelled drawing his crew's attention. "Waste your time on me? Is that what you've been doing? I'm sorry, I thought we were going somewhere with this."

"We weren't, and we aren't. Good bye, Pax."

"So that's it? You're walking out? You're going to walk away from me and my family like none of us meant anything to you? I never knew you to be so callous."

His words stung, but his angry response meant my arguments hit their mark. "It's not that big of a deal. I'm sure the man I end up with will have a family as welcoming as yours has been." At the end of my control, I didn't give him a chance to respond and turned on my heels. I speed-walked out of the station and he didn't stop me.

And just like that, I walked out of his life.

Chapter Twenty-Eight

Pax

"Fuck!" I bellowed. What just happened? Jagged edges bit my insides. Nausea rose in my throat as I tried to make sense of her actions. One minute the future was mine for the taking, the next my world dissolved around me. How had I been such a fool? I let myself believe we had something. Apparently, she never loved me, and my family was replaceable after all. She grabbed my heart in her hands, decimated it, threw the remains in the ground, and stomped on them on her way out the door.

My building anger needed an outlet. I grabbed a heavy helmet from the closest bench, stepped outside, and headed for the empty parking lot. I reared my arm back and threw it like a baseball. My shoulder protested, but I didn't care. My anger didn't dissipate, and I spun around looking for another way to find relief. I spotted a tree in need of a good trimming.

With a one-track mind, I stomped over and punched the daylights out of it. I ignored my aching, bloody knuckles and beat it until I couldn't anymore. Arms wrapped around my chest and hauled me away from the tree. Heavy bodies dragged me to the ground. A heavy weight landed on my back and legs.

"Son, Pax, stop it. Right now." Billy's commanding voice broke through my violent haze. I slumped, the fight leaving me, replaced with numbness. I quit struggling against Rob and Beck's holds. They were either courageous or downright stupid. I wasn't in the right mind to decide.

Billy knelt beside me and placed his hands on my shoulders. "You need to calm down, son. Let Rob take a look at your hands."

I nodded even though I didn't care about my injuries. The pain in my hands kept the pain of my broken heart in the background.

Rob replaced Billy. "Shit, Pax. You've done damage here. Maybe even broken a few bones."

"Call Morgan and have him meet you at the hospital," Billy said. Beck helped me up and guided me to Rob's car with a hand on my elbow. Not forceful, but unwavering.

"Whatever has you worked up ends now. You are no good to yourself or anyone if you can't figure your shit out. Broken hand or not, I want you back here first thing tomorrow morning. Be ready to talk," Billy said, and I got in the car.

"Yes, boss." I didn't recognize my own voice. It was the voice of a broken man.

I grunted my responses to the hospital personnel and Morgan when he arrived. I didn't have it in me to care about my broken bones or the resultant stitches. All I wanted was to drown my feelings in a bottle. I would take one night of sorrow and tomorrow I would move on.

Love had no place in my life. In fact, happily-ever-after was a fallacy. One I refused to fall for again.

I refused Morgan's help until he promised not to call Mom. When my phone rang, I threw it to him to deal with. How she sensed something was amiss was beyond me. Probably Caden.

"Mom, he's fine. He substituted a tree for a punching bag. The tree won." I wanted to beat the smirk off his face but glared at the floor instead. "Sure. I'm sure he'd love it if you came by my place. We're heading there shortly."

I groaned. I wasn't ready to tell anyone anything, but in my family, Mom's word was law.

We arrived at Morgan's minutes before Mom. I figure she'd waited by the window and raced over after seeing Morgan drive past my parents' house.

She marched into the house and straight for me. I braced for her hug but instead a sting from her hit landed across the back of my head. "You're a fool." Of all the things I expected to hear from my mother, that wasn't one of them. "I called your boss, and he said Susan walked out on you."

"Mom. I can't believe you called my boss. I'm not five."

"Funny you say that since you had the temper tantrum of one."

Morgan laughed from his perch in the corner of the room. My glare only made him laugh harder.

"Tell me what happened," my mother demanded, and sat down on the couch beside me.

Groaning, I relented and told her about Susan dumping me. About how she said she didn't love my family or me. How she walked out as if I meant nothing to her.

Morgan burst out into raucous laughter when I finished. Mom gave him a scolding look, which only produced the opposite effect. He covered his mouth but failed to contain his amusement at my expense.

"If you have nothing to contribute, then sit there in all your tattooed glory and keep your mouth shut. Obviously Pax is confused, and I need to set him straight." Morgan winked at me as if he knew what was coming. "Susan loves you. You love her. She wouldn't have walked away without good reason and hers are most definitely not good enough."

Mom turned to Morgan, and he nodded. "Mom's right. She was crying when she called me. I was on the way to your place to find her when Beck called."

I swung my head back and forth between them, but I couldn't focus. My mind exhausted from the battering it endured. "I don't understand. Why would she say the things she said? None of this makes sense."

"Dig deeper. Did something frighten her? She moved in with you. Those aren't the actions of a woman not in love."

"Whatever her reasons, it doesn't matter. I never thought she'd be so callous."

"Susan isn't. She watches out for the ones she loves," Morgan said. He knew her better than I did, and although I wanted to hold onto my anger, I envied their relationship.

"But what would she be protecting me from? I don't need it."

My mother tilted her head and silently waited for me to answer my own question. I thought past the sludge in my brain and reevaluated the situation. As I would a fire, I viewed the break up and subsequent information Morgan and Mom gave me from a different angle. One moment I was confused and the next I wasn't.

"Julie," I whispered.

Morgan and Mom shared a look.

"Probably/" Mom said.

Nodding in agreement, I played out different scenarios. The truth behind my thoughts rang out. "She must have gotten to her somehow. But why wouldn't Susan tell me?"

"The only one who can answer your question is heading home to pack and leave you. Might I suggest you head her off?"

I hugged my mom. She was right. I needed answers. Susan had them. If she thought she could walk away from us because of Julie, she was wrong.

****

Susan

I got back to Pax's in record time, stuffed my clothes into a bag, and booked out of there. Instead of returning to the van, I left it parked in the driveway and headed to my car parked in the carport beside the house.

I called Ann Marie as I made my way through Bellevue, heading to the Evergreen Point Floating Bridge to cross Lake Washington to Seattle. I couldn't think beyond the pain and drove on autopilot. At the last minute, I realized my mistake. I drove past the Andersons' and Morgan's. Before I knew it, I looked toward Morgan's and my heart dropped at the sight of Pax wearing a sling.

I stepped on the gas getting away before he spotted me.

"Hello…? Susan…? Hello?"

It took me a moment to register Ann Marie's voice.

"I'm on my way to Seattle," I said, as a way of

greeting in between tearful sniffles.

"What's wrong? What happened? Where are you?" Ann Marie rarely lost her composure but her rapid-fire questions hinted at her unease.

"I'll tell you when I get there." I wiped my tears with the back of my hand. Definitely not one of my finer moments. "Please don't tell anyone. I need to hide out for a few days. Okay?"

"You're worrying me."

"I'm sorry. I promise I'll tell you everything when I get there. I know I'm asking a lot of you. Please, don't tell anyone where I am."

"Bitch, your secret's safe with me, but you better call your dad and let him know. He'll go out of his mind if anyone comes looking for you at his house."

"He's my next call. I'll be at your place soon."

"You still have the key I gave you?"

I sniffled out my yes.

"I have a couple of meetings, but I'll finish up early and meet you at the apartment."

"Okay. See you soon," I said. I waited to call my dad until I passed through the tollbooth. I didn't want to worry either of them, but I needed a place to get myself together away from the Andersons. Especially Pax and Morgan.

My dad wanted me to return home. To work it out from the safety of his house, but in the end, he understood my need to leave. I asked him to keep my destination secret and sighed in relief when he agreed. My final call was to the shelter. I didn't give them any information other than I was taking an impromptu vacation. With my calls completed, I shut down my phone and threw it on the passenger seat.

After five hours in grueling traffic, with my wayward thoughts, I was exhausted. I parked a few blocks away from Ann Marie's high-rise and lugged my bag to her building. A doorman greeted me, but I raced past him to the elevator. The ride up to the twenty-fifth floor took forever. I was drained, but I looked forward to a hot bath, a couple glasses or bottles of wine, and Ann Marie's shoulder.

Ann Marie opened the door as soon as I stepped off the elevator, still dressed in her business uniform of a pencil skirt, button down blouse and blazer. She pulled me into a fierce hug, which prompted a new round of the water works.

"I have ice cream and wine. Let's go." She grabbed the bag from my hands and dropped it in the foyer before leading me to the kitchen.

True to her word, two tubs of Ben & Jerry's pistachio ice cream stood defrosting on the kitchen counter. Next to them, several bottles of wine and two glasses waited for us. We gathered everything and plopped down on the couch in the living room.

White walls, white slate floors, and white furniture decorated the room. Purple and green pillows and throw rugs gave the space pops of color. Although the room resembled a showroom, it was comfortable and welcoming.

Ann Marie filled the glasses, sat back with her feet plopped on the table, and dug into her ice cream. I mirrored her stance, and we ate in silence.

A half-pint and a glass of wine later, I relaxed. My stomach ached, but my mind cleared. I took the containers and put them in the freezer. I returned to the couch and sat closer to Ann Marie. She reached for my hand and waited me out. It was time to talk.

She listened as I told her about Julie, the threats, hurting Pax, and my uncertainty. The farther I got away from Bellevue the more doubt set in. I was no longer sure I had done the right thing. Hours later, I had yet to come up with an answer.

"So let me get this right. You broke up with Pax, the man you've lusted over and loved for more than half your life? You did this because you thought if you didn't, Julie would hurt him? Have I got it?"

"When you say it like that, it sounds stupid. But this woman's crazy. I don't doubt for one minute she'll hurt him or his family. I did the right thing."

"Huh? Are you trying to convince me or yourself?"

"I'm not...I'm...I don't know," I said, placing my head in my hands.

"You know what I think? I think you got scared and took the first chance and ran."

"That's not true...Is it? I don't know." I stood and paced the living room. Ann Marie's gaze tracked me from the couch. I hated feeling unsure. Was she right? Did I run because my relationship with Pax was too good to be true? No. I left because of Julie. Right?

"Okay. Nothing's getting solved tonight, and we've already polished off one bottle. Unless you want to be hungover as well as confused tomorrow, I think it's time to go to bed. I have a meeting tomorrow morning, but I'm taking the rest of the day off. We can figure this out together."

I hugged her and for the first time since I walked away from Pax, my heartache receded for a second or two. With her by my side, I knew I could get over him.

Chapter Twenty-Nine

Pax

Morgan drove us to my house. My broken hand confounded my feeling of uselessness. I couldn't even get to my girl without help. I told him about my suspicions, and he listened with a scowl.

"What's the plan?" he asked.

"No idea. Get her to tell me the truth then lock us in a bedroom."

Morgan's glower deepened. "Shit, man. Keep your bedroom antics to yourself. You're talking about my best friend here."

We pulled into my driveway and my stomach rebelled. There was no sign of her car, only the shelter van. I was too late. It didn't stop me from running through the house looking for any sign she was still there. I hoped against all odds she was sitting in our bedroom, rethinking the break up. When I found most of her belongings gone, I couldn't deny the truth. She had left me.

I called and texted her, and when I didn't get a response, I called her dad.

"Mr. Hayes, I need to find Susan. We had an argument earlier and I'm worried, sir."

"Pax, son. The way I hear it, it was more than an argument."

I gulped, unable to explain.

"Don't know as I can say I understand why she broke up with you. Her explanation was a little, how do I say this? Ridiculous? But I still can't tell you where she is. I'm sorry." His voice wavered, and I wondered if he was hiding her in his house. "She's not here," he said, answering my unspoken question. "Give her time, son. She needs to get her head on straight."

"I don't know if I can. I need to see her. It feels like a part of me has died, sir," I confessed.

"I get that, I really do, but you will only push her away if you don't give her space. Take my advice and wait a day or two. She'll come around. If you haven't heard from her in a week, I will personally take you to her."

I nodded even though he couldn't see me. "Morgan said the same thing. Sir, please just tell me, is she okay?"

He breathed deeply before answering. "No, but she will be."

Hanging my head in surrender, I bid him goodbye. Between my aching heart, the adrenaline from my tree fight, and acknowledging Susan's departure, I was done. I sank onto my couch and closed my eyes taking stock of my body. My hand ached, my heart bled, and my soul wounded.

My home was empty without her. In the brief time we lived together, Susan managed to put her personal stamp on the place. Everywhere my gaze landed were traces of her.

I took her throw from the back of the couch and pressed it to my nose. It smelled of coconut and sunshine. Her happy scent.

I missed her. Her smile, her laugh, her shining

hazel eyes, her small hand in mine, her out of control red hair. Her everything.

The cushions dipped, and Morgan sat beside me. He hung up his phone and shook his head without looking at me. He too was unable to locate her. Lost for ways to find her, I heeded Mr. Hayes' advice and took a step back. Give her a few days and hope she came back to me. But if she didn't, then I was going for her. Deep down, I knew where she had run off to, but if she needed that kind of distance, I would give her the time she needed.

Morgan left me alone, and I closed my eyes again fighting off a headache. A minute or twenty later, he pressed a cold beer to my hand.

"As long as you promise not to drive, I think a beer and your pain meds will help you sleep."

"Thanks." I took a couple of swallows before I was able ask the one question that plagued me. "What am I going to do?"

"Nothing."

"How can I do nothing? I feel like I've been ripped in two."

"Yeah? Bet she's feeling the same."

"I know where she is. I think you do too."

"Her cousin's."

"Yep, that's what I'm thinking. I can get Simon to get me the address. I can go get her. Bring her home."

Morgan laughed. If my hand wasn't already broken, I might have punched him.

"Sorry. First, you're going to ask your friend to break the law, and then you're going to barge in and what? Take her by force? Kidnap her so you can mend your bruised ego?"

I stood up abruptly, rubbing my hands down my face. "No. I don't know. It's not a bruised ego. I need her with me. I've wasted ten long years. I don't want another single day without her by my side."

"Pax, your career is on the line. Between your outburst today, ignoring commands, and Julie showing up at the station, you're giving the department a reason to fire you. Take time to get things back in order and if she hasn't returned by then go get her. Give her the best you."

He was right. I never broke the rules. My job was my life. Yet since our first kiss, I had changed. Having her in my life soothed my soul. Her presence calmed me, but at the same time excited me. I wanted to be with her to the detriment of all the other things important in my life. I needed to learn how to balance who I was with whom I was becoming. Susan brought light to my life and made me break out of my box. I liked the change in me, yet I needed to find my middle ground if I wanted to be the best person for her.

I agreed to sit tight, work on my career, and wait her out. I saw him out, locked the door and set the alarm. In my Susan-empty room, too tired to undress, I plopped on the bed. I forwent my pillow, opting to use hers instead. With her scent filling my lungs, I fell asleep.

****

Susan

Five days was a long time when your world's thrown off its rails. Two days in, my quiet time ended. Pax texted me hourly. He wished me good morning and good night. Asked about my day. Told me about his. His stories about the firehouse and his crew made me laugh. He took pictures of everyday things he thought I'd enjoy. Pictures of my shelter, animals, and the progress they made.

I cried with each message, and when he asked me to come home, or told me he missed me, I couldn't control the tears. My throat hurt from the number of hours I spent breathing through my sobbing. Permanently swollen and red, my eyes scared off people as I walked around Volunteer Park.

After two days of holing up in the guestroom, Ann Marie threatened to call Pax if I didn't at least get out for a couple of hours each day. I walked the trails of the park, always ending up at the Reservoir. I sat for countless hours gazing out over the water, thinking, evaluating, and reviewing my options, yet I couldn't decide on what I wanted to do.

I had to return home if for nothing else but my dad and the shelter. I spoke with Dad nightly, and he told me Pax called him every day. Although he wouldn't tell me what they discussed, he confirmed Pax broke his hand punching a tree. I wanted to check on him but knew I would run back as soon as I heard his voice.

However, I did the next best thing. I called Morgan.

"Hey, Red."

"Morgan, I'm sorry."

"What for?"

"For hurting your brother."

"I'm not the one you should be apologizing to then."

I didn't have an answer, and I stayed quiet fighting against the threatening tears.

"Red, what are you running from?" Morgan asked,

the longer I remained silent.

"If I stayed she was going to hurt him."

"Who? Julie? She could try, but Pax would never let that happen. You're not giving him enough credit."

I debated telling him the rest but decided against it. If he knew Julie threatened his family, he would have agreed with my choices. Yet I didn't want him to carry any of the burden.

"Do you love him?" he asked, before sighing quietly. "Because if you do, you need to come home. Come back to him."

"Of course I love him. How can you even ask me that? But I can't live with knowing he got hurt because of me."

"Don't you think…?" He stopped mid-question, and I knew what he was about to ask. I didn't have an answer he would like.

My fractured emotions switched back and forth between misery and fear, and I didn't need Morgan to add to my guilt. I acted with everyone else's best interests in mind. Not mine.

"What? Just ask? Didn't I cause him enough pain already? Is that what you were going to ask?" I huffed.

"Red, you're my best friend, but he's my brother. I'm not taking sides, but I think you hurt him when it could have been avoided. You love him, and he feels the same way about you. Why are you standing in your own way?"

Pushing my fingers against my eyes, I used the pain to focus on breathing. All the reasons for giving into my feelings for Pax smacked me in the face. My fear of losing those I loved was no longer just a fear. It was my reality. I was also forcing Morgan to choose. I was going to lose my best friend.

"Listen to me, I'm saying it again. I'm not taking sides. I love you both," Morgan said. "You're hurting. I can hear it in your voice. But you don't need to be. There's a solution here."

I breathed in and out, concentrating on conquering one emotion at a time. "I want to come home, but I'm afraid."

"He'll leave you alone if that's what you really want. But if I'm standing by you, then you better be damn sure that you're willing to let him go. Pax and you both deserve a chance at happiness. He will move on, eventually. Can you handle that?"

I sucked in a breath, losing all semblance of control over my erratic tears. Morgan waited me out. "I don't…I don't know," I answered honestly.

"I miss you, Red."

"I miss you too. When I come home, can I stay with you?" I knew it was unfair to ask, but I needed my best friend and I couldn't bear to see my dad's disappointment in me if I stayed with him.

Morgan hummed, and I worried he would turn me away. "You can stay with me, but the sooner you face him the better. He's not going to like you staying here."

"I know, but it's for the best."

We hung up and my stomach churned. Whatever I hoped to achieve, talking to Morgan I didn't. I was more confused than ever and stuck between a rock and a hard place. If I stayed away from Pax both of us hurt. If I returned to him, he could be hurt worse. Which was the lesser evil? I didn't know, and until I figured it out, I only had one choice. Stay away.

Chapter Thirty

Susan

Ann Marie slammed the door shut, storming into the apartment. I'd been in bed since I returned from the park. After my conversation with Morgan, my heart felt heavier. I wasn't making these decisions for myself; I was doing it for Pax. Throughout the day, my mood seesawed between sadness and anger. Why did nobody understand I was looking out for Pax? Since I couldn't come up with satisfying answers, I returned to bed and hid from the world.

Ann Marie walked into my room without knocking and hauled the covers off. I groaned and reached for them only to have my hand swatted away. A few minutes of tug-of-war and I gave up. I didn't need covers after all.

"Enough is enough. We're going out tonight," she said. She stomped her way to my bag and haphazardly pulled out my clothes. "Did you bring anything you can wear to a club? Jeez, woman, do I need to teach you how to pack?"

Ignoring her, I buried my head under the pillows and picked up my phone. I scrolled through the past three days of texts from Pax.

"What the hell are you doing?" She yanked the phone from my hands, threw it on the dresser, out of my reach. "If you're so over him let's go dancing tonight, have a meaningless hook up, then you can go home and get on with your life."

I huffed out in anger. "I'm not going out tonight, but if I've become such a nuisance, I'll pack and leave."

Turning away from my bag, Ann Marie stalked to the bed, straddled me, and tickled my sides. I writhed and bucked. For a small woman she was strong.

"Fine. Fine. You win. Get off me."

"Go take a shower. You stink," she said. "You know you can stay with me as long as you like but staying in bed all day is not healthy."

"I went out today. Not my fault you weren't home to see it."

"Yeah? Did you change before you crossed the street to go to the park? Did you talk to another human being or just the birds hovering for handouts? No? I didn't think so. Get up. If I have to drag you into the shower I swear I'll do it."

I glared at her and yanked the underwear dangling from her finger. Her laughter rang out as I slammed the bathroom door, and I did my best to ignore my creeping smile.

The water sluiced over my skin washing away the grime, and my spirits lifted. My new reality didn't include Pax, but hopefully, over time, he and his family would forgive me. By the time I stepped out, my resolve solidified. Dancing, people watching, and laughing with Ann Marie, I decided, was exactly what I needed to move on. No hook ups for me, but a chance to simply be. It was time to lock my past away and look to the future.

I dressed in skintight jeans and didn't allow thoughts of Pax and his love for those particular pants penetrate my rising mood. A green silk tank and gold strappy-heeled sandals completed my outfit. I twirled in front of the mirror liking what I saw. With the help of makeup, my eyes no longer looked red or swollen. I left my hair to air dry, allowing the waves to fly naturally.

Ann Marie waited for me in the living room and I didn't fight back the smile when she whistled her approval. "Come on, let's paint the town red." She hooked her hand in the crook of my arm and walked us out of the apartment.

We walked out onto the busy streets of Seattle, hailed a cab, and were on our way to what she promised was one of the hottest nightclubs in town.

A long line of people, corralled behind red velvet ropes, wrapped around the building. Ann Marie grabbed my hand and led to me to the front instead of the back of the line. The bouncer spotted us coming and his eyes lit up. Ann Marie stood on her toes and gave him a quick kiss on the cheek as he opened the rope, letting us pass.

"Thanks, D. This is my cousin, Susan," she said, and pulled me closer. "Susan, meet Daniel. Anything you need, he's your man."

Daniel wrapped an arm around Ann Marie's waist and hauled her to his side. He whispered in her ear and she giggled before slapping his chest. "Behave," she said to him and winked at me.

I beamed at her. There was no way to stay sad when she was in a playful mood. Which, to be honest, is ninety-nine percent of the time. We stepped inside the club and were greeted with loud, undulating music. I squinted against the strobe lights dancing across the room. Gyrating bodies moved along the wood floor, many doing things I wished I could unsee. Ann Marie laughed at me before leading us to one of two bars on either side of the vast space.

Dim lighting overhead gave just enough illumination to see the gorgeous bartenders. The two men and one woman pranced around behind the bar, putting on a show as they made the ordered cocktails.

Ann Marie caught the attention of one of the male bartenders and lifted two fingers. With a nod of his head, he moved away and filled her order. He returned with two craft beers in one hand but didn't place them in front of us until Ann Marie stood on the foot bar and leaned over. He smiled and pulled her closer to kiss her on the cheek. She smiled at him when he let her go.

He reached over the bar and shook my hand and tugged me closer. "Any friend of Ann Marie's is a friend of mine. I'm Colt. You are?"

Ann Marie yelled, "Taken," before I gave him my name.

He sighed, and stepped down, but a twinkle remained in his eyes. Holding his hands up, as if in surrender, he laughed at Ann Marie's scowl.

"And so are you," she said to him, over the roar of the music.

The female bartender came by, placed her arms around Colt's waist, and extended her hand to me. "Don't mind him. He's the biggest flirt."

"Come on, let's grab a table," Ann Marie said.

With a nod, I followed her to a private, closed off section toward the back of the club. We skirted around tables filled with people laughing, couples kissing, and friends enjoying a night out. "Colt owns the place. Stone is his wife. Their relationship is strong and secure, but they flirt with the clientele because it brings in more tips, which they give to their staff," she said, as we sat on a black velvet couch facing the dance floor.

People moved about, either lost in their own world, or vying for attention. Images of Pax and me dancing, wrapped around each other, unconcerned with the world around us swam before my eyes.

I shut down the visions and focused my attention back on Ann Marie. She watched me carefully, and with a shrug, I silently told her *I was fine, and it would take time to keep Pax from infiltrating my every thought*.

"Sorry, go on," I said, and rolled my hand for her to continue.

"What I was saying before you zoned out, was Colt and Stone came to me for marketing help when they bought the place. The club had a bad reputation, and they wanted to turn it around." She waved her arm around. "We made it the club to be and became good friends. Drinks are always on the house and the staff knows me. I love coming here to unwind."

I glanced about the room and smiled. For the first time in a week, I relaxed. "You want to dance?" I asked, surprising myself.

Ann Marie drank the last of her beer, took my empty bottle from me, and placed them both on the table. "Let's get some booty on, bitches!" she said, and we walked arm in arm to the dance floor.

I laughed as she shook her small butt, waving her arms in the air, and, in general, losing herself to the music. Men turned to watch her, but she ignored all their leers. The longer we danced the more I got into it and soon was lost in the rhythm.

I ignored hands pulling at me, deftly moving away each time it happened. Four dances in, Stone joined us.

Pax was never out of my mind, but I was able to push him back far enough to let go and have fun. My spirits lifted as we laughed and one-upped each other. We voted on each other's best dance moves, which Ann Marie won. Sweaty and exhausted, we marched our aching feet back to our table. Four fresh cold beers and Colt appeared as we sat down.

He pulled Stone onto his lap and nuzzled her neck. She melted into him and I envied the ease of their partnership. Trailing his mouth over her skin, he ended at her mouth and kissed her with fervor. Their kiss so hot I turned away.

"They're always like this," Ann Marie said.

Stone and Colt pulled apart, and Stone turned to Ann Marie and me. I guessed her flushed cheeks were not due to embarrassment.

"Sorry. I can't keep my hands off him," she said before reaching for her drink.

"First stages of a relationship are fantastic," I said, remembering the times Pax and I had been together.

"Oh, we've been together for six years, but if you count the years in high school, it's been nine altogether," Colt said, slipping his hand inside her shirt and rubbed her back.

"Wow. I'm sorry...I thought with the way...just forget I said anything," I said.

"It's okay. I nearly lost her once, and ever since I've held on tight," Colt said, pulling Stone to meet his mouth again.

I watched, this time unable to look away. Their love shone through, and I struggled with feeling both jealous and sad.

"What happened?" I asked, too curious to care if my question was intrusive.

Stone focused on Colt as he answered. "I come from a rich family. My college roommate, Gus, was jealous. One weekend before Stone visited, he threatened her life if I didn't pay him. I figured if she was no longer my girlfriend she would be out of harm's way."

My stomach dropped. Ann Marie's knowing smirk confirmed she brought me to this particular nightclub to meet these two people.

"Colt broke up with me and told me to stay away. Instead of fighting for him, I walked away with my shattered heart. We were apart a year."

"I thought by breaking up with her Gus would leave us alone. Sophomore year, I got a new roommate and life continued. I missed her every day, but I didn't want to risk her safety. Gus got expelled, and I thought that was the end of him."

"It wasn't. He found and kidnapped me for ransom."

I lifted my hand to my mouth stifling my gasp.

"Stone's sister called me looking for her. No one had seen Stone for two days. In my panic, I forgot about Gus, until he called demanding money in exchange for her. Thankfully, the police were able to tag his location through the phone call."

"They found me in a closet tied to a bar screwed to the floor. I wasn't hurt but had gone without food or water. Colt hasn't let me out of his sight since. But," Stone said and cupped Colt's cheek, "because of my kidnapping we found our way back to each other, and we're stronger because of it."

I sat silently absorbing their story.

"Hey, we need to get back to the bar. One of our bartenders had to stay home with his sick daughter, so we've been working all night. Come back when we're fully staffed. We'd love to get to know you," Stone said. She and Colt left hand in hand.

"How come I feel you had an ulterior motive bringing me here tonight?" I asked Ann Marie as soon as they were out of sight.

"Huh? Who? Me? Nah. I brought you here for you to hook up with Daniel. He's exactly what you like. Big, strong, loyal, and great in bed. A perfect distraction to get your mind off you-know-who."

"I don't need a distraction and I'm not sleeping with Daniel."

"Who said anything about sleeping?" Ann Marie laughed and winked at me.

I sat back on the couch and people-watched, thinking. Could I go back to Pax and tell him what Julie intended? I didn't think so. No matter what Stone and Colt said, their circumstances were different. Gus wanted money. Julie wanted Pax. That deep-seated desire for another human being was far more of a threat than money.

No. Pax was better off without me.

****

Pax

Five long days, five sleepless nights. It sucked. My hand was healing but returning to full duty was a few months out. Since I couldn't lose myself in work, I spent hours at Kisses and Paws, playing with the animals, helping the construction crew when I could, and fighting my instincts to find Susan.

I texted her, so she knew she was my first and last thought every day. She didn't answer. I didn't like it, but I understood her need for space. I'm not going to lie. It was one of the hardest challenges I ever faced.

Each day, my agitation grew, partly from the loss of her from my life, but mainly because of Julie's reappearance. She kept her distance, but I couldn't turn a corner without her being there. She hung around the coffee shop in front of the firehouse, and I caught her following me in her car. At night, I locked every window and door, set the alarm, and drew my blinds.

More and more I became a prisoner in my own home. During those moments, I was grateful for Susan's absence since it kept her out of harm's way. When Billy gave me the keys to my now official office, I spent time cleaning it out instead of going home. Mike held onto reports dating back over ten years. I sifted through the piles, shredded documents, and packed the ones I couldn't discard and moved them to the archive room in the main building.

If I kept my hands and mind busy, then there wasn't enough room for thoughts of Susan. At least that's what I told myself.

"Any word?" Billy asked, leaning against my office doorframe.

"No." I rubbed my hands across my face.

"You're looking haggard."

"Haven't been sleeping much."

Billy nodded and observed me quietly. "Did I ever tell you Janice ran away from me?"

Looking up, I shook my head. Billy entered my office and closed the door behind him.

"If you ever repeat this to anyone, I'll deny it." Intrigued, I nodded. "Janice and I have been together for thirty years. We have kids and grandkids to fill up the house on any given day. But thirty-three years ago Janice hated me."

I laughed, but at his scolding look, I shut up quick.

"Interrupt me again, and I won't share my words of wisdom." I stayed silent and tracked him as he got up and paced my office. "Janice hated I wanted to be a firefighter. Said that she couldn't live with that kind of fear. I convinced her I would be fine, and she finally agreed to date me. I never told her when I went out on a call. One day, I responded to a house fire in her neighborhood. I did my job. We stopped the fire quickly, but I was injured. Janice forced her way under the line when she saw them loading me onto the ambulance. I sat up too quickly and threw up all over the EMT. She yelled at the guys keeping her from me. Man, was she fierce." Billy stared off into the distance. "Freaked them all out," he said, around a grin. "They let her ride to the hospital with me. She helped take care of me and waited 'til I was given a clean bill of health. My first day back on the job, she left me."

Billy sat down in one of the metal chairs facing my desk.

"What did you do?" I asked. Technically, I didn't interrupt him.

"Nothing. I was an idiot. I left her alone. She found someone else, dated him, and almost married him."

I sat back, dumbfounded.

"Almost?"

He hung his head in shame. "She started dating the damn doctor that operated on me. I didn't find out for two years. Not until they announced their engagement."

"Wow."

"Tell me about it." Billy's gaze wandered, lost in his memories. "Anyway, the day of the wedding I couldn't take it anymore. I showed up at the church, draped her over my shoulder, and booked it out of there. Her bridesmaids ran after us, shouting. I threw her in the back of my car and hauled ass."

I laughed, picturing the image he painted.

"What did she do?"

"She laughed. The. Entire. Way." Billy's smile widened at the memory. "I drove around for hours. I apologized, told her I loved her, and I forbade her from marrying the bumbling idiot. She didn't like the forbidding part, but when she calmed down, she admitted she was miserable with him. She didn't know how to get out of her predicament.

"Janice hung a picture of me with her across my shoulder running out of the chapel in our living room. Apparently, her mom thought the moment was romantic and instead of stopping us, she took photos. It's one of my best memories, but I almost didn't have it, or her, because I was too proud or too scared. Either way, I could have lost out on the love of my life."

Billy stood and rubbed his hands on his pants. He walked to the door but stopped.

"I'll kill you if you tell any of the crew."

"I won't. I get what you're saying, sir, but…"

"There should be no buts at the end of that sentence. Either you act or lose her forever. Which is it going to be?"

Billy walked out, leaving me alone with my thoughts.

Chapter Thirty-One

Pax

We sat on the deck, taking it easy. The sun beat down on us as the boats on Lake Washington sailed by. The quiet moment should have been relaxing, but it wasn't. It was Caden's second to last day at home and Morgan had us all over for a few beers.

It was also my birthday. Morgan and Caden convinced Mom to hold off on celebrating until the following day at Sunday lunch. My brothers and cousins hugged me when they first arrived, murmured happy birthday but otherwise left the festivities for another day.

Parker and Dustin rode Morgan's jet skis across the water while Foster sat at the end of the deck, his feet dangling in the lake. Morgan, Caden, and I sat in the lounge chairs laughing at our brothers and drinking beer. Jesse disappeared soon after his arrival, and Morgan found him asleep on the couch inside the house. We let him be considering he needed the rest. Medical residencies were a bitch.

With Mom and Dad at dinner with friends and Kate in class, our grown up asses were left without supervision. It gave us the perfect opportunity to behave stupidly, which we did in abundance.

Although my family's antics kept me distracted, I thought of Susan. I missed her, and my patience was at its end. Once Caden left, I planned to hunt Susan down, convince her to come home to me.

"I have to tell you something," Morgan said. His tone indicated it was something I wouldn't want to hear.

Caden sat up, hearing the same hesitancy in Morgan's voice.

"Susan's coming back today."

I stood up abruptly, excited at the news, yet upset she told Morgan instead of me.

"You've been talking to her?" I asked through clenched teeth.

Morgan stayed on his lounge chair, relaxed, without a care in the world. It grated on my nerves. I wanted to grab him and haul him out of the chair and deck him. I was jealous. However, I kept a tight hold on my aggressive thoughts and waited him out.

"She's my best friend."

"That's it? You have nothing else to say?"

Morgan cracked open one eye, stared at me for a moment, and closed it again. "Sit down, and I'll tell you what you need to know."

Taking my seat, I sat on the edge, leaning into him. My body vibrated with unspent energy and I swore under my breath.

"Morgan, just talk already," Caden said, and I sighed, grateful for his support.

"She's coming home today, picking up her stuff from your place, and then coming here."

Smiling, the tension eased from my shoulders. She was coming back to me.

Then it clicked.

"Wait? What? Why is she getting her things then

coming here?" I asked, although I already knew the answer.

"She needs a place to crash."

Knocking my chair back and phone to the ground as I stood, I threw myself at Morgan. Caden stepped between us. "She has a place. My house. Our home."

"That's what I told her."

My anger deflated. I fell back into the seat Caden righted. "She doesn't want to see me." Statement more than question.

"She's being stubborn. She admitted Julie threatened her, but there's more to the story. If she's here, I'll get it out of her."

Dustin popped Parker with a wave and Parker gave chase, their laughter loud and boisterous as they outmaneuvered one another. Foster came over to sit by Morgan.

"I don't know what to do," I finally admitted. "Someone please tell me what to do."

My brothers and cousin sat silent.

"You know what? Don't tell me. I know what I'm going to do. I'm going to be here when she arrives. I will tie her down if I have to, and insist she tell me everything."

My phone dinged alerting me to a problem at my home. Retrieving my phone from the ground, I opened up the security app. I expected to see Susan. It wasn't.

"Damn it. I have to go. Julie's just triggered my alarms," I said, and slipped on my sneakers. Caden and Morgan did the same and followed me out the door. I didn't argue with them, appreciating their support.

****

Susan

I arrived at Pax's relieved he wasn't home. I only intended to grab the clothes I left behind and head over to Morgan's. He expected me but the drive through Seattle and the bridge went faster than anticipated. I laid awake the previous night after returning from the club, thinking through my decisions, and with the early morning light, I became eager to act. To move forward. I called Morgan far earlier than acceptable, but he didn't complain, and Ann Marie insisted on taking me to breakfast before I left.

Six hours after calling Morgan I was home. At least my Bellevue home. I didn't have a place to live yet. With no signs of Pax, I rushed through the house after resetting the alarm. I hustled to pack my belongings into a suitcase and ran down the stairs.

I took my house key off the key chain and left it on the kitchen counter. I rubbed my hand on the surface, remembering how Pax had taken me there. I jerked back and shook my head to get rid of the memories. I avoided looking at any of the other christened surfaces. I had to keep one and only one thought in mind.

Get away.

Staying was not an option. Tears sprang. I took one last look around and said my final goodbyes.

I hurried out of his house without the caution I promised Pax. I didn't see Julie on the front porch.

****

Pax

As we climbed into my truck, my phone dinged again. My stomach dropped as Susan walked into our house. I didn't have cameras inside and lost sight of her as she crossed the threshold. I cursed, angry I hadn't installed internal cameras. The hits kept coming, and I nearly lost my mind when Julie returned to the front porch.

She looked directly into the camera and smiled. My heart thumped against my ribcage. She knew I was watching her.

"Step on it. Susan's at the house and Julie's waiting for her."

Morgan's gaze turned animalistic as he cursed and floored the pedal. We weaved through traffic and Caden and I had to brace ourselves from being tossed around.

****

Susan

"What the hell are you doing here?" she sneered, startling me.

I bit my tongue and walked past her. "Don't worry, I'm just leaving."

Fear, not jealousy, ran through my veins. I was certain Pax hadn't invited her. I calculated my next moves. Do not engage, get to my car, leave, call the cops, and get to Morgan's.

One minute I was walking, and the next I was on the ground. My suitcase lay open beside me, my phone a few feet away. I thought I tripped. Julie's weight settled on my back; ostentatious perfume permeated my nose. She pushed my face to the ground.

I had miscalculated. I should have never turned my back on her. I knew she was a threat. I didn't act accordingly. Mentally slapping myself for my own stupidity, I lay still. I needed time to think.

"Why are you here? This is my home now and you're not welcome," she shouted. Spit hit the back of my neck. I dared not move.

I kept my voice steady. "I left a few things behind. I came to get them."

"I don't believe you. Give me your key."

Ha, like that would ever happen. "I left it in the kitchen." Thankful I wasn't lying. "I did what you wanted." I let my anger run freely through me. Every decision I made until that point was due to fear. For the first time since the break-up, I stopped thinking about him or his family. I thought about how Julie used me and that made my blood boil.

"You got what you wanted. I broke up with Pax and I'm leaving." I bucked. It was time to fight. She slammed her fist into my back. An action I didn't expect. Again, I was a fool for not recognizing the threat. I coughed and sputtered, pulling air into my lungs only to inhale dirt.

She wrapped her hand in my hair and yanked twisting my neck awkwardly. "Not good enough. I have to make sure you can't interfere."

"I'll stay away." I remained still. She didn't need another reason to hit me.

"No, you won't…"

When she didn't continue, I chanced a glance. Her gaze focused on something in the distance. She shook her head and anger glinted in her eyes. Her scowl deepened the longer she thought.

I studied her changing expressions and my mind calmed. I finally saw the situation clearly. The terrorizing would never end. I was a threat as long as she thought she had a chance with Pax. She would continue to pursue him.

In that moment, I acknowledged the mistakes I had made. I gave her too much credit. I figured if I did what she wanted she wouldn't hurt Pax. I figured wrong.

With a goal in sight, I re-evaluated my situation. My small stature did not diminish my strength. If I gained her trust, I could fight.

"Let me up and I'll go wherever you want to go."

"No. The minute I do you'll run."

"Where would I go? The closest house is a mile away. I'm not stupid. I know there's no way out of this, but if Pax comes home and finds us here, it won't be good." Her hold loosened, and I knew I was getting through. "My phone's been ringing. I'm sure it's Morgan. He'll also come looking for me. We need to get out of here."

"You're right." Her voice was low and her body weight shifted. "Fine, get up and don't try anything funny."

She climbed off me. Light reflected off a knife in her hand. My situation grew grimmer. I had one chance to take her down. Ensuring my survival hinged on my ability to disarm and fight her. Pax's safety compelled me forward and confirmed my plan of action.

I stood slowly making sure I had my footing. I took stock of my injuries. I ached but not enough to slow me down. She waved her hand toward the van and ordered me to get in. I complied but calculated the steps I needed to take, turn, and attack. I planted my left foot and kept my knee loose like I learned in my monthly self-defense class. Using my arms for balance, I pivoted and kicked out with my right leg.

See the target. Kick. Punch. Repeat. I repeated the mantra and swung with all my might.

With a satisfying crunch, I landed a direct hit. Not sure if I broke her hand or temporarily incapacitated her, I readied for her retaliation. She screamed, dropped the knife, and cradled one hand in the other.

I didn't give her a chance to regain her footing. I cocked my elbow back and swung. An uppercut my best option for maximum damage. My knuckles connected with her jaw, spinning her on her feet.

She recovered quickly. With a scream rivaling a banshee's, she charged me. I stumbled back, my foot caught where grass met blacktop. My arms pin-wheeled, fighting for balance.

I hit the ground; the impact rattled my brain. I fought to catch my breath for a second time. The lack of oxygen made me woozy. My stomach revolted. I turned on my side. Pulled my knees to my chest as Julie lifted her foot. Time slowed down.

I lifted my arm bracing for the hit. I grabbed her calf. She lost her balance, fell backward, and hit the pavement. Adrenaline pushed me forward, and I dug deep for strength to tackle her.

I wrapped my knees around her ribs, bracing my ankles against her calves. I pinned her to the ground. Her hands lay limp by her side. I didn't take her unresponsiveness for granted.

A noise in the distance caught my attention, and I turned. I sighed in relief at the glorious sight. Pax's truck barreling down the road.

Chapter Thirty-Two

Pax

In a matter of fifteen minutes, Morgan pulled onto my street. I couldn't sit still. We spotted the women fighting. Morgan's curses grew louder and hateful. I stared. From our distance, I couldn't tell if Susan was injured, but she smiled when she spotted us.

I hate to admit it but seeing my woman in action turned me on.

Morgan pulled into the driveway tires screeching. I flew out of the passenger side. Morgan and Caden right behind me. I hauled Susan into my arms, and Morgan quickly subdued Julie. Caden was on the phone, talking to nine-one-one dispatch.

I pulled Susan tightly into my chest. Clutching her to me, I carried her to the porch and set her down on the first step. I ran my hands over her body.

I focused on her ripped clothes. And she pulled the hem of her tattered shirt. With a light tug, I pulled her to me once again. Our shuddered breaths matched, and I leaned my forehead against hers. Our breaths mingled and slowed. Tears wetted my eyes, and she ran her thumb along my cheek. "Never do that again," I said, meaning less about my heartache than my fear of losing her.

I sat with her in my lap on the porch steps and relished her weight in my arms. I rubbed my thumb on her forearm and goosebumps popped along her skin. I smiled at her response. I couldn't keep my gaze off her. She was a sight for sore eyes.

Susan gasped. "Pax. She's wearing boots." I followed her gaze. I had never seen Julie in anything other than heels, but seeing her boot clad feet cemented loose ends. It was her prints in the dirt outside of the house.

I turned my attention back to Susan to find her fixated on Julie. I shifted so my body obscured Julie from Susan's view. I lifted her hands to inspect them. "Look, we match," I said and showed her my cast. She laughed, and the tension of the past five days dissipated.

I couldn't ask for anything more. Hearing her laugh, seeing the sparkle in her eyes, and feeling her body against mine afforded me serenity. They were gifts I would never again take for granted.

"Baby, I missed you so much."

"I'm sorry. I didn't mean anything I said. She wanted to kill you. I wanted you safe but, in the end, I hurt you. I'm so sorry. I love you."

I stilled. "Say it again."

"I love you," she kissed my forehead, "I love you," my nose, "I love you," each cheek, "I love you," and finally my lips.

I grabbed her face and held her to me. I met her kiss with my needy one. She moaned in my mouth, and at the taste of blood, I pulled away.

"Shit. I hurt you."

She planted her hands over mine, keeping our faces close. "Never."

"I love you. I should have told you every day. I'm

sorry," I said, looking her deep in the eye.

Her fingers caressed my cheeks. "I knew."

I hunched and laid my head against her chest. I needed to feel her heart beat, listen to her breathe, feel the warmth of her body against mine.

"If you ever do that again in the name of protecting me, I'm going to—I don't know what I'm going to do, but you won't like it."

She giggled and rested her chin on the top of my head. "Oh, dang it. I was hoping you were going to say you'd tie me to your bed."

"Baby, now that's something I can definitely do."

We sat in silence for a few minutes until Susan gasped. "Happy birthday, Pax. I can't believe I forgot. I swear I'll make it up to you."

"Sh, baby. You in my arms is the best birthday gift I could ever hope for." I cupped her chin and brought her lips to mine, kissing her slowly, mindful of her cuts.

Pulling back, I rested my forehead against hers again and ignored everything around us. I didn't care about the police in the driveway or when they hauled Julie away in handcuffs. I appreciated Morgan keeping the cops and EMTs at bay. I made a mental note to thank him for giving Susan and me more time in our cocoon.

Eventually, Morgan pulled us out of our bubble. I hovered as the cops questioned Susan, and the EMT guys patched her up. No broken bones and no stitches needed. After everyone, including my brothers, left I led her back into the house.

Morgan and Caden promised to call and update Mom. They assured me she would not call that evening, but all bets were off for the morning.

I led her to the bedroom where I stripped us both of our shirts and shorts. Laying her down on the bed, I crawled in and spooned her from behind. Feeling her skin against mine gave me much needed comfort.

"I love you," I whispered into her hair. "I want to be inside you right now."

She sighed, her breath tickling the hairs on my forearm. "Do it. Take me."

Pulling my boxers off and then her panties down, I ran my fingers along her seam. Susan pushed against my touch, moaning quietly. Reaching back, she palmed my erection and guided me to her entrance. I barely got a word out before she seated my head inside her. "Condom."

"Birth control. I'm clean."

"I'm clean too." I pushed forward giving her every inch of me. Fully encased inside of her we stilled, and I waded through the myriad of sensations surging through my body. She felt incredible without a barrier between us.

"Pax, I'm close. You feel…"

"I'm taking you slow tonight, baby."

"Yes," Susan whispered, as I moved. I pulled out slowly, wanting to feel everything. The walls of her pussy quivered around me, sucking me right back in. I wasn't going to last, but we had all night and if I had my way, the rest of our lives to be together.

"I love you, Pax." She turned her head and our gazes met. Leaning down, I kissed her deeply as I rocked into her body.

"Marry me." The words came out unbidden, and I didn't regret them.

Susan teared up but kept her gaze on mine.

"Asking or telling?"

"Doesn't matter. You're mine. Always will be."

She closed her eyes nearing her orgasm, and I flattened my palm against her stomach. Dragging my hand farther south, I played with her as I pumped into her from behind. She clasped my arm and screamed through her release. My name on her tongue along with her milking walls tipped me over the edge.

"Always yours," she whispered, seconds before her breathing evened out. She fell asleep in my arms, with me still buried deep inside her.

****

Susan

I waited for Pax on the front porch of our home. Life returned to normal two weeks after Julie's arrest. Her lawyer sought an insanity plea. I had mixed feelings, but as long as she left us alone, I didn't care what the courts decided. Julie needed help, and I hoped the City of Bellevue provided her the necessary counseling.

Since his lust fueled proposal, Pax hadn't brought up marriage again. Yet he bought me a dresser and emptied half of his closet, making space for my ever-growing wardrobe. Slowly, I rebuilt my life, filling my new space with things Pax and I loved.

My phone rang in my lap as I sipped my coffee.

"Hi, baby." Pax spoke as soon as I answered. "I'm going to be a few minutes late. Need anything?"

"No. I'm good, just sitting on our swing enjoying the morning air. I'll see you when you get home."

I loved referring to our house as home. We packed it each day with love and respect. I saw us having children, raising them here. I could see us as a family.

A few minutes later, I stood, returned to the kitchen, and made Pax a cup of coffee. I grew accustomed to his schedule faster than I thought I would. When he was at the station, we talked throughout the day, and I brought him lunch, and cookies for the crew. On his days off, he came to the shelter to have lunch with me.

The days he visited, after we ate, he often disappeared with Darth in the new courtyard. I didn't mind. He had a special bond with the dog, and I left them to play outside while I tended to the daily grinds of the shelter.

When he wasn't with me or at the fire station, he spent long hours fixing the dining room and the other bedrooms in our home. We bought a table large enough to fit our families around, and we made plans to have them all over as soon as it was delivered.

We christened the majority of the house, and Pax's feisty side wanted to explore christening the land. With no neighbors and only wildlife for company, we had sex and slept on the back porch many times.

Nights frightened me most, and when he wasn't home, one of his brothers stayed in the renovated guest bedroom. With each passing day, I grew less afraid and hoped when Julie received her sentence, my worries would diminish.

Pax was patient with me and held me when I needed it. Or he distracted my mind with the things he did to my body. The best moments of the past two weeks were the hours we spent talking after we explored each other, giving and taking, bringing each other pleasure and contentment. I already knew so much about him, but with each moment we spent together the more I learned. With each shared story, he showed me more of his soul. My love for him grew stronger each day. He told me about his fears—losing his family or losing the ability to do his job. I told him about mine. He didn't laugh or cower when I went on about having my own brood of children. Instead, he waggled his eyebrows and said he was on board, making me laugh. His hopes and dreams became mine, and mine his.

His truck rumbled up the driveway pulling me from my thoughts. I stood from the newly added porch swing and waited for him. Pax exited the truck but leaned back in. My heart swelled, and tears broke free as he pulled an unleashed Darth from the front seat. He followed Pax's commands without hesitation.

I stepped off the porch to pet the dog I loved but hadn't a home for. Pax gave me more than he realized. As I approached them Pax signaled, and Darth sat, stretching his front legs out in front, as if in a bow.

"I couldn't get him to learn to bend on one knee." My gaze shot up, questioning him, hoping my conclusions were correct. "He has something for you on his collar."

Shaking, I knelt before Darth and reached for his collar. I found a small velvet pouch and pulled it off the clip. Pax took it from my hands and knelt beside Darth facing me. "Good boy," he said, petting him and I swear Darth beamed at the praise.

Lifting the bag, Pax tipped a shiny object out into his palm. He held a sparkling ring, and my eyes watered. The simple yet elegant ring glimmered in the early morning sun. A marquis diamond surrounded by small, round green diamonds mounted in yellow gold. It was my mother's ring, and it was perfect.

"I love you. Always and forever. Marry me?"

Love and devotion shone through his eyes and his proposal, although simple in its delivery, was everything I loved about Pax. I threw myself at him, unbalancing both of us. We fell backward a tangle of arms and legs. Darth danced and barked, wanting to join in the fun.

I cried into his shoulder and Pax held me tightly against him.

"Baby, I'm sorry. If it's too fast, we can wait. I just wanted you to know…"

In between sobs of joy, I kissed every part of Pax's face my lips could reach.

Pax adjusted so I straddled his lap. He caressed my hair and wiped the tears with his knuckles. "Baby, I love you. There's no one else for me. There never has been. I want to spend the rest of my life showing you how much I love you. Your beautiful face and smile, greeting me in the morning and tucking me in at night, are more than I deserve. You are the light in my life and you shine brightly bringing me home to you. And, although I fear this is going to sound cliché, considering my job, you are the fire that drives me. I will run into a burning building any day of the week for you, and I will fight your demons with you. Please say you'll marry me."

I cried through his speech and couldn't control my voice to say yes. I nodded instead.

Pax beamed and took my hand in his. He slipped my mother's ring over my finger until it came to rest against my knuckle. Lifting my hand to his mouth, he kissed my palm, my finger, then the ring, before kissing my mouth.

Darth quieted down and lay beside us as we lost ourselves in each other.

Pax's phone dinged with incoming texts.

Pulling it from his pocket, he held it, so I could see the screen.

Mom: *Did she say yes?*

Mom: *Of course she did. How silly of me*

Mom: *Welcome to the family Susan. Pax tell her I said that*

Mom: *Better yet, tell her she has always been family, but now she has to call me Mom*

Mom: *I like that. Do you think she'll call me mom?*

I took the phone from a laughing Pax and texted her back

Pax: *Hi, this is Susan. I said yes, and I am honored to call you mom, Mom*

Pax pocketed his phone and lifted me with ease. Darth followed us to the house. He sniffed around as Pax carried me to our bedroom. Closing the door behind us, he made his way to our bed and undressed me.

Without a word, he conveyed his affection in every touch, caress, and whisper against my skin. He trailed his lips down my neck, licking the swells of my breasts. I raked my fingernails along his side, digging into his butt cheeks when he sucked a hardened peak into his mouth. I parted my lips in a silent scream the more he toyed with my nipples. Too impatient, I wedged my hand between us and grabbed him, positioning him at my opening. He slowly entered me, teasing me with shallow thrusts. My gaze locked on his. Sweat beaded his forehead. I reached up and swiped away a droplet.

Pax groaned, lowered his chest, pumped his hips, never once looking away, and brought us both to climax.

The moment was perfect.

He was perfect.

My love for him absolute.

Falling asleep in his arms, I knew my dreams were only just beginning.

Rasha Selim

About the Author

Rasha Selim was born in Cairo, Egypt and was raised in both Cairo and Dubai, United Arab Emirates. She moved to the U.S. to attend college and pursue a career as a Forensic Psychologist. She left criminology behind to become the mother of three wonderfully active boys.

Rasha has spent her life engaged with books and as stories of her own began to develop, she knew that she had to get them down in print. She is extremely excited to be sharing her stories with the world. She lives in upstate New York where she is blessed to be surrounded by her loving and supportive husband, children, great friends, and incredible books.

~*~

Visit Rasha at

www.rashaselim.com

~*~

To chat with Rasha Selim and other Wild Rose Press authors of erotic romance, join us at
www.groups.yahoo.com/group/thewilderroses.

Taste Me
By Cali Caliente

One impulsive tryst…one unforgettable fling.

Culinary columnist Aurora Daring adores creating desserts with fresh fruit and dreams of becoming a pastry chef. Always on the lookout for new food places to review, she visits Love's Farmer's Market, an old barn converted into a 'green store' with all the wonders a gourmet cook could possibly want. She finds something else as well—a ruggedly handsome man who fulfills all her sexual fantasies in one impromptu encounter.

Bryce Lovella loves his family's farm. His idea of expanding the farm to include a produce market is just the beginning of his aspirations. He also wants to start a family. When his twin brother, Brent, challenges him to find the perfect woman in two weeks' time and get her to say I love you, Bryce eagerly agrees to play. He's already seduced the woman of his dreams. There's only one problem—he never got her name.

Also Available
from The Wild Rose Press, Inc.
and major retailers.

Revving Her Heart
A Blacke Brothers Novel One
By Cadence Vonn

After the sudden death of Allison Lorde's father in a motorcycle accident, she vows never to love a man who rides the beastly machines. But when a memory from her past rides up on his bike, looking all bad-boy sexy, the sweet promise of a shared kiss long ago makes it difficult to deny his steamy seduction.

Nick Blacke's number one passion is motorcycles until the gangly girl he'd kissed as a teen shows up with womanly curves that beckon to be explored. She seems eager to let him and even embraces his penchant for kink, but when he wants more, he realizes revving her engines might be easier than revving her heart.

Thank you for purchasing
this publication of The Wild Rose Press, Inc.

For questions or more
information contact us at
info@thewildrosepress.com.

The Wild Rose Press, Inc.
www.thewildrosepress.com

To visit with authors of
The Wild Rose Press, Inc.
join our yahoo loop at
http://groups.yahoo.com/group/thewildrosepress/